THE
ARTIST
AND THE
SOLDIER

A NOVEL

ANGELLE PETTA

Copyright © 2018 by Angelle Petta

Author photograph and cover photo by
Sharon Hallman Photography

ISBN: 978-1-943258-72-7

Edited by: Amy Ashby

Published by Warren Publishing
Charlotte, NC
www.warrenpublishing.net
Printed in the United States

For Kim, the shiniest of women, who read my words
from the beginning and still kept reading.

And for my husband Ryan who redefines patience and love.

"We shall not cease from exploration
And the end of all our exploring
Will be to arrive where we started
And know the place for the first time."

—T.S. Eliot, "Four Quartets"

ACKNOWLEDGMENTS

Reading an entire novel is an undertaking. Reading it and offering helpful critique and feedback—an even more challenging endeavor! Some of my readers have been with me for many years: A deep and abiding thanks to those who have read for the last fifteen years: My mother Mary Ann Cook, Kim Tapper, and Tom Sweitzer. Thank you to those who have been with me for almost as long, my husband Ryan Bascom, my dear writing group—Lauren Nalls, Anna Carner, Theresa Murphy, Mary Follin, each so talented in their own right, and my early readers Carla O'Brien, Tami Erickson, Tully Satre, Ann Northrup, and Tina Jenkins.

Some of my readers joined my writing career for *The Artist and the Soldier.* Thank you to Beth Meeker, Malissa Cadwallader, Susan Tapper, Leah Lederman, who edited an earlier version of the book, and my editor at Warren Publishing, Amy Trainor Ashby.

Each page is better because of each of you. Thank you for the enduring support and love during this journey.

PART ONE

1938, LONG ISLAND, NEW YORK

CHAPTER 1
CAMP SIEGFRIED

MAX TRUDGED UPWARD behind the rest of the campers, stopping only when the group crested the hill and was lost from sight. He swiped his hand across his forehead and smeared perspiration onto his black shorts. The sig rune insignia, in the shape of two lightning bolts, brushed against his palm. The New York sun bore down on him; his sweat, once only beading here and there, now made a trickling stream from his hairline to his ankles.

At the start of the race, they had been in a line, one by one like good little soldiers. But Max had fallen behind, as he often did in athletic endeavors. No one seemed to notice when he began to trail the group, first by paces, his stride taking him from the front, to the middle, to the back, and then by yards as the pack of boys surged ahead, step by step. He'd never catch up now. The uniformed man with the dark eyes and loud voice made it very clear that every boy must finish the race. He didn't say, "or else," but it was implied in his tone.

Max cursed his father for sending him to this place. He thought he could get away with lolling around the apartment all summer, wishing away the months until school began again—his senior year, finally. But Herr Amsel had been adamant.

"This camp was recommended to me by my colleagues. It will be good for you. It will teach you much needed skills in areas where you … are lacking," his father had insisted.

In Herr Amsel's opinion, his son was lacking in many ways. Max was not athletic, avoided physical confrontation, spent all of his free time watching films, and seemed to have no friends. It didn't help that each time Herr Amsel looked at his son, his own image was not reflected back. Max looked like his Italian mother and not his German father. Was it too much to ask for his only son to be made in his image? Instead, Max, with his black curly hair and olive skin, looked nothing like him. This disturbed the man and he took it out on Max: never allowing him to get too close, avoiding after-dinner conversation, and by looking at him with general disapproval.

"This camp will teach you strong German ways. End of discussion," he'd added.

In Max's case, those words were always final. He was used to his father speaking to him this way. Herr Amsel could not address his wife with this tone, however. He had to be so much gentler with her, such a delicate creature, undone, as she was.

Max glanced behind and saw a handsome boy around his age, walking the path, approaching. Max picked up his pace. It would be better to avoid possible confrontation.

***

The dirt trail was hard under Bastian's aching feet. To hell with running, he'd walk to the finish line—maybe not finish first for a change. When he looked up, he saw a dark-haired boy a few yards ahead. The young man didn't seem to belong at Camp Siegfried. He drifted while the others stomped, was dark and brooding, and wandered alone while the others lined up like cookie-cutter militiamen. Bastian himself looked like all the rest, a perfect German specimen with cropped blonde hair, square shoulders, and a long stride—enough to make any father proud, except his own, of course. The boy faltered, stopping for a moment, seemingly overcome by the dust cloud at his feet. Bastian smoked a cigarette as he approached with his usual saunter.

"Hey kid," Bastian called. He typically reserved the endearing nickname for his baby sister, but the boy looked easily riled and Bastian lived to provoke.

"Kid? I'm your age, looks like," Max answered.

"Oh yeah? How old are you?" He stopped beside Max and gazed down at him.

"Seventeen. How old are you?" Max asked.

"When's your birthday?"

"April fourth." Max took a step back.

"Ha! March twenty-eighth. So, technically I'm older." Bastian held out his half-smoked cigarette, offering it over.

"No thanks," Max said, looking back up the hill.

"You'll never catch them now." Bastian tossed the butt to the ground, stubbed it out with his boot and stuck out his hand. "What's your name? I'm Bastian."

Max shook Bastian's hand and nodded, though he never took his eyes off the hill. "I'm Max. I really should try to find them."

"I'll show you a shortcut," said Bastian. "We can join back up with the group. No one will even know we were missing."

Max was uncomfortable with Bastian's liberal use of the word "we" but decided that joining forces with this stranger might be the best option. If he were kicked out the first day for not finishing the race, his father would never speak to him again.

They moved off the path and into the woods. Long ago fallen leaves from previous winters crunched under their feet. Mosquitos buzzed around their heads and landed on their legs, arms, faces, and necks. The bugs were undiscerning, as long as there was fresh blood to be found.

Neither boy said a word, which was all the same to Bastian. He was happiest in silence, to delve into his own thoughts. His mind was on his aching feet. He'd had to hoof his bags halfway across New York City from his apartment, all the way to Penn Station, to get to Yaphank and finally walk through the gates of this miserable place once more. He didn't have the money to take a cab or train to the main terminal, and he'd left the house in less than ideal circumstances.

The first day of camp was the same every year: a grueling, sweaty, tedious, six-mile race. The boy who won was celebrated for the duration of the eight-week stay; the boy who came in last was chastised until picked up by his parents on the last day. Bastian won every year. This was his fourth summer of hell and by now he knew many of the tricks, most of the adults, and every kid who'd ever been there. This Max who trailed behind him—he was new, fresh.

A light breeze echoed through the woods. Both boys inhaled deeply. It was a gift, this faint wind. Hot sticky days and humid restless nights were not pleasant for anyone, but here at camp, the weather felt like part of the plan instilled by the rigid officers, meant to stiffen the boys' constitutions.

Max watched Bastian ahead of him. His black shorts hung at his hips and he wore no shirt. Where Max was thin and slight, Bastian was strong and well-built. His stomach was taut, defined muscles running up his torso like railroad tracks. He looked like a man instead of a boy. Max imagined the two of them in a movie scene together, trudging up a hill toward battle, Bastian looking like Johnny Weissmuller from the *Tarzan* films, square-jawed and full-lipped. Side by side they'd fight for what was right. In the end, they'd meet the president of the United States and he'd shake their hands.

"How do you know about this shortcut anyway?" Max asked as he lagged further behind, his imagination running.

"This is my fourth year at the camp." Bastian was there the day they hung the Camp Siegfried sign and opened the gates to its first initiates.

"Does your dad make you come?" Max asked.

Bastian turned toward him, stopping mid-step. "My dad is dead. I come because it's something to do and the city is too damn hot in the summer. Even hotter than this hell-hole." It was mostly true, anyway.

"I'm sorry about your father," Max said.

"Don't be." Bastian turned forward and kept walking.

Max scrambled to catch up. "How much farther?"

Bastian pointed to the right, a ways into the woods. "See that dense set of trees over there?"

Max nodded.

"On the other side is the finish line. The group should be close to the end by now."

"So, we'll just blend into the back of the crowd?" Max asked.

"Screw that. Haven't you read the tortoise and the hare?"

Max thought about this before he answered, trying to figure out what Bastian was hinting. The sweat continued to pool in every available dip and crevice of his body. Bastian looked slick with sweat too, but it didn't seem to bother him.

"Yes. The tortoise wins because he keeps going. Slow and steady wins the race," Max said. "I don't think that applies in this case. It's the opposite of what we're doing. The hare loses because he slacks off and falls asleep."

"Exactly. But don't you think the hare should have won?"

"Not really," Max answered.

"But the hare was far stronger and smarter. A mightier breed than the tortoise." Bastian sighed, exasperated, as if talking to a child. "It's just a story, meant to teach a useless lesson. In reality, strength and cunning intellect will always prevail. If you are smart enough to figure out how to cheat, you should—if it means you come out on top."

Max frowned. All his life, he had lost, fair and square. He excelled in his own way, in his own interests, but not in any arena that was considered worthy. Not by his father anyway. What a surprise it would be for Herr Amsel to learn that his son had won something.

Eclipsing a small hill, they were almost past the clearing. They could hear footsteps on the dirt trail in the distance.

Before Max knew what was happening, Bastian grabbed his hand and pulled him onto the path and into the crowd. They wove in and out of runners, gaining speed. With all the jostling and excitement, no one noticed the boys join the race and wrench through. Bastian ran faster, yanking Max behind him. They knitted themselves into the fabric of the determined and exhausted boys until, somehow, they broke free of the pack, pulling ahead. The finish line was in sight.

"Hey! Stop," Max huffed in a whisper, attempting to jerk his arm free. "We can't do this. It's cheating."

Bastian yelled back, his grip strong on Max's arm. "We can and we will. Come on, Max. When was the last time you won a race?"

Max had never won a race.

He raised his head and saw the finish line ten yards ahead; hunger swelled in his eyes. Bastian saw it too and a smile spread over his face. Max thought it made him look wicked. With a surge of energy, Max propelled himself forward to meet Bastian's stride. Sweat dripped down their faces and their feet pounded the dirt path. Clouds of dust billowed from every footfall. The boys looked at each other. Together they ran, shoulders forward, the rest of the runners now on their heels.

Never had Max been so close to winning something. Never had Bastian shown another camper his shortcut.

With one final swell of energy, they launched themselves across the finish line; Bastian's hand once again found Max's, giving it a tight, hard squeeze, and— just as fast—let it fall.

Within seconds, the rest of the boys had joined them, drenched and huffing. A few of the runners, upset about losing, plodded forward, whispering and not looking back. Those who knew Bastian slapped him on the back and cheered for him. He grabbed Max's hand again and thrust it into the air. Max's heart flapped in his chest, a terrified bird confused by its newfound freedom.

Max looked around. His triumph, however undermined by the cheating, glimmered in front of him. Older boys, bigger boys, cheered for him, reached out to touch him, just to get a piece of the glory. He closed his eyes and thrust his arms higher into the air, yelping in delight.

Bastian had helped Max do something he'd never thought he'd do.

Win.

***

The shrill screech of a whistle startled Bastian awake. Moonlight streamed in through the cabin windows. All around him, boys sat up groggily. Hans Mandel, last year a camper and now a superior, wore a smug expression as he blasted the whistle into the boys' ears and woke them from their sweat-soaked slumber. Bastian watched, holding himself up in bed on his elbows, as Hans paced the room. The young man wore a self-righteous grin that Bastian swore he would have him eating before the end of camp. The last three years, Hans and Bastian had marched in the same lines, raised the same flags. Now, Hans had graduated from the camp and thought he had earned the right to boss everyone around.

All over the room, boys scrambled from their beds, throwing T-shirts they'd tossed to the floor only hours before over their half-naked bodies. It was obvious who'd been through this before and who was afraid of the barking superiors. Those who were new this year looked terrified. Bastian scanned the room until he found his new friend, Max, looking panicked. He flashed a smile at Max and winked at him.

Hans appeared at Bastian's bedside. He kicked at the thin, unstable frame, pulling Bastian's attention away from Max.

"Up, Bastian. Don't want to have to make an example out of you."

"Wouldn't want you to have to do that," Bastian answered. He dragged his feet from the bed to the floor.

Those who'd been in camp last year pulled out dress uniforms from their trunks. Starched white shirts filled the room. The newbies took notice and mimicked the action. Bastian saw Max give him a nervous glance. Bastian picked his shirt out and stretched a sleeve over each arm while the rest of the room fell into order, the boys lining up for Hans without being asked. Bastian told himself this was the last year he'd be coming to Camp Siegfried. Screw all of the "good, like-minded German people," as his father called them. Screw politics and The Depression. He was going to make something of himself.

Bastian wanted a cigarette, but had smoked his last one before bed. If he'd thought ahead, he would have raided his mother's stash before packing his bag. But he hadn't really planned to come back this year, had he? In the end, he would have done anything to escape that house. He only regretted leaving his younger sister again for the full summer. She'd always been able to take care of herself, though. It was better for him to be out of the house, away, where he could not incite anyone's anger.

Bastian glanced up and found himself face to face with Hans. Why they'd given this shithead a position as a supervisor he didn't know. Bastian was smarter, faster, more shrewd and still, no one had asked him to join the ranks.

Hans leaned into him. "Come on, man. You're making me look bad. Get your shit together and fall in line."

Bastian smirked.

When Hans received no response, he said quietly, "Okay, asshole, what will it cost me?"

"Three packs of cigarettes."

"You know I can't get my hands on that many."

Bastian began to fall backward, into his bed.

Hans grabbed his arm. "Okay. I can get you two. Deal?"

Bastian nodded and finished dressing, pulling on his heavy boots and straightening his tie. He palmed a coin, his lucky penny, from under his mattress and slipped it into his pocket. Instead of heading to the back of the line, he found Max and shoved his way between him and another boy. Max wouldn't look at him.

"The wind is good tonight, boys," Hans said. "It's time to raise the flags."

A slow murmur spread through the crowd, chests exhaled and shoulders dropped down to normal heights. The raising of the flag was a tradition that occurred on the first windy night. In this case, it was also the first night of camp.

They marched, single-file, into the humid evening. Bats swooped over their heads, and Max saw some of the younger boys ducking away from them. Behind him he could feel Bastian's body pressed lightly against his own. Max's heartbeat pulsed through his body, his wrists, his neck, his gut, pulling him backward against Bastian, but he quickly recovered himself.

As Max marched, he thought of his mother, Francesca. She had said nothing, nothing at all in the year of "Hitler this and Hitler that." While his father seemed to be living one reality, his mother lived a different one, totally separate from father and son and often separate from the world at large. *My demons*, she'd say on the days when she couldn't get out of bed. *They've taken over again.* She'd shove four pills into her mouth on those days, the bad days. Only two pills were necessary to get through the others.

Hans's shrill whistle sounded again, lasting longer outside as it echoed against the trees. The farther they marched into the woods, the denser the darkness. Max was afraid he would trip and fall, so he stayed close to the boy in front of him as Bastian stayed even closer behind.

"Pick those boots up, boys. This is a march," Hans yelled.

Why were they marching again? For a flag? The more Max learned about the camp, the less he believed he would last the full eight weeks. Two months of night marches, getting little sleep in a muggy room with boys who smelled far worse than he. Day after day of physical competition and exertion. Could the whole camp really be this excruciating?

And what of this Bastian character—what did he want from Max? Based on what he'd seen of the other campers, Max did not fit in. Maybe Bastian was setting him up for a joke—pretend to be his friend and then, when the opportunity arose, humiliate him. Things like that happened all the time at Max's prep school. High school was a delicate hierarchy, and this camp would be no different.

A few paces in front of them, the trees fell away to reveal a clearing. The open sky, full of thousands of stars, beamed above them, lighting up the field. Max smiled and reveled in the beauty, despite the marching boys surrounding him. In the city, it was hard to find a night with so many visible stars. He drew his face upward and closed his eyes to see if the starlight reflected in his vision behind his eyelids. Another piercing whistle and an abrupt stop brought Max almost tumbling to the ground. A hand gripped his elbow and he turned to see Bastian. Somehow, he was always there when Max needed him.

They'd stopped at the edge of the clearing. Ahead of them, in the center of the field, was a tall flagpole. A weak fire burned in a pit to the left.

A group of men stood in a semi-circle around the pole. Bastian knew all but one of them. Last year they'd brought in a special guest for the raising of the flag. It upped the intensity of the ceremony and helped spread the word about the camp; bring some hotshot officer over from Germany to impress the boys who told their fathers, who, in turn, were equally impressed.

Hans led the group forward once more, their knees reaching waist height as they marched. When they stopped, he yelled a command; like geese they fell into formation, a semi-circle mimicking the adults. Those who didn't know what was happening caught on soon enough. The boys faced the men. When the officer in the middle of the pack that Bastian didn't know, made a motion with his arm—from his chest to the air, each man and boy mimicked the gesture in turn.

"Gentleman, I am Fritz Kuhn." A quiet murmur spread through the crowd and Kuhn was pleased so many of the boys recognized his name. It meant their fathers were acting as they should, educating their children about important figures in their movement. "As many of you must know, it is a special treat that I am here tonight. Though I am very busy, I've heard of the good work being done at Camp Siegfried the last few years. This is one of our largest youth Bund camps and you should feel honored to have the opportunity to be here at this momentous time in history." He paused and the man beside him leaned forward and whispered in his ear. Kuhn addressed the crowd, his voice booming in the open field. "Ich bitte Maxwell Amsel und Bastian Fischer, sich zu melden."

Max and Bastian looked at one another. Both spoke enough German to understand what was being said, Herr Kuhn had told them to step forward. Fear flashed in Max's eyes as the crowd around them erupted into a soft murmur. Both boys did as they were told, Max with trepidation in his step. They joined together in front of Herr Kuhn. Max wanted to ask Bastian what was happening. Bastian looked calm and collected; a slight smirk danced at the edge of his mouth.

"I am told the two of you tied in this afternoon's race. Is this true?"

Bastian spoke first. "Yes, sir," he said in a crisp voice Max had not heard him use before.

"And how did it happen that you *both* won?" Herr Kuhn asked.

"Neither of us pulled ahead of the other, sir" Bastian answered.

"Not even a step?"

"No, sir," Bastian said.

The man looked at Max, who could not swallow. His throat felt unbearably dry, as if he would die of dehydration before anyone spoke another word. They knew. Max and Bastian had cheated and they knew and now they were going to make an example of them. His father ... what would his father say ... what would he do?

There was an almost imperceptible nod of the head from Bastian. Max took a shallow breath, forced himself to speak. "No, sir," he said in agreement. Max wondered if too much time had passed; he didn't know if his answer was still relevant. "No, sir," he said again, "not even a step."

A smile appeared on Herr Kuhn's face. "Teamwork. It was how we Germans captured the most medals in the '36 Olympics. It was how you won the race today. Congratulations."

Kuhn shook each of their hands. Somewhere in the crowd, a bright flash and pop of a camera went off, capturing the moment in the star-lit field.

"To honor your victory," Herr Kuhn said, raising his voice against the excited murmur, "the two of you shall lift our flags!"

Max and Bastian were each handed a pile of heavy fabric and led to the pole. The men and boys made a wide circle around them. Dozens of eyes set upon the two boys. Max was thankful his shaking hands were buried under the heavy load. Herr Kuhn looked on with a satisfied smile.

"Just do what I do," Bastian whispered to Max.

He folded the flag over his arm so the metal grommets were accessible. Max did the same. In a fluid motion, Bastian attached one end of his flag to a fastening on the halyard. Max fumbled, almost dropping his prize. He saw Herr Kuhn lurch forward then stay himself as Max regained his grip. He tried to mimic Bastian, but it was a struggle to get the grommet inside the hook, as both parts were rusted. He jabbed himself in the palm and saw blood well up instantly. Max felt his body waver as the blood pooled in his hand and dripped over his fingers. He hated blood. He glanced up, his face white as the starched sheets the maid brought. Everyone was staring at him, including Bastian whose own flag was prepped and ready to be raised.

"Sir?" Bastian said in question to Herr Kuhn.

The man nodded.

Bastian went to Max, took the other end of his flag and fit the hook inside the grommet. Buoyed by this action, Max tore his eyes from the blood and repeated the step. This time it slid in. Max realized he'd been holding his breath and let out a sigh, relief filling his chest. The color began to return to his cheeks and once again he felt steady on his feet. Bastian returned to his own flag. He ran the lines between his fingers and the flag began to rise. Max did the same, thin smears of blood speckled the white rope with each pull. Soon it waved above his head, its red background seemed to catch fire in the starlight, burning into the night sky. The red matched the burnt flush of his cheeks while the black swastika blazed against the white circle.

The flag that flapped gently in the wind on Bastian's side was the grand old stars and stripes. Max wondered if they'd given him the Nazi flag intentionally. He was the new kid. Were they testing his allegiance? He didn't know. Though it was not the time to bring his feelings on Nazism to anyone's attention, Max felt a burning rage inside. He'd avoided the talk in his household when he could. But when he was made to sit for dinner with his parents and his father's colleagues, his mother drinking, eyes almost closed, he had to pinch himself under the table to stop from objecting to the disgusting conversation. It was as if the men at the table were born without morals, without empathy. To hate one race of people so completely, it defied all logical thinking, felt more dangerous to Max than being lost in the wilderness.

During those dinners, he'd felt like he was lost, the cruel jokes and retold stories forming thick stands of trees around him; the meanness of the men's words flung like a lion's claw inches from his face. Max had said nothing at the table, just as now, the fire hot against his skin, he would say nothing.

Herr Kuhn turned to Max and Bastian, bringing his right arm into the air and giving a "Sieg Heil" first to the boys and then to the group. Arms were thrust forward on all sides, then the song began.

The world seemed to slow. Max felt like he was in a movie. At home, he often pretended he was in a film, either as the star actor or sometimes the director. Each imagining was like a dream. But this, this was a nightmare. All around him the voices swelled in the night, singing Hitler's national anthem. Everyone seemed to know the words, even in German. And everyone appeared to be staring at him, as if they knew his secret: he was not meant to be here.

He was not one of them.

CHAPTER 2

MAX SLEPT IN FITS and spurts that night. When his body allowed him to drift off, images pierced his dreams: the flag being raised, the pooled blood on his hand, the firelight catching in the men's eyes.

Waking the next morning, the first thing he felt was throbbing in his palm. On either side of him boys slept, sheets kicked to the side, their legs sticking together. The room was thick with sweat and body odor. His own body was beginning to stink and he hoped there would be time to shower today.

Max sat up. His breath felt sharp when he thought of Herr Kuhn, the way the officer looked at him as if he were an impostor.

Max *was* an impostor.

He stood and dressed quietly, not wanting to wake the other boys. Across the room, Bastian lay wrapped up in himself, his limbs looking too big for his body. Lying there, he was like the other boys, golden skinned and muscular.

Next to Max was a narrow table with camp brochures spread across it. The officers wanted the campers to take them and distribute them to friends when they returned home. He opened one and read. *Send your boy to learn how to camp, hunt, shoot, and learn his place in the order of the world. He will be taught the same ideologies you are teaching him at home. He will meet people who think like you.* There was a photo of shirtless boys, smiling, with their arms thrown around one another's shoulders, the Nazi flag waving in the background. Max tossed it back onto the table with disgust.

His stomach churned from hunger. He tiptoed through the room. The door creaked when it opened and soft early morning light streamed in, but he didn't bother to look back to see if anyone awoke.

The air was cooler than it'd been in the cabin. Less stagnant. By noon the sun would bear down on them as if it were burning out. In front of him loomed the oversized clubhouse, adorned with a Nazi flag and an American flag, both fixed securely between windows. He'd seen the men in uniforms gather there last night, before the campers had gone to bed, before the nightmare flag raising had taken place and Max realized just how much trouble he may be in. People from town had joined the officers, drinking pint after pint of beer and talking loudly. Their words carried from one table to another in the light breeze that wove through the place as Max and a few other boys huddled together at their own table, playing chess.

Max thought of his father, who had dropped him off only yesterday. Herr Amsel greeted each of the officers while Max stood nervously by the car until his father commanded him to grab his bag and line up for registration with the other boys. His mother had not joined them on the journey from Manhattan to Yaphank. When Max left her, she was in their living room, listening to a record and smoking a cigarette. Her gaze was fixed to a far-off place only real in her mind. It may have been a four-pill day. On those days, she didn't even acknowledge him.

"I'm leaving now, Mother," Max said, wishing beyond measure she'd snap out of her trance and ask him to stay. To say, *No, darling, you can't leave your mother. You must stay with me and keep me company*. But she only offered up her cheek for him to kiss, never putting her cigarette down, never changing her gaze.

"Have fun, darling," she'd said and Max didn't know if she even realized he would be gone for eight weeks. Perhaps she thought he was just going out to a movie? She knew how much he enjoyed those. He was always asking for extra pocket money to go see the talkies.

***

Max heard voices from the clubhouse and slowed his step. Some of the uniformed men were already sitting at the tables. He kept his head down, fearing interaction with anyone, but when he approached, no one bothered to look up. He moved inside, a fly following him in and buzzing by his ear until he swatted it away.

In front of him was a long serving table with an older woman behind an oversized pot. The bottom had char marks from years of use on an open flame. The woman did not smile, and barely acknowledged Max at all. If it weren't for the bowl of porridge she handed him, he'd have questioned whether she'd seen him.

"Morning," he said.

She grunted at him and he left.

To get to his seat, Max had to pass by the men. Some were standing, talking, and smoking. Others sat and ate. This time when Max sat, leaving as much space between himself and the group as he thought appropriate, he felt noticed. When he looked up, one of the older men was pointing at him. The man spoke in a thick German accent.

"You were one of the boys from the race?"

Damn Bastian. What had he gotten Max *into* by winning that thing? He gulped and tried to answer, but the words stayed inside. So, he nodded his head in affirmation. The man stood and came closer. Max drew his body back, a natural reaction. The man didn't seem to notice and leaned over Max to pat his shoulder.

"Good job, young man. Is this your first year?"

Max regained his speech. "Yes, sir."

"And your father, he is a good German man who understands our mission, yes?"

"Yes, sir," he answered again.

"Good, good. He will be very proud of you for winning, yes? You must write him a letter. Do it after breakfast and I will be sure he receives this news."

Max's silent nod was enough to satisfy the officer, who went back to his group, sitting down heavily enough that Max's body bounced on the bench. As he ate, he heard bits of the men's conversation.

"Kuhn is only staying on until lunch. He wants to observe and then must move on."

"How many Bund camps is he visiting?"

"As many as he can in the coming weeks. All of the ones near here, certainly."

Max had heard the name Kuhn before last night but could not place where. He was someone important, that much he understood.

Several of the men laughed and Max trained his ears again, eating a bite of the tasteless porridge.

"You mean Franklin *Rosenfeld*? Him and his dirty Jew deal. We have come just in time to help stop this nonsense." The men were all nodding. Max found himself staring openly. Were they talking about the president? He couldn't imagine his parents speaking of their country's leader in that way.

One of the men caught him gaping and said, "Don't worry, son, win some more races and they will give you eggs too."

Max realized the officer was talking about the men's breakfast, which looked far heartier and well-rounded than his bowl of mush. They had heaps of eggs, bacon, and sausage; it was more than they would be able to eat. Before Max could respond, Bastian plopped onto a bench across from him.

"Morning," Bastian said, a yawn in the back of his throat.

"Morning," Max answered.

"How's the hand?"

He touched his palm instinctively. "It's all right."

"When we go to the cabin to change into our dress whites, I'll show you where the first aid kit is kept."

"Why do we have to change?"

"Rifle practice." Bastian said. "If you bleed, they want to be able to see it on you." He smirked at Max's white-faced stare. "Kidding. Kidding. It's their same old ceremony shit. First time you shoot, they want you in your dress uniform. Who the hell knows why, really."

Max's face was still drained of color. Bastian gave him one swift pat on the hand. He supposed the kid had never shot a gun. Bastian's father had given him his first rifle when he turned twelve. *Every boy must learn how to shoot to become a man,* he'd said. Target practice was something Bastian excelled at; he never missed a shot.

Hans had shown up for breakfast and was chatting with the other camp leaders. "Shithead," Bastian said, only half under his breath. Hans looked up and strolled over to them.

"Well, well, well. If it isn't the two musketeers."

Bastian wanted to say, *it's the three musketeers, you illiterate dumb shit.* But he held his tongue. Though last year they were camp mates, Hans was now a superior and in front of the other adults, Bastian had to treat him with respect, veiled as it was.

Max stared at Hans. "Yes, sir. Good morning," he finally stammered.

Bastian puffed out his cheeks but said nothing.

"And how do we greet a superior, Bastian?" Hans asked with a slick smile.

The other men looked at the trio, silent. Bastian knew what he must do. "Good morning, Herr Mandel. I hope you slept well."

"Oh, very well, thank you for asking. You don't happen to have a smoke, do you?"

It was clear Hans had no intention of following through on his bargain with Bastian from the previous evening. He wasn't going to get him those cigarettes.

"No, sir. Sorry." Bastian answered, tight lipped.

Hans smiled in a way Max did not understand, tipped his head to the other uniformed men, and left.

Bastian swore under his breath. "Let's go, Max. I want to be there first."

Max looked down at his half-eaten breakfast, still hungry. He gave in. They cleaned up their bowls and headed for the cabin. When they entered, most of the others were dressed in their uniforms, somehow, just like Bastian, knowing what was coming next. Each nodded his head at Bastian and Max in turn. Max liked the acknowledgment, liked that people noticed he was there. He pulled his clothes from a trunk in front of his bed and changed while the other boys filed out for breakfast. The room was quiet and then Bastian was behind him, his hot breath on Max's neck. Max was still, his own breath caught high in his chest, a choke.

"What are you doing?" Max asked him.

"Nothing." Bastian took one step back. Something in his gut, just below his bellybutton had pulled him forward to Max. "Are you ready? I want to pick out a good gun."

Bastian took another step back so Max was able to turn around without stepping on him. They exchanged a glance and set off into the woods, using the same path they'd taken on their night march. The mosquitoes were out in full force, armies of them swarming.

When they reached the clearing, they saw six or so uniformed men, already near the rifles, chatting. One of the men was Hans Mandel. Bastian's face tightened. He led Max to where the men stood and picked out a Winchester .22 for each of them. Both rifles looked new; the barrels glinted in the sunlight. An officer handed them each a small box of bullets.

Bastian swung his rifle over his shoulder. Max copied him, glad he had someone to mimic while handling a weapon for the first time. The gun was heavier than he'd expected. Max adjusted and readjusted, attempting to make the firearm comfortable against his body. Across the arena, a seemingly impossible distance away, stood targets.

Max looked nervously to Bastian as they walked through the field. "We're supposed to be able to shoot that distance?"

"It's easier than it looks. Trust me." Bastian flashed Max a smile and then jogged the last twenty yards until he reached the middle of the range. Bastian got down onto his belly and Max followed his lead. They both leveled the Winchester .22s, the barrels long, the dark marbled stock against their shoulders, and looked into the sights. Max knew there was no way he'd reach the target. He'd never been good at sports, or anything that required coordination or aim. What if he accidentally shot someone?

Beside him, Bastian was at ease. He leveled and re-leveled the gun, looking through the sight. Then he pulled out his case of bullets and loaded the weapon. His finger rested on the trigger.

Footsteps sounded in the grass behind them. Max turned to see who it was as Bastian's gun went off. Max's body jerked against Bastian in surprise; their shoulders bounced into one another. For a moment, he heard nothing but a ringing in his ears. Bastian swore and jumped to his feet. He was face to face with Hans.

"Why did you do that?" Bastian said in a heated whisper.

"No idea what you're talking about," Hans answered.

"Bullshit," Bastian raised his voice and the other officers looked over at them. A couple took tentative steps toward the boys. They stopped when Hans put his hand up. "You kicked my foot just as I was taking aim," Bastian said.

Max didn't understand why Bastian's face was so red, why he was so angry, until he looked around and saw the other boys had joined them in the field and were chiding and pointing at Bastian for his missed shot.

"Boys," Hans said, addressing them all. "Do you think maybe Bastian has lost his faithful aim?"

The boys nodded, not meeting each other's eyes. Hans and Bastian were two powerful forces and no one knew whose side to be on. From the ground, Max tugged at Bastian's pant leg, willing him back. Bastian obeyed, lying on the ground again.

Hans sauntered away. While the boys gathered their rifles, he came to rest against a fence several yards from everyone else. Hans knew he was testing his new power, but he did not care. That asshole Bastian had humiliated him more than once in the years they were in camp together. This year it would be different. This year, Hans had the power to get even. He grinned and waved at Bastian to taunt him.

Once everyone joined Max and Bastian, clambering to the ground, Bastian took sight at a target. If Max had noticed his friend's gun was not pointed in the same direction as everyone else's, he would have stopped him. Again, Bastian's rifle went off; again, Max's ears rang. This time, though, there was a splintering sound and a yelp of pain.

All eyes were drawn to Hans, standing near the broken fence, to the left of the target field. Blood trickled from his forehead down his cheek. Bastian's bullet had blown apart the fence, and splinters of it struck Hans on the face and arm. Hans licked the blood from his mouth as he waved the officers away who raced to his side. "I'm fine," the boys heard him say. "Bad aim is all."

Max stared at Bastian, open mouthed.

Bastian stood and said so everyone could hear, "There must be something wrong with this gun. That's the second time my aim was off." He looked at Max who was a pale shade of gray and gave him a quick smile.

Under his breath he added, "Oh, stop it, Max. The fence barely grazed him. Now he'll know how good my aim is for next time."

CHAPTER 3

THE BOYS RAN TOWARD THE LAKE, Bastian surging to the front of the pack. The rest fell back; no one could match his stride. It had been a week since he'd shot at Hans and they either admired him or feared him. Either way, most were keeping their distance.

Bastian catapulted from the dock into the lake, beads of sweat flung away from his body. When he crashed into the water, the cold lake engulfed him in a way that brought him comfort; to be so encased felt safe. All around him the other boys dove, cannonballed, or tentatively dipped one foot at a time until a friend pushed them in.

Bastian wanted a cigarette so badly and cursed himself for smoking the last one from the pack he'd stolen. The kid he'd taken them from hadn't even noticed. When he found the stash, he counted at least ten packs. He figured the boy must have stolen them from someone else so it was fair game. But now he was out, and wasn't sure if he could get away with pilfering another pack. Of course, enough of the boys were afraid of him now he could probably just ask and they'd hand them over.

Bastian dunked his head under once more and looked for Max. There he was, fully dressed, making his way at a snail's pace to the water's edge. The other boys had thrown off shirts and shorts as they ran toward the lake, or stepped out of them with ease before plunging in. Bastian himself hadn't even bothered to dress, donning only his Jockeys as he ran from the cabin to the water. He watched Max sit at the edge and remove his shirt, fold it, set it aside. More than a week in, the kid still looked bewildered to be there, as if he didn't know how he'd gotten to camp. Bastian decided it was Max's innocence that reminded him of his sister, Ilsa. Despite all they had been through together, she still believed in the good in people. Bastian didn't know why, but he suspected Max was the same way.

Bastian had left his house the week before in deep bellowing anger. He didn't want to come back to camp and had told his family as much. There wasn't a choice, though; he had nowhere else to go. He'd tousled his sister's hair as he ran out, one single bag shoved under his arm.

"Be good, kid. I love you. I'll see you when I can."

***

Bastian eased onto his back, floating, then swimming. With his fingers, he traced the faint, long, thin scar running up his right side. The mark was a consequence of the first time his father used a belt on him. Perhaps Herr Fisher didn't realize the belt would cause more damage than his hand, though Bastian tended to think the man had known exactly what he was doing. Still, the blood that trickled down his son's stomach had given him pause. He'd withdrawn from the room, leaving Bastian to cower. It made Bastian wish the man drew blood each time. Maybe it would shorten the beatings.

He flipped onto his stomach and dove under. The water filled his ears with a comforting, rushing rage.

It reflected the chaos he always carried inside himself. Bastian swam deeper, trying to reach the bottom. It was too far down. If he kept going, he may drown. *Not the worst thing,* he thought. When he rose to the surface, he spotted Max across the way. Something stirred in him, making him dive under again, trying to reach the bottom a second time.

Max looked around, uneasy about getting into the water with the other boys. He left his shorts on and stayed at the edge. Maybe no one would notice him. Bastian had been the first one in, Max saw, and was now doing backstrokes wearing only his underwear. He watched as Bastian's strong, sinewy legs kicked in rhythm with the stroke of his arms. Max thought he looked beautiful in the water; graceful yet somehow dangerous, a merman, a movie star.

The little bit of fame Max had enjoyed after his win faded by the week's end. Bastian was all they talked about now. That shot had been amazing. It made the boys fear him. It made Max fear him. He waited for Bastian to quit paying attention to him, but each morning they had breakfast together, they walked together, had even begun to share pieces of themselves. Pieces Max had guarded closely; like his mother's decline into madness and his father's ignorance of what was important to his son. Max didn't talk about his family with anyone at school. Telling Bastian about his parents made Max's home life feel truer, as if speaking it aloud concretized it into reality.

Bastian had shared with Max that he had a little sister, and he felt like it was his duty to protect her. Protect from whom, Max was not sure. Perhaps more pressing, he still had no idea where Bastian stood on the topic of Nazi ideology. They didn't talk about it, though it pressed in around them—the uniforms, the propaganda brochures, the anti-Jewish rhetoric that was not whispered. He was afraid Bastian agreed with Hitler's dogma. Where would that leave the pair?

Max slid into the water, the cold shocking his limbs. There was an area to the far right where some boys were talking quietly to one another, and Max swam over, figuring it would be his best chance to be part of the group without having to interact. When he arrived, they nodded their heads and grunted, but ignored him otherwise. He dunked his head under and wished for a comb to tidy his hair back into place. Max took comfort in cleanliness and appearances. They were things he could control: how he dressed, how he wore his clothes, how he carried himself.

A small pack of boys joined their group, shouting and pushing, rough housing with one another. One boy dunked another's head under the water until Max was sure he meant to drown him. The boy resurfaced sputtering and slapping at his assailant in a playful way. It made Max's stomach turn. What if he was next? As if reading his thoughts, the group looked his way.

"Hey kid," one said.

Max hated that everyone called him 'kid.' "Yes?" he said.

"You're the one who won the race with Bastian, right?"

"Yes."

The boy was sneering. "How'd you manage that?"

Max shrugged his shoulders. "I ran, I guess."

The boy swam closer to Max and the pack took the cue, coming closer in turn. "Doesn't look like you'd be a very good runner. Doesn't even look like you're

German." He turned to look at his friends. "You know, boys, I think we have a dirty Jew in our presence. Yeah, I think he's snuck into our camp and is taking intelligence on all of us."

"Is that true, you dirty Jew?" another said.

Max looked at them, confused by the onslaught. What had he done to stand out?

The boys moved in closer, and a few others swam over to see what all the fuss was about.

"This kid doesn't look German at all," one said, addressing the crowd that was forming.

They eased closer to him. Somebody spat at him, the saliva landing and bubbling in the water close to Max.

"Come on you dirty Jew, give it up." This boy was two heads taller than Max and used his height to dominate him. He shoved Max deep into the lake so that water streamed into his nose. Max pulled himself out, choking. The boy was reaching for him again when they heard a voice in the distance.

The crowd cleared and Bastian swam through until he was treading water beside Max, who looked gray. Bastian's heart raced. Conflict exhilarated him.

"Who's picking on my friend?" He moved toward the boy who'd pushed Max under. "You. What's your name? Why haven't I seen you before?"

"It's Klaus," he answered, steadying his voice. "I'm new this year."

"And what gives you the right to pick on *my* friend, newbie?" Bastian bore his teeth like an animal about to pounce.

Klaus looked around. All of his friends were abandoning him; one by one they each inched back from Bastian or swam away.

He was practically on top of Klaus when he said, "You've seen me shoot, right?"

Klaus nodded.

"Well, if you don't want my gun trained on you, I'd better not see you near him again, unless you're paying him a compliment about his fine German features. His last name is *Amsel*, asshole. When was the last time you met a Jew named Amsel?"

Max watched all of this, hoping that if he didn't move, they'd forget he was there. Bastian had stepped in to save him once again. While the boys swam away in opposite directions, Max made his way to the steep ledge and lifted himself from the water. He was still out of breath. Moments later, Bastian joined him, using his long arms to pull himself from the lake.

"You didn't have to do that," Max mumbled.

Bastian didn't say anything.

"Okay, maybe you did. Thanks, I guess."

"You're welcome, I guess," he answered.

"Why did they think I was Jewish?"

"Oh, I don't know. Dark hair, darker complexion. You don't look German, that's for sure. I just figured you took after your mother who is …?"

Max looked up. "She's Italian."

"Oh, well that's okay." Bastian looked to the water, where all the boys were swimming to the dock and pulling themselves out.

"You cleared out the whole lake, huh?" asked Max with a nod toward the water.

"Nah," Bastian said inhaling sharply and coughing. "It's time for our next sport, kid."

"What's that? And can you stop calling me kid?"

"Okay. It's time for our next sport, *Max*," Bastian corrected.

"More shooting?" His stomach gave another lurch. He'd been terrible at target practice. If he were to redeem himself it would not be there.

"No, even better. Boxing."

Max didn't think he could feel more terrified, but there he was.

They collected their clothes, Max's at the water's edge and Bastian's from the cabin. Max took the opportunity to change out of his wet bottoms.

"Should I wear white again?" Max asked, attempting a joke. "So they can see the blood?"

Bastian's face was serious. "No, that shit will never wash out of your dress whites."

***

They were in another clearing, this one consisting of five small boxing rings made of dirt and one large ring of sand. The boys surrounded the biggest circle, most wearing only their black sig rune shorts, while the rules were explained. Some of the boys were smaller and thin like Max, but most were built more like Bastian, thick shouldered and tall. The fights would take place in the smaller rings first and each winner would fight another winner until one was championed. Each match only lasted three minutes and the person who came out still standing—or, if both were standing, was better off— was the winner. Max hoped he would not be beaten too badly in the first fight, but badly enough he would not have to move on.

The rings around him filled and the boys jostled one another. They were having more fun and landing fewer punches than Max expected. Perhaps this part would not be so bad. The two officers who had explained the rules walked away together, bored by the lack of blood after three rounds. They handed their stopwatches over to a couple of the older boys to keep time.

Bastian joined a ring with another boy around his size. They bounced from foot to foot, throwing a few punches. When there were fifteen seconds left, Bastian punched the boy in the nose, causing it to bloody and knowing it would be enough to move him on. The crowd cheered. They stepped out of the ring and someone threw Bastian's hand into the air in victory. Max felt like he would vomit. What would happen if he were placed in the ring with Bastian?

Bastian winked at Max. He was laughing, enjoying himself.

At the far end of the field, a man in uniform walked toward them. When he was closer, Bastian saw that it was Hans. He was smiling in a sick sort of way, as if he knew something they didn't.

"Doing a little boxing, boys?" he asked, addressing no one in particular. Hans moved toward Bastian. The boy who'd been holding his arm up in victory let it drop and stepped away. The three stitches on Hans's forehead were almost healed, but the incident at the fence would leave a scar.

Instead of stopping in front of Bastian, Hans moved forward into the big sand ring. He gestured to Bastian, welcoming him into the pit. They locked into a dead stare while the other boys shot cautious glances at one another.

"Come on, Bastian," Hans said. "Don't I get a chance to get back at you for the cheap shot?"

"I don't know what you're talking about," Bastian said in a quiet voice. He stood stiffly, not looking at Hans.

Max didn't understand why Bastian didn't just fight him. He was bigger than Hans and far stronger. Hans was built more like himself, not quite grown. Max looked at Bastian in question and then watched him step into the ring. All around them voices and gasps exploded like tiny firecrackers through the crowd.

"What? What is happening?" Max asked the young man next to him.

"Don't you know?"

"Know what?" asked Max.

"Bastian can't fight him," the young man explained. "We're not allowed to fight a superior unless we want to get kicked out. Technically, officers aren't allowed to challenge campers, but sometimes it happens anyway."

"So, he gets kicked out. What's the big deal?" Max asked, wishing he could be booted himself.

"You don't know anything about Bastian, do you? If he got kicked out—that would be the end of him," the boy said, shaking his head.

Before Max could ask another question, Hans took his first swing. Bastian's arms stayed limp at his side. Max wove his fingers together, prayer like, and felt his pulse beat steady against his palms. He closed his eyes and when he opened them again, Bastian was looking at him and smiling, a small trail of blood already dripping from his nose.

Bastian turned his attention back to the ring and smiled instead at Hans. It infuriated Hans and he swung again, this time striking Bastian in the eye.

"Come on, Herr Mandel. You can do better than that," Bastian taunted.

Hans hit him again, harder this time, and Bastian's lip split open. The blood swelled and dripped onto the sand, congealing the tiny particles and creating a lump. The pain was blinding, but Bastian forced a smile, knowing what infuriated Hans the most—the impression that his beating was doing nothing. With each punch, Bastian heard the crowd suck in their breath in unison. He knew some of them had never liked him and were enjoying the show, and that made him smile all the more.

Bastian had learned to take a beating from his father, a connoisseur of the belt. He knew which belts cut and stung the most, a lesson Herr Fischer had been taught by his own father. Bastian carried the beatings on his skin, day to day, as the scars faded but did not disappear. To take a beating was nothing. Early on, he'd found smiling angered his father and took some of the joy out of the act for him. And smiling reminded Bastian that eventually it would be over and he would be on his own again, in his room, safe.

A kick to the stomach brought Bastian to the ground. He crouched on all fours like a dog and took two more kicks, the first to his abdomen and the second to his side. He waited for the next, hoping it would finish him so he could be done with the show.

A pair of shoes appeared in his vision, but they did not belong to Hans. He heard a voice, familiar, but it sounded like it was coming through a thick fog.

"Stop it," Max screamed, protecting Bastian's body with his own.

"So, you'd like a beating too?" Hans said. His face was slick with sweat and he was enjoying himself more than he thought possible. He was exorcising every aggression that'd built up over the years against the young man, against the population at large.

"I just want you to stop," Max repeated.

"I'll make you a deal. I get to take three shots at you and then I'll be done with him."

Bastian gripped onto Max to pull himself up. His body was covered in blood and cuts; his right eye was half-closed so he had only partial vision.

"Max, go. This is not your fight," he managed to say.

Max stepped in front of him again, not even covering half of Bastian's body with his thin limbs. He spoke to Hans through clenched teeth. "Take your three shots."

"No," Bastian half-whimpered behind him. He was clutching his side. Trying to concentrate on something other than the pain.

The first swing hit Max so hard, he stumbled backwards into Bastian, who fell back to the ground with a groan.

"Stand up!" Hans yelled, his voice echoing through the field. "I still have two more to go."

Max managed to get to his feet, only to be knocked off them again with a blow to his jaw. His molars loosened in his mouth and his body slammed against the sand. He looked over to Bastian who had succumbed to the pain and passed out. Max was aware of the crowd of boys knitted around them, covering them in a blanket of shadow. No one spoke.

Max rolled over onto his side. "Bastian," he said, hoping he would wake up. Trusting when this was over, his friend would be okay.

In the distance, he heard the pounding of boots running—other officers coming too late. Max said Bastian's name once more before the final blow came.

The kick landed so hard on Max's face that there was a flash of hot, bright white light before he passed out and there was nothing.

CHAPTER 4

WHEN BASTIAN AWOKE, it was with throbbing slowness, knowing that as his body fully came to life, the pain would light up each curve of it. He lay in the dark at the camp infirmary and touched his body, feeling around for bumps and bruises. He had a vague recollection that he'd been there for several days and they were keeping him sedated. He recalled moments of feverish pain, followed by needles piercing his skin, then darkness. They were probably keeping him knocked out to avoid getting into trouble with his parents. *If they only knew.* No one was supposed to come to real harm at the camp. It was designed to toughen them up, not kill them.

He continued to explore his injuries. Both of his eyes could open, but the right was still swollen. Bruises covered his face. His nose was bumpy, like a crooked road. Likely broken, he'd need to have it fixed. After running his tongue along the path of his teeth, he found them all still intact. That meant he could still smile at Hans when he recovered and the swelling went down. The thought made him laugh, but the laughter hurt and turned to bitter mirth. Hans would not get away with what he'd done. The man would need far more than a few stitches to the forehead to fix him next time. Bastian felt his face with two fingers and found he had stitches too, four above his right eye. He would make Hans pay.

He sat up in bed and clutched his stomach. Most of the bruises to his chest were on his left side.

"Bastian." He heard his name in the dark room.

"Max?"

"You're up then?"

"What time is it?" Bastian asked.

"Past midnight I'd guess," Max answered. "The last nurse left hours ago and camp has been quiet."

"What are you doing here?" Bastian asked, confused again.

"You don't remember?"

Bastian recalled the end of the fight. Max had stepped in to help. The wrath he felt toward Hans compounded until it threatened to rip his chest open.

"I'm going to kill him," Bastian said.

"You're not," Max answered, sitting up in a bed across the room from Bastian. He'd pretended to be more injured than he actually was so he could stay in the infirmary. After several days of healing, it no longer hurt to screw his face up in different expressions. He could have moved back into his own room two days ago, but the thought of rejoining everyone, without Bastian, was not tempting. He'd allowed himself the luxury of drifting in and out, dozing all day. It was the best part of camp so far. When the nurse came in to check on them, he'd feign sleep until she left. After, he'd watch Bastian's chest rise up and down in steady succession. He looked bad, but not as bad as Max thought he'd be. His handsome features were still visible behind the cuts and black and blue marks. They'd kept him sedated most of the time so his injuries had time to heal.

Bastian sat up, winced, and looked toward Max. His voice was clear in the quiet room. "Yes. I am going to kill him and I'm doing it tonight."

The moonlight streaming through the window cast shadows upon Max's face. Bastian couldn't tell how badly off he was. He stood and hobbled over to a chair where the nurse had set out clean clothes. All he'd been wearing during the fight were his shorts, which must have been covered in sand and blood because they were nowhere to be found. He put on the new pair of black shorts and white T-shirt and turned back to Max. He hurt, but not unbearably. It was like the day after a beating from his father. Everything was stiff, sore. "Are you coming?"

Max didn't think he had much of a choice, so he joined Bastian. They walked into the cool night together. The camp was tranquil. All the drinking men had gone home for the night and the only sounds came from nature. For a moment, they simply stood and breathed in the night. Max hoped Bastian had already abandoned whatever crazy plan he'd concocted, but Bastian was only thinking about the best way to go about it, the best way to kill Hans and get away with it. Supervisors had large tee-pee tents made of hard canvas or, when they were older, a small cabin to themselves. Bastian knew exactly where Hans would be.

First, he would need an igniting agent. He led the way to the storage building where he located a jug of gasoline and a few boxes of matches.

Max looked at him with alarm but said nothing. They walked side by side toward Hans's tent. Their arms grazed each other as they strolled through the night, quiet as owls on the hunt. It wasn't until Bastian snapped the lid off the jug that Max grabbed him by the arm and pulled him silently away from Hans's tent.

"What the hell are you doing?" he whispered to Bastian.

"I told you. I'm going to kill him."

"Jesus, Bastian! I thought you were just kidding, just playing at one of your games."

"Why would I do that? He's only getting what he deserves," Bastian shot back.

Max tugged at the gas can in his hands. "You can't."

Bastian tore away, taking the gas with him and pouring it onto the ground. Max trailed him around the tent, equally scared of Hans waking to find them and not waking to stop them. Bastian tripped over a branch and fell to the ground with a soft thud. Max seized the opportunity and snatched the matches from him, then took off running, box in hand.

Bastian scrambled to his feet and swore, stashing the jug of half-spilled gasoline behind a tree. On a normal day, he would have caught up to Max in seconds, but each step shot pain through his chest. He ran all the same. When he caught up with him at the dock, Max had flung the box of matches into the lake. Bastian collapsed onto the ground.

"Are you going to kill me now?" Max asked.

Bastian gave him a wry glance. "If I was going to do that, you'd be dead."

"That's reassuring," Max said, attempting a smile.

Bastian pulled off his shirt and pants, paused a moment and then also removed his Jockeys before he slid gently from the dock into the water. "Shit, this is cold," he yelped.

"The matches are ruined. You can't get them now."

"I know that, you asshole. I just thought the water would numb my wounds. It hurt like hell to chase after you," Bastian winced.

Max took his own clothes off, keeping his underwear on, and joined Bastian in the water. The night was cool and the water was cooler. Above them the stars were out in full force, armies marching side by side to battle the darkness of the night. They could see each other in the starlight, in soft silhouettes.

They were silent for a time, Bastian floating on his back and Max leaning against the edge. Each boy was consumed with his own thoughts. Max thought of his father. If he saw Max, covered in bruises and breaking rules, would he be proud? Would he see him as a man finally? In less than a year he would be eighteen, could join the army and fight in a war if he wanted. The thought made his body spasm in fear. If a war were to come, he'd want no part in it. And what of Bastian? Max looked at him in a way he'd never looked at a boy before. As if the two of them could have a future beyond friendship. It was equal parts terrifying and exhilarating, though he didn't dare say it out loud. It was enough to let the edges of these thoughts come into consciousness.

"Bastian, do you believe in war?" Max asked.

"Believe in it or not, it's a real thing."

"Okay then, do you think there will be a war?" Max clarified.

"I think there already is one."

Bastian found the idea of war exhilarating; to be on the field, open and free to do as he wished, to take control of his future. War was barbaric; there were no rules. That was what he liked most about it.

He tilted his head and looked at Max. "Why?"

"I just don't want anything to do with it—the war," Max said.

"You'll be lucky if that's the case. Most people don't get the option." The water numbed Bastian as he'd hoped it would. The box of matches floated by and he swatted them away.

"Were you really going to do it?" Max asked him. He gingerly pushed away from the dock wall and swam toward Bastian.

"What do you think?" Bastian asked.

"Dunno." Max was now by his friend's side, treading water.

Bastian moved his feet downward so the two were facing one another. "I guess we'll never know."

Max took that to mean his vendetta was tamed, at least for now. There was comfort in the now. Comfort in being so close to Bastian, their limbs grazing one another under the water.

"Where do you live?" Bastian asked him.

It seemed an odd question. Something they ought to know about each other.

"On Park Avenue."

Bastian whistled. "Money bags. Why am I not getting smokes from you?"

Max laughed. "First off, I don't smoke. Secondly, we live in tenement housing. It's not the worst of them, but it's not the best either."

"Whatever you say," Bastian answered. His fingers surfaced on top of the water, did a little dance and then submerged again.

"Where do you live?" Max asked.

"On the lower east side in a tenement building too. But mine's a shit-hole." He turned his body from Max and leaned backward so that his head was almost resting in Max's hands. He kicked out his feet and made tiny waves in the water.

"Who do you live with?" Max asked.

"Who do *you* live with?" Bastian asked back.

"My parents. My mom is from Italy, which you know, and my dad is German of course. Amsel. They met in Europe in 1918 and then came over. They've been married a long time."

"Are they happy?" Bastian asked.

The question felt out of place. "I don't think so," Max said. "I don't think they're unhappy though. They're just … there. They do their own thing mostly, go out with friends sometimes and come home drunk." In his head, Max added, *when mom isn't devoured by her demons, anyway.*

Bastian smirked at him. "Do you break into the liquor?"

"Only once. It made me sick." He looked at Bastian and thought about what the boy at the boxing rings had said. That he didn't know Bastian at all. "What about you?"

"Do I drink, you mean? That would be an affirmative. I drink. I smoke." He turned around so he was facing Max again and said, "I'm a bad boy, Max."

They stayed looking at one another. Max said, "Tell me something else."

The air around them felt hot, sticky all of a sudden, as if a webbed blanket had set upon them. Each treaded water lightly under the surface, pockets of air bubbles kicking out at the other. They seemed impossibly close.

"What do you want to know?" Bastian asked.

"Something I wouldn't guess."

Bastian contemplated him. Max's dark eyes blended into the night so they looked the color of the water. It was a curious thing, how translucent water could take on the characteristics of the world around it—clear blue in the day, green at sunset, and black at night.

"You wouldn't guess that this is my last time coming to this shit-hole."

He was right, Max would not have thought that. Bastian was an institution at Camp Siegfried. And the next summer he'd be eligible to become an officer.

"Why?" Max asked, letting his body dance an inch closer to Bastian. Whether it was the darkness or the almost drunk giddiness of being close to him with no one else around, Max felt emboldened.

"Because I'm done," Bastian sighed. "When I go home I'm going to start making my own choices and that will be the first."

"I thought you already made your own choices," Max said.

Bastian closed the small gap between them. Their chests touched. Under the water Max felt something like seaweed lap against his leg. He kept still as the dead.

"Why do you think that?" Bastian asked.

Max felt himself quiver, his heart thudded so powerfully through his body that it must have made waves around him. Water shone on Bastian's lips.

Nearby something came to the surface of the water, making splashing sounds, disturbing their moment. Like a switch, Bastian backed away from Max, swimming toward the dock. Max followed. Bastian climbed out and then reached for him, helping Max out.

In the moonlight, they watched a snake glide on the surface of the water, coiling and lengthening. Max could see Bastian's heart pulse in his neck and placed his hand on his own neck. They stood together in the silence of the night, their rhythmic heartbeats reminding them they had more moments to live.

CHAPTER 5

THE MONTH OF JULY was rounding out and the boys' bruises had all but faded. Bastian's stiches had been removed the week prior and he was looking more like himself. Max could not believe they were almost done with camp, just a couple more weeks to go. Their time since the boxing match had passed without incidence. There were two more night marches, more shooting and boxing and swimming, but the initial buzz of the camp had settled. Hans and Bastian avoided one another and Max kept his head down.

One day during the previous week they'd all joined together in the clubhouse to listen to a lecture and watch a reel about Germany's efforts in Europe. Max was so excited to see a film that it took him partway through to realize it was a propaganda piece glazing over much of what was being whispered about in the city. Max had heard of camps, of Germans rounding up Jews from all over Europe; it was something people referenced without anyone really saying anything. Halfway through the film he'd claimed a headache and was allowed to go back to the cabin to sit in the quiet, alone.

The friendship that formed between the two boys grew in layers each day. Though Max still did not have a true understanding of Bastian, he felt he knew him better than most. They played cards and chess in their off time and had even snuck out for a second night swim. But the intensity of that first night never showed itself again; they were pals, splashing and swimming under the starry sky. Max found himself looking forward to the next two weeks, whatever they may bring.

Bastian on the other hand dreaded each passing day, because with it he came closer to having to leave. He doubted that after he and Max parted ways they'd still be friends. Max went to a prep school on Park Avenue and Bastian was finishing his last year in a place that didn't have enough books to go around. Here at camp they were equal; out there in the real world, whatever bond that held them was sure to break away.

Bastian worried at night, in that space between sleep and wakefulness, about his sister, about what he would go home to. He'd left her alone plenty of times, but this time had felt different. As if he'd walked out his front door for the last time. The only person who could make that a reality was himself. He would have to choose to go home or not. To face it or not.

***

It was a shooting day. Bastian was glad for it. He enjoyed the buck of the gun against his shoulder, the slight pain as he sent a bullet spinning through the field to the target. He'd become even better with his aim; as if firing at Hans was all the assurance he'd needed that he was a capable shot.

Before they headed to the range that morning, Bastian peered at Max from his bed and was about to say something when a uniformed officer came into the cabin. Most of the boys were getting dressed and a dozen heads turned to look at the man who stood in the doorway.

The officer was one Max had seen around, though he didn't know him by name. He was older, with graying hair at his temples. He looked determined as he scanned the room for someone. An older boy offered his help and a moment later, they were pointing at Max. Bastian moved in beside him.

"Max Amsel?" the officer asked.

"Yes, sir," Max answered.

"I need you to come with me."

Bastian said, "What is this about? Max hasn't done anything."

"Bastian, this does not pertain to you," the man said. He gestured toward the door. Max led the way and felt Bastian on his heels. The officer let out an exasperated sigh but said nothing. They walked in silence to the clubhouse, dust kicking up around them into the dry air.

"Come in please," the officer said. He led them inside the building, toward the back, and into a small room that served as an office. On the light wooden desk sat a pile of papers and a telephone. Max's family had recently installed one just like it, though he was not allowed to touch the thing. If he wanted to make a call, he still had to go down the street and use the payphone for a nickel.

"Max, we've had some news," the officer said.

"What kind of news?" Bastian asked.

The man moved his gaze from Max to Bastian and back to Max. "We've had a telephone call from your house," he said. He placed a hand on the boy's shoulder. "I'm sorry to tell you your father is dead."

Max sank into a chair. He looked up at Bastian but his friend was unable to offer anything. "How …?" he managed to get out.

The officer went behind the desk and sat. He cleared his throat. "A heart attack they think. They'll have to do an autopsy to confirm." After a silence he added, "I'm sorry."

Max was disgusted—with this officer, with this cruel joke. His father was the strongest man he knew. A weak heart was inconceivable. "You must be mistaken. It was not my father. Is there another Amsel in the camp perhaps?" His voice came out cold and not like his own at all.

"No, Max. I know your father. Knew your father. I spoke to your mother on the phone. She asked for me and requested I deliver the news myself."

Max's world went wavy and he leaned back in the seat. His mother. She would be devastated. Herr Amsel did everything in that house. His mother could barely get herself out of bed, let alone run a household. "I need to get home to her," Max said and the officer nodded his head in agreement.

"One of the men can drive you there. You will have to begin making arrangements when you arrive. Your mother, she sounded at a loss as to what to do next." He looked at the watch on his wrist, gold and silver with a square face and leather band. "Go pack your things and you can leave in about a half hour. Someone will meet you at the front of the clubhouse."

Max was unable to move. He felt Bastian's hands on his shoulder. "Don't worry," Bastian said. "I'll go with you and help."

The officer stood. "I'm afraid that's not possible, Bastian. Your family would not approve of you leaving camp. You can see your friend in two weeks once camp season is finished."

"Bullshit," Bastian shot back.

Even in his state, Max knew Bastian had crossed a line. Why let Hans beat him to a bloody pulp if he was going to get thrown out for disrespect?

"It's fine," Max told him, getting to his feet.

"Listen to your friend," the officer said. He put a hand on Bastian's shoulder to make it clear he was not going anywhere.

"Max," Bastian said, "go pack your stuff, okay? I'll meet you in the cabin."

Max obeyed. The world around him seemed altered, yet all the same. In the clubhouse men sat in oversized chairs, drinking. Outside, boys ran and played and shot guns. As he left the clubhouse, he ran into Hans, bumping into his chest and almost stepping on one of his feet.

"Watch where you're going, kid," Hans sneered.

Max looked up at him but didn't bother to respond. With luck he'd never have to see the guy again. He made his way toward the cabin in a daze. It only took him five minutes to place his belongings in his trunk, mostly uniforms and camp clothes he would never wear again. Then he threw a few more things into a knapsack, a copy of *The Hobbit*, which he'd read three times already, an old suit shirt that was too small for his father to wear anymore, and a pocket watch that had belonged to his mother's father, whom he'd never met. She gave it to Max on his sixteenth birthday and told him the story of how her father died in the war.

She was fourteen when the news came. Max's mother, Francesca, believed her father to still be alive. For an entire year, during the Italo-Turkish war, she' sat in the front of their stone house waiting for him to return. It wasn't until after the fighting stopped, when one of the men who'd served with her father had visited, that she knew he was truly dead. She'd sat in the room with her mother as the man told the story of her father's death; how he'd seen the whole thing. With him, he had brought her father's pocket watch.

Francesca's mother was so heartbroken she left the watch where the man laid it down; not wanting to touch it, believing it was cursed. While her mother saw the man out, Francesca leapt from her chair and snatched it up. Her mother never asked about the watch. Francesca had carried it with her to America. When she gave it to Max, he too had wondered if it was cursed. At first, he'd put it away in his bedside table, listening to it tick as he fell asleep each night. A few months later his father's company had an event. He'd worn a suit and his mother asked him to wear the pocket watch.

"So handsome," she'd told him, straightening his tie. "You look just like him, you know. Just like Papa." She kissed him on the forehead. Max could not recall the last time she'd done that. At the work party, she drank too much and they had to leave early, before they'd even had cake.

***

Max snugged up the contents of the knapsack, slung it over his shoulder, and took a final look around the cabin. He was about to leave for the clubhouse when Bastian tore into the room with a bloody lip that was already starting to swell.

"What the hell happened now?" Max asked.

"We've got to go."

"What?"

"We have to go now, Max."

"But—"

"Do you need your trunk?" Bastian asked.

Max touched the straps of his knapsack. "What? No, I guess not right now. What is happening?" Outside Max heard rising voices. "What did you do?"

Bastian reached under his mattress and pocketed something. He gave Max a wicked smile. "They wouldn't let me go with you. So, I had to change their minds." Voices cut through the outside, they sounded closer. "*Now*, Max!"

Bastian grabbed his hand as he had that first day at the race. They wove through the camp toward the trees, boots behind them pounding the pavement and then the dirt. Max allowed himself to be pulled as if in a dream. The trees blurred past them, one after another, like on a movie reel. His life was moving in fast motion.

After some time, the footfalls faded. They stopped to rest in the forest that bordered the camp and Max reached over to wipe the blood from Bastian's split lip.

Bastian winced. "Ouch."

Max furrowed his forehead in apology. He didn't think he'd be able to face his mother or his dead father alone. He wanted to tell Bastian as much, but admitting it made him feel weak. His father would not approve. Then once more it hit him that his dad was dead. He would have to keep reminding himself until it sunk in. "Thank you for this, for coming along," he said quietly.

They moved forward, deeper into the forest. Bastian had spent much of his free time prior to this year wandering these woods. He had memorized several ways out of the camp, somehow knowing he'd have to escape one day. He'd left all of his stuff back in the cabin, but he didn't mind. The thrill of the fight and the chase was enough to keep him going. Besides, he'd managed to grab the one thing that was most important to him, his lucky penny. Usually he wore it at the bottom of his shoe, but it'd begun to wear a hole, so he'd taken to tucking it under his mattress instead.

They walked for just under an hour before the trees parted and they entered onto a side street in town.

"Told you I'd get us out."

"No, you didn't," Max said.

"I implied it."

"I'm hungry," Max told him. Bastian looked at him and Max shrugged. They had the same thought, *you're thinking of food now?*

"I'm just as surprised as you are. Should we stop there?" Max pointed down the road at a little store.

"Don't you want to get home?" Bastian asked.

"Yes, but we can take five minutes." Max brought his bag from his shoulder and dug around, extracting his grandfather's watch. "The train only runs on the half hour. It's one thirty now so we've missed this one. We have time to grab food and then find the train, right? We're not that far from the center of town."

Bastian shrugged and relented. "Up to you, my friend."

Max took the lead, walking to the small market store. Bastian caught up and they walked side by side. In the near distance a train whistle blew and people were transported from one place to another—from one life to another, in Max's case. His next chapter had begun. There was a sick thrill to it. To the possibility.

CHAPTER 6

THEY BOARDED A TWO O'CLOCK TRAIN and found it almost empty. A young girl and her mother boarded at the same time and moved to the far end of the car. Bastian and Max sat side by side, not talking. The walls were painted a mint green color that reminded Max of his parents' bedroom. Their room was a shade darker and after years of pictures being hung and taken down and rehung, it needed to be painted. His mother used to do those sorts of things, but had lost the energy in the last few years. She used to take pride in their home, but lately Herr Amsel had hired someone to do the painting and repairs, as well as a woman to clean the house every two weeks. The dust would build up in between her visits but they would all ignore it.

It was hard to imagine how Francesca would function now that her husband was gone. Some days the woman seemed barely alive. Now, one of the two people who held her upright was dead.

The weight of taking care of his mother brought tears to his eyes. He knew that soon enough he'd cry for his father, for the years of unmade memories that were taken away. Harald Amsel would never see if Max filled out. Max would never know if his father would treat him like a man. Max would never be able to tell him about winning the race, as stolen as the victory was.

He would never watch his parents dance to a record in their living room again. All of these facts were just that to Max, facts, bits of information he could not process. He only thought of what this meant for his life, for the people who had to go on without the man, and his new obligations that would abound. This was not only the last summer before he turned eighteen, it was his last summer as a child.

Bastian wrapped his arm around Max and pulled him closer. Max took in the comfort and allowed himself to break down. He buried his face into his friend's warm chest and cried.

"Shhh, shhh, shhh," Bastian said, as his mother had done in times of loss and comforting. Max shook and he held him closer. The kid looked tiny next to him. Bastian brought his right arm to meet his left and encircled Max. This only made him cry harder. They would wait it out together.

Bastian ran his tongue near his split lip. That blow was the last one he'd take from Hans, from anyone at that place. He'd left Hans bloody and swearing on the stone floor of the clubhouse. After Max left, Officer Müller had reprimanded Bastian for talking back and made it clear that he would not be leaving. Hans stood outside the office and overheard the conversation.

"Oh, little crybaby. You were told 'no' for once in your life? Poor baby."

It was impossible to hold it in. Bastian had not even registered that his fist was flying toward Hans's face until the man stumbled backward and landed with a thud on the ground. The commotion brought the attention of the commanding officers. Bastian climbed on top of Hans and hit him three more times. Someone pulled him off and Hans was able to get to his feet and land one punch to Bastian's face. With it, the officer lost hold of Bastian who took off, running away while the commotion ensued without him.

***

Max lifted his face from Bastian's shirt. He'd left it wet with tears. "Sorry," he sniffled.

"For what?"

"For being a crybaby," Max said.

"You'll never hear me say that about a boy crying over the death of his father."

"That's what mine would have said."

The train stopped. The child and her mother left and no one boarded to replace them. "Well, I need to get it out before I arrive home anyway. My mother can't see me like this." Max pulled his knees to his chest and rested his chin on them.

"Why is that?" Bastian asked.

Max sighed. "Because I have to be strong for her. Strong as me and my dad combined."

"You think she'll be that torn up?" he asked Max.

"She hasn't been whole for a while. I'm afraid this will just chip away at her." Max remembered when it started, the sleeping for days, the manic moods in which she'd clean for fifteen hours straight into the night while he and his father tried to sleep.

His baby sister Christina had died three days after she was born. There didn't seem to be an explanation. Francesca had gone to bed, the baby in a cradle beside her while she dozed. When she awoke, her screams pierced the house, the building. Neither Max nor Harald had been there, but the neighbors came with the sound.

Hours later when Max and his father arrived home, she was clutching the baby to her breast, rocking. She'd gone from screaming to crying to whimpering. Max had watched her, as if he could see pieces of his mother fall away. Pieces that would never fit back together. She'd been so happy they'd had a girl, had wanted a daughter so much more than a son. Francesca and her mother had been close and she wanted to feel that way again, the way only a daughter could make her feel.

"I love you," she'd told Max. "But it's not the same."

Max didn't know Christina. He hadn't even been trusted yet to hold her. Hadn't spent hours gazing at her as his mother had. Hadn't carried her inside his body for almost a year, bonding to her before she even breathed air for the first time. No, the death of Christina only affected him in what it had done to his mother. It was like she'd lost two children that day, like she no longer saw Max.

***

Max could not think on it anymore. He needed something to distract him. They were still an hour from Penn Station and then would have to walk the eleven blocks, take a cab, or transfer to another line. "Bastian," he said after another stop, "can you tell me about how your father died?"

Bastian moved his arms to rest in his lap and laced his fingers together. "Yeah, I guess."

"You don't have to. I just thought … since we have it in common."

A family of five boarded the train and sat in the middle. Once they were settled, Bastian spoke. His voice was different. Max could not pinpoint what it was. Perhaps this was the quality a voice takes on when speaking of a dead parent. Max wondered if his voice would do this too.

"There was an accident. He worked at a factory. Was one of the managers. It was a terrible place. Everyone had to work long hours, including him. There was a fire that started in a trash can." The trained lurched and stopped. Bastian paused until it started back up. "He tried to put it out but the hose was rotted through and the valve to turn the water on was rusted. It was useless. The flame spread so fast, that's what they say anyway. Half of the workers, including my father, exited into the stairwell to escape the burning. The fire followed them in. They raced to the top of the stairs, to get to the roof, but they'd all forgotten that the doors in the stairwell locked once closed. It was a precaution implemented by the owner." Max tilted his head at Bastian in question. "You see, some of the girls would go into the stairwells to take breaks because the owners didn't really allow them. So, they installed locking handles. When one of the girls was missing, if she was found on the stairs, she was fired straightaway."

"That's terrible." Max said. He was transfixed by the story, and remembered hearing about it years before.

"They were trapped in the stairwell and eaten alive by the flames. That's what they say anyway. Others jumped out of windows and died when they hit the ground. The fire ladders only reached to the seventh floor, see, and the fire itself was on the eighth floor. They just couldn't get to them.

"I was there. With Ilsa—my sister. When I heard all the fire trucks so near our house, I grabbed her and ran outside in case our building was on fire. The factory was only a few blocks away. We ran toward the flames, the chaos. I watched as people jumped from the windows and I searched for my father. He was nowhere. Hundreds of people crowded the streets. There was screaming, so much screaming. And cameras flashing and people pushing. I got Ilsa out of there. I'm still not sure what she remembers."

"How many died?" Max asked, his voice wavering.

"One hundred and forty-five in all. Lots of innocent lives." He looked up and added with disgust, "The owners made it out, of course. Made it onto the roof and to the next building over. They were brought to trial but nothing came of it."

Max asked, "Was he a nice guy? Your dad, when he was alive?"

Bastian said, "I was lucky enough."

***

The farther they traveled into Manhattan, the more crowded the train car became. Toward the last stop, they gave up their seats to an older couple. It was impossible to talk without shouting so they rode the rest of the way in silence. They climbed the dirty stairwell hip-to-hip and emerged onto a busy street. After more than a month in the country, Max and Bastian both felt overwhelmed by the city, the noise, traffic, and blaring horns. They exchanged a glance and began walking toward their destination. A block into the journey Max said, "You don't mind walking, do you?"

"No. I walk everywhere."

When they stopped at a corner to let traffic pass Max said, "Thank you again. For doing whatever it was you did back there in order to come with me."

"I wanted to." There were a few flecks of blood on his shirt. He saw Max looking at them. "Maybe I can borrow something of yours when we get to your house."

"Will it be okay?" Max asked. "When you have to go home? I mean you can stay with me as long as you like. My room is pretty big so we can share it."

"I'll be fine. Of course, I'll be fine. Why are you asking me that?"

They crossed the street and kept walking, pushing through small crowds here and there. "It's only that someone at the camp said if you got kicked out you wouldn't be able to go home again. And that's what happened, right? You got kicked out?"

"Who said that?" Bastian said sharply.

"Just one of the boys."

"Well that guy had no idea what the hell he was talking about. I can go home any damn time I please. Do you want me to go home now? Is that what you're telling me?" His volatile tone caught Max off guard.

Max slowed and grabbed at Bastian's hand. He didn't pull away. "I need you, okay?"

They broke away from one another and continued. When they were less than a block from Max's house and the crowds had changed from dirty factory workers to men in suits and women in soft skirts that fell past their knees, Max stopped mid-step.

"What's wrong?" Bastian asked.

"How was your mom? After."

"She held up okay. German women are tough."

Max didn't want to move. His mother was not tough. Even before Christina she had not been a sturdy woman in that way.

"Come on. You can do it." Bastian placed a hand on Max's back and they walked like that for the final block until they came to Max's apartment building and he pulled away. The structure was made of white brick and loomed, gleaming in front of them. A doorman greeted them, giving Max a nod of the head. Bastian's cheeks began to burn. Why had Max downplayed where he lived? A tenement house. Bullshit.

They took an elevator to the sixth floor. Bastian fingered the coin in his pocket. Max was straight-faced and rigid. The elevator dinged and the doors opened directly into his apartment. Bastian gave him a look and Max said, "Okay, maybe it's a little nicer than tenement apartments."

They stepped into a large living and dining room area with shining wood floors. As the elevator descended, Bastian looked back at it, no longer sure he should be there. A woman came pouring into the room, moving like water over stones. She was about to fall forward. Max did not reach out to catch her, did not have the instinct, but Bastian stepped in front of him and stretched out his arms. She fell into them, clutching Bastian's white T-shirt. There was no way for Bastian to extricate himself from the embrace, so he allowed the woman to hold onto him and wail.

"Shhh, shhh, shhh," he heard himself saying for the second time that day.

Francesca looked up as if aware for the first time that the boy she clung to was not her son. She let out a fresh moan and like water again, flowed from one to the other. Max was knocked to his knees. He wrapped his arms around his mother. He felt trapped. He felt like she would never let him go again.

CHAPTER 7

THE FOOD BEGAN ARRIVING two days later; pasta dishes meant to be served cold and warm, desserts of pies, custards, and cookies, platters of meats and cheeses, fresh bright fruits and vegetables. Max and Bastian took each one in hand, thanking the giver, while Francesca lay down in her bedroom. Yesterday she hadn't come out at all. Max had brought her soup, and this morning, when he went to retrieve the bowl, he found it full. On her night table was a bottle of pills. The lid was off. Max picked them up, screwing the cap back on and read the label. *Francesca Amsel, Barbiturates, Take one to two pills a day.* He'd read the same label many times over the years, ever since his mother started seeing that doctor downtown.

It was two p.m. when Francesca emerged from the bedroom; the kitchen was full of food and void of mourners. Stepping into the room, she saw two young men. It wasn't until they turned around that she realized one of them was her son, Max. And the other? What was his name? The young man, tall and fit, was wearing her husband's slacks. They were too big for him at the waist.

Max saw how his mother eyed them and stepped forward. "Mom, this is Bastian. Remember, from when we arrived? He came home with me to help."

She nodded and continued to stare at her dead husband's pants. She reached out and grazed her hand against one of the pockets.

"I'm sorry, ma'am," Bastian said. "I didn't have a chance to bring along any clothes and Max's pants are a bit too small. I hope you don't mind."

She shook her head back and forth several times, not speaking.

"The vigil is in two hours," Max said. "You should change clothes. People will start arriving soon. The body …." He stumbled over his words. "Dad's body will be here by three o'clock. You should be ready."

She stared at them, numb.

"Let me," Bastian said, taking her elbow.

"No, I should," Max said. He made no motion to move.

"It's okay. I can do it," Bastian told him again.

With too much force, Francesca yanked her arm from Bastian's grasp. "I'm just fine, boys. Max, please make sure your father has on that suit he likes. I can't remember which one we sent along."

Max couldn't swallow and he found his mouth too dry to speak.

"We'll make sure, Frau Amsel." Bastian said.

They watched her go. Max walked into the living room where his father's body would be arriving anytime now and slumped onto the couch. "What am I going to do with her?" Max asked.

"We'll figure it out." Bastian sat down and patted Max's leg.

***

When the mourners arrived, Herr Amsel was laid out in the living room, Francesca, wearing a black dress, sat on the couch, and Max stood near the center of the room, greeting everyone and listening to their condolences. Max watched as each person approached the casket to kiss his father's white face, or squeeze his lifeless hand. It was more affection than Herr Amsel would have ever allowed in life.

It was surreal to Max, watching all these faces say good-bye to his father and then turn to him and greet him like a man. They asked him about schooling and if he would follow in his father's footsteps and become a businessman. Those who knew about the camp he'd attended asked about his experience in excited tones. Max kept all of his answers polite and short. In truth, he had not given much thought to what would happen after his last year of prep school; college was certain, where he would study something he had little interest in but that would make his father proud. His life had been laid out for him, but now, adults were asking him what *he* wanted, what his life would become.

Whenever there was a break in the crowd, Max would look up to find his only real friend in the room. Bastian hadn't known what to do, so he placed himself in a quiet corner. If Max was overwhelmed with two dishes, a vase of flowers, and three crying women, Bastian would intervene, taking the objects and leaving the mourners to Max. Mostly he watched from a distance. From the people who flooded in through the elevator door, it was obvious that Herr Amsel was a loved, or at the least, a respected man. Bastian had a hard time mustering any respect for his own father.

He listened to the small groups that gathered near him and heard snippets of conversation. Most were the same, consisting of similar topics and comments throughout the room.

"Oh yes, he's been doing very well for himself."

"The house looks wonderful. I had heard other things. I hadn't seen Francesca in ages."

"Yes, they never went out with us anymore. Maybe they knew he was sick and didn't tell anyone."

Some people spoke of Max, wondering idly what he would do now.

"He'll finish high school, he told me. Didn't seem to know what was next."

"Poor boy. He must be so lost without his father." Then they would throw a furtive glance Francesca's way. "I don't think she's doing very well. Poor woman."

"After Christina, she was never the same."

Bastian didn't know who Christina was but several of the guests used the name. Whenever a group of German men gathered, Bastian was sure to hear something of the Fuhrer and the impending war in Europe. They all seemed certain it would happen.

"But America will never join. It will not reach us. Hitler will want it contained."

"Yes, but he is growing more powerful each day. Someone is sure to take note."

"Our American armies were depleted after the Great War. There will not be another. No one's enlisting now. They still remember the last war."

Bastian wished he had something to do with his hands, something to fix or clean. Each person at the vigil seemed to have a purpose, the mourners going to the casket to visit with Herr Amsel, the priest blessing and saying prayers, and Max offering and receiving comfort. Francesca, that's what she told Bastian to call her, sat on her own on the couch, allowing the line of people to kiss her cheek and say words of sympathy. She was stony, unlike yesterday when she poured like a fountain, she now seemed inanimate.

"I'm so sorry for your loss, Francesca," they said, one after another.

Once in a while she would nod her head in acknowledgment. She mostly just offered her cheek without a word. When there was a break from the mourners, she would turn her face in a calculated way and look at Bastian, as if she were trying to figure out who he was. He'd catch her gaze, offering her a smile each time. She had put herself together, bathing and dressing in a black dress that clung to her body. Bastian imagined it was one she'd worn out dancing with her husband.

He also caught Max sending glances his way. With each one Bastian would lurch forward to see if he needed anything, but Max would give him a weak smile and shake his head to indicate, *I'm fine, just looking for a friendly face in the crowd.*

In the moments when he was not catching an Amsel's eye, Bastian was forced to burrow into his own mind. He did not want to give so much thought to what was next, but the concept followed him. When he'd left home before the camp, it was made clear that if he came back, it would have to be with contrition. Now, with his unfortunate exit from Siegfried, he didn't know if even contrition would get him through the door. To be unwelcome somewhere you didn't want to go in the first place, with no choice but to return—that was his current hell. There was nowhere else for him to go. He had no money to live on. And could he really abandon his sister like that? Perhaps he could blend into this corner forever. The mourners would clear and Max and his mother would move on and he could stay, just where he was.

He looked up to find both mother and son staring at him. Bastian went to Max.

"How are you holding up?" he asked.

Max leaned in for just a moment to rest his head on Bastian's shoulder. He was not holding up; he was exhausted, and felt like at any moment his legs would give way and he would have to lie on the floor, the mourners stepping around him to get to the casket. "I'll be okay," he said quietly to Bastian. "I just want this to be over."

Max removed his grandfather's pocket watch from his suit jacket. "Five thirty."

"Almost over, just a half-hour longer," Bastian said. He was wearing one of Herr Amsel's suits. It fit him better than he'd expected.

Father Anthony approached Max, and Bastian faded back into the corner.

"Maxwell," the Father said, "it is time for me to lead everyone in the rosary prayer. Would you like to start with the Apostles' Creed? Or you could lead the Eternal Rest prayer after the first decade of the Rosary. Would you like that?"

"I—I don't think so," Max answered. "Thank you for asking."

"Very well," Father Anthony said, nodding in agreement.

He gathered everyone together. Francesca would not move from her spot on the couch. Max tried to cajole her forward but Father could see that the woman would not come. She was in shock. He'd seen it countless times in the vigils he proceeded over. The hysteria would come sooner or later.

Father Anthony began, "I believe in God, the Father Almighty, Creator of heaven and earth."

The crowd joined in with murmurs, each saying the prayer. Bastian stood off to the side near Max and it gave Max comfort. All he wanted to do was lay in bed with his friend and have Bastian hold him. Max found himself missing his muscled arms and earthy smell.

They'd completed the first set of ten Hail Mary's and had moved on to the Eternal Rest prayer—*Eternal rest grant unto him, O Lord; and let perpetual light shine upon him*—when, from the corner of his eye, Max saw his mother lunge forward. Before he knew what was happening, she'd made it to the casket and was pulling on its side and wailing.

She was on her feet, her hands running along her dead husband's face, rocking back and forth. Her son and the priest were by her side, trying to calm her, but she could not be calmed. Her husband was dead, the man who fathered her children, who had brought her to America and given her a life she did not appreciate; he was gone. Behind her, she felt a set of hands curl around her waist. Francesca allowed herself to fall backwards into them and be carried away from the casket.

When he placed her in bed, she saw it was Max's friend—Bastian. That was his name.

Max appeared at the foot of the bed. His mother shook as wide, fat tears rolled down her cheeks.

"Your father is dead," she said over and over.

Bastian turned to him. "Go, you should be out there. Finish the Rosary with them and I'll put her to bed."

Max hesitated.

"It's okay, really."

What Max wanted was for Bastian to send everyone away. For he and Bastian to leave the confines of the stuffy house and go into the woods together where no one would bother them and Max didn't need to answer countless questions he'd had no preparation for. But he agreed and left the two of them in her room.

Bastian watched him shut the door and turned back to Francesca. She was still murmuring. He brushed hair from her face and made soothing sounds. He'd done the same thing for his mother after the fire. Though with his own mother, it was a different kind of mourning and hers had lasted hours, not days.

Francesca grasped at Bastian's elbow, taking comfort in this strange boy near her bed. She reached her arms up and touched his face and then pulled him in toward her. Her lips brushed against his for a moment. He was a beautiful boy, much like her husband had been in his youth. He looked like the man she married on her wedding day, nineteen years before. He was her Harald.

Bastian extricated himself from her embrace and pulled the covers from the bottom of the bed up to her shoulders. He was numb to the kiss, it had meant nothing at all.

She burrowed into her pillow and said, "Thank you, Harald. Thank you for putting me to bed. I am so tired. So tired. I will get to it in the morning. I will take care of things then."

"It's okay," Bastian told her. "There's no rush."

She turned from him completely and within the minute she was sleeping.

CHAPTER 8

S T. JEAN BAPTISTE CHURCH hosted the mourners the next morning. It was a magnificent building. Max had spent many Sundays staring up at its vaulted, muraled ceilings and out of the colorful, stained glass windows. The hemispherical ceiling, lined with stained glass as well, seemed to be built so high as to reach the sky. The gold leafing around every edge made the light blue paint appear heavenly. These were the things Max concentrated on as he sat between his mother and Bastian in the front pew, Father Anthony at the pulpit giving the funeral liturgy and Mass. Before he'd left the vigil the night before, Father asked Max if he or his mother would like to deliver a eulogy at the funeral. Francesca lay in another room, sleeping away the events of the day. Max knew she would not be prepared to speak, and he would rather she resume her stone-like silent stature for the whole of the funeral day so they didn't have another episode of wailing and throwing her body at the casket.

"I can say something," Max had told him. "Though I am not sure what."

"Speak from your heart, my son, and you cannot go wrong."

Max doubted that very much, however he agreed to try.

After everyone had gone home, he and Bastian were left to clean. Max could not imagine spending another evening tidying, so after they'd put just enough of the food and dishes away to discourage hungry insects, they retreated to Max's bedroom. Herr Amsel was laid out in the living room and would stay there until the morning when people from the church would load the body into a horse-drawn hearse. Max would walk the four blocks from the house to the cathedral behind the casket with his mother. The fact that his father's body was in the next room while he slept made him uneasy, as if the ghost of the man would finally pay attention to his son.

They sat on Max's bed, leaning against the headboard.

Max sat up straight. "Do you need to call your mother? To tell her where you are?" He realized that Bastian had not contacted his family in the three days since they'd left the camp.

"We don't have a phone." As if that was enough information to end the conversation, Bastian lay back against the headboard.

Max wanted to know more, but he was drained from the day and the constant talk to family and friends. He decided not to push. Instead, he laid his head on Bastian's shoulder and thought of his mother. She'd been falling apart for years; he was afraid she would not recover from this loss. It was like she didn't even know he was there. Bastian had tended to her more in the last few days than Max had.

On his night table was a photo of Christina, the only one that existed. Francesca had thrown it away and he'd dug it out of the trash. Ever since, he had hidden it in a drawer, displaying it only at night while he slept so his mother would not find it.

After a time, Max put his head against his pillow and shut his eyes. He had no idea what he would say the next day at the church and only hoped it would be revealed to him before he had to stand there in front of everyone.

Bastian thought that Max had fallen asleep and was moving from the bed to the floor, where he'd slept the previous nights, when he felt Max's hand on his elbow.

"Stay with me here, please. I don't want to be alone."

"I was just going to the floor," Bastian said.

"I don't even want to be that alone."

Bastian consented and lay down next to his friend. Their skin stuck together in the hot room until they were both covered in a thin layer of perspiration.

"Is this what it was like when your father died?" Max asked.

"Not exactly," Bastian said.

"I don't know what to say tomorrow."

"You don't have to say anything." Bastian could not imagine what he would have said at his own father's funeral. "Tell a story. Don't you have any nice stories about the two of you? The first time he took you to a ball game?"

"We didn't really do things like that. He worked a lot. And after Christina ...." Max had not said her name aloud in years. Once someone died and was buried, his mother said, their spirit would haunt you if you used the person's name. Christina's name was forbidden in their household.

Bastian wanted to ask about her, having heard the name during the vigil from some of the guests, but decided not to pry. Beside him Max's body began to shake. The tears he cried were silent, only the tremor of his body giving away that he was weeping. Bastian moved his arm around Max to pull him in. Max came willingly, burrowing into his friend for comfort yet again.

They fell asleep like that, wrapped in one another's bodies. When Max awoke in the middle of the night, Bastian had moved onto the floor. It made him angry and sad; as if the death of his father was not enough to deal with, his feelings for Bastian over the last weeks had confused him. He wanted to be next to him, wanted to maybe even kiss him. But that would not be right and Bastian would never allow it. Max wanted to scream and wake him, wanted to ask Bastian to crawl back into bed with him, to climb on top of him and wind their bodies together.

He didn't. He let him sleep on the floor as he lay awake above, writing and rewriting in his mind the words he would deliver for his father.

***

A hand on his own brought him back into the church. It was Bastian. He gestured toward the pulpit where Father Anthony stood and his father's body lay.

"It's time," Bastian said.

Max looked to his mother. She did not move. She stared off into the distance as if she were watching a film. Max squeezed her hand and, receiving no response, stood up and moved toward the altar. The suit he wore was one of his father's, to big for his thin frame. That morning he'd ironed it, poorly.

Max thought he knew what he would say; he would talk about how his parents met, how they fell in love and came to America together. About their dedication to the church and family. About his father's successes in life. He would not talk about Herr Amsel's evolving ideology, about the loss of his little sister, about his mother's constant breakdowns. Max would speak only of the good things.

When he took his place and looked out among the people in the church, he felt small and inconsequential. Many had come to honor his father, yet because of the immensity of the space, it appeared all but empty. They were one set of people, filling only a small space in a mammoth church, one among many churches in the city, a city of seven million. His pain and grief could not transcend this place. He was a piece of dust in the world, much like the dust he'd swept away from the apartment. This world would grow and move on and his father would never see it. He would never see Max and what he would become.

"My father and I were not close," Max began. His mother looked at him, did not move. "This fact will never change. As we age, I've learned in the last few days especially, we begin to collect regrets. Things we wish we had done." He faltered and Bastian offered him a smile.

"I regret that I was never the son my father seemed to want. I regret that even if I become that person, he will never be able to see me. I regret that I never thought to give my father a chance, to see what he was looking for in me that I was lacking. I never truly knew him, nor him me, and now we'll never get that chance." He saw his mother reach across the pew to grasp Bastian's hand.

"I regret all of these things, but to honor the man who is before us, I will work very hard in my life to lessen further regrets. To ask when I am curious, to take the chance even if I think I may fail, and to not let the people I love float through my life in ways where we never truly connect." Max was crying now, openly. He didn't wipe away his tears; they felt good on his cheeks. He finished with a prayer Father Anthony had recommended, stopping every few words to sniffle and take deep breaths.

He moved from the pulpit to the casket and Bastian joined him. They acted as pallbearers with his two uncles to carry his father from the church to the graveyard around the back of the building. A train of people trailed behind them as they transferred the casket. It was heavy and going down the stairs of the cathedral, Max was afraid he might drop it. He stole a glance at Bastian, who looked to be carrying more than his share of the weight.

When they'd made it to the cemetery and placed the body into the burial vault, Bastian breathed a sigh of relief. The weight he'd been made to carry over the last few days, both physical and emotional, had him at a loss. His body felt bruised from the impact. All the while, he put a smile on his face. He was good at that part.

Aside from being present for Max and Francesca, he had to think of his own life, how it was about to change and not for the better. He'd need a place to live, money to do it with. Bastian felt a gnawing suspicion that he was lending himself to Max this fully so that Max in turn would be obligated to fill this void. With Herr Amsel gone, maybe they'd need help around the house. There was a third bedroom and Bastian imagined that Max would be thrilled if he stayed around.

Father Anthony was saying another prayer over the casket.

"Amen," everyone echoed around the grave. With Max and his mother in the lead, each person threw a handful of dirt onto the ground where Herr Amsel lay.

The funeral ended without incident. There was a moment when Francesca looked like she would lose herself again, but Max was able to catch her in his arms and comfort her into a place of quiet submission.

As everyone scattered from the gravesite, making their way back to the house, Max's Uncle Franco, his mother's brother, approached him and Bastian. He hugged his nephew and shook the hand of the boy who'd been so helpful the last few days. He had a specific intention for approaching Max, though, and got right to it. "Max, do you know what you will do now?"

"Honestly, I have no idea."

"May I make a suggestion?"

"Yes, please," Max said. It was the first time anyone had offered this. His father had always told him what to do in life.

"Much of our family is still in Italy. What do you think of going there? With your mother and her *condition*," he said in a whisper as if everyone was not aware of Francesca's *condition*, "it may be better for you to go and we can take care of her. You will almost be ready for college and will need to learn how to be a man." He leaned in closer. "You will not be able to do that while taking care of your mother."

"Italy, really?" Max said in surprise. "Do you think with—"

"Yes! I think it would be the best thing for you."

"I'll think about it, Uncle Franco. Thank you for the suggestion."

The man nodded and left. Max realized that Bastian held very still while his Uncle was there. He glanced over and Bastian looked like he would be ill.

CHAPTER 9

THE SUN HAD SET by the time the last of the mourners left. Max had willed them to go, becoming sullen and quiet toward the end. Uncle Franco talked with his mother for a long time; she nodded her head a lot during the conversation, not saying much.

When Max walked past them on the way to the kitchen, he heard his Uncle say, "It's settled then, Francesca. It will be taken care of." Max assumed they were talking about his father's business affairs. Max already had to care for his mother and go to school; he would be happy for someone else to pay the bills and manage the money. If the family could take care of those things he'd be okay.

***

The house grew dark, one room at a time, as Max and Bastian turned off the lights. His mother went to bed before the last people left, claiming a headache. Max let her go.

When the boys went into his room, Max did not have to ask Bastian to join him on the bed; he did it on his own. Everything was quiet. Even their breathing was almost silent. They lay on their sides, facing one another, their noses inches apart. The intimacy of their bodies beside each other, the power of it, overwhelmed

"What's wrong?" Max asked, touching his shoulder.

Bastian cleared his throat and came out of the trance. "Nothing. I just … not feeling well, I guess."

"I'm not going to go, Bastian."

"Go where?"

"Italy, of course. I couldn't." They watched as Uncle Franco gently took hold of Francesca and loaded her into his car to take her to the house. Knowing he didn't have to get her home helped Max relax. He took a breath.

"Max, it's your life. Do what you want with it." Bastian looked around at the almost empty graveyard. "We should get back to the house, don't you think? People will be arriving soon."

They moved together down the crowded streets, Max's shoulder bounced against Bastian's arm with each step and Bastian in turn allowed his body to ease in and out of the rhythm of their walking.

them both. There was guilt in it for Max, feeling so content next to his friend only days after his father had died. In the last weeks Max had changed, had begun to grow into a different person. It was an evolution he'd wanted. He felt as if he'd spent his whole life in one skin and now he was shedding it, seeing who he was one layer down.

Bastian too had changed, allowing Max to sway his opinion when before his decisions were like concrete, unmovable. He'd never had the opportunity to care for someone like he'd cared for Max, not even his sister Ilsa. It felt dangerous and unsure, as if everything they'd built together in the last two months could melt away like wallpaper in a fire. Everything good in Bastian's life had been taken away, eventually. Lying next to Max, Bastian realized he'd never allowed someone to see him as Max did. For the world he was strong, clever, unbreakable. For Max, he was vulnerable, intimate. His consent to have Max near him, to touch him, to need him, was unprecedented in his life. For the first time, he was open. He was available. He wanted to see the possibilities.

Max wrapped an arm around Bastian and put his face on his chest. Because he was a head shorter than Bastian, their bodies could be tucked into one another like puzzle pieces. Bastian returned the gesture and put his own arm around his friend. He circled his finger on Max's back. The movement caused Max to shudder and Bastian pulled him closer still. Their chests beat against one another as if the two fleshy hearts could touch.

Bastian felt himself rise against Max and he pressed harder into him. The movement was subtle, each feeling if they stirred too fast, the moment would be broken.

Max pressed his flat palm into Bastian's back to weave them tighter. His own groin ached with the pleasure of it, a pleasure he'd never known before.

Bastian was the first to risk it, to pull his body enough away so that his lips pressed to Max's in the dark of the room. The action was like a start button, winding the boys up to take their passage together. Max had never kissed a girl before. Had never kissed anyone. He could not imagine how he'd gone his whole life without knowing the feeling. His body was awakened from a sleep it didn't know it was in.

Bastian had kissed plenty of girls, but never like this, where the sensation had built up in such a way that he felt he might explode if he didn't keep kissing Max. His body was compelled to make contact with Max's. They reached and tumbled, moaned and groped and they released—their breath, their inhibitions, their wildest imaginations, the pieces of themselves each held so closely, they may have not existed.

***

It was Bastian who fell asleep first afterward. Max's body had awoken in such a way he wondered if he could ever sleep again. He breathed deeply and smelled the sweet musk of Bastian. He wanted this.

All the questions he had about who or what he was becoming over the last eight weeks had been answered. This was who he was. A boy who could lie next to another boy and feel alive. Before Bastian had awoken this in him, Max didn't give consideration to either gender. He'd thought of himself as asexual, above it all. His life was film and imagination and an unreal world beyond his own. Max hadn't felt his own needs until that first day of camp when Bastian sauntered up to him.

Sure, there may have been clues through his lifetime that he was not like other boys. Before, to entertain those ideas in the light of day was ludicrous. But now, the faint suspicions about himself that he'd encountered through his childhood were shining beacons of what made him who he was. That night in the lake, he'd been too afraid to consider what could have happened between them.

Max no longer cared about his responsibilities. With Bastian by his side, he'd be able to do anything. The last few days had proven it. In the most crucial time in his life, they'd transformed into a team. One that could conquer anything. Bastian would stay there, live with them. Francesca would not care. It was doubtful she would even notice him. Maybe they could finish out in the same school together. Max wanted to spend every waking and sleeping moment with Bastian. If they were apart, his heart would surely break into pieces so small they would swim in his blood stream until they dissolved and he was no more.

The thought of them not being together caused Max to wrap his arms around Bastian again. He moaned but did not wake. Max wanted Bastian to feel alive with him, to experience the sensation. He would never be the same and he never wanted to be.

Bastian turned in his sleep and Max clung closer to him. He fit his body against Bastian so they created one long, curved snake. It was in this position that he finally relaxed and released some of the quaking energy that had taken him over.

Tomorrow they would start a new day, a new life together; one Max never thought possible.

***

The dim hallway light cast a shadowy glow in the kitchen. It was dark enough that Bastian didn't see Francesca until he was next to her. She sat slumped over the table, holding half a glass of wine. She did not look up at him and he turned away, going to the sink for some water. He drank slowly and deliberately, waiting for the woman to speak. The house felt still, even with his movement; their combined heartbeats, though resounding in each of their ears, did nothing to fill the room.

"You are a good friend," she said after a time.

"Not likely." Bastian had awoken in Max's embrace hot and confused. What had happened? What had he done? What would his father have said?

"Yes, I see my son takes comfort in you. You are a great comfort to him."

He turned toward her. "I've done what I can to be helpful."

She stood. Bastian could see her wet lashes as she cast her face in his direction. "Helpful … you could be helpful to me, too."

He took one step toward her. And then another. He was a *man*. He would prove it to his father. He wanted to erase what had happened with Max. Francesca's feet stayed in place, but she reached toward him, a subtle flick of her wrist beckoning him forward. She touched his bare, taut chest. With the next step, he saw the moist rims of her eyes. Her pain seemed insurmountable, as if enough of her lay in the living room where her husband's body had been that she was no longer even human.

Bastian didn't think she would—he would have bet his life on the fact that the final step toward him was impossible; but there she was, hands on hands, lips on lips. She cried into his mouth and he took in her pain, feeding off of it, its momentum drawing their bodies into her bedroom, with the photos of her dead husband and the wrinkled sheets and the faint smell of men's cologne.

He did not object when she removed his shorts, but did not move to undress her either. She did it herself, sliding her thin nightdress from her shoulders. Her body did not stir him in the way he'd hoped. That made him take another step to her, and another until he'd pushed her onto the bed. She uttered a small cry—of pleasure? Of pain? He didn't know nor care.

She was the leader, his guide, and he followed her. Her will did not need to overtake him. He had no will and no drive, no desire for her to take hold of, but he reached for her all the same. Bastian pressed his face into her neck and bit down. He was hard against her. That had never been the problem. He operated on autopilot. Neither of them wanted it; neither did anything to stop it. Francesca's mind was on her husband, Bastian's on her son.

When Bastian was with a woman, he'd do it without thought, eyes closed and mind compartmentalized until he was somewhere else. Most did not notice and those who did, didn't seem to care. He was a body, tender and full. His hands explored, groped, did all of the right things, and in return the other set of hands delivered the same for him. It did not matter who lived in the shadow behind his eyes in these moments, only that he was defying them.

Bastian's mind drifted to Max; his soft black curls, to his liquid blue eyes that always looked as if they'd just had tears in them.

Francesca moaned her dead husband's name into his ear and he squeezed his eyes shut. He blocked out the woman, the bed, the room, his thoughts, and his feelings; the reality he'd chosen to live was cast in front of him and he was a petulant child, turning away from it.

***

Max woke in the middle of the night with a thrill and then a sinking heart when he realized Bastian was no longer beside him. So many excruciating and exhilarating thoughts raced through his head. He imagined Bastian was feeling the same way. He lay in bed for a long time, listening to his own breath and not quite believing he was alive, that he was the same boy he'd been the night before. Yet he was not. Max was another person altogether. Self-actualized. Maybe Bastian was feeling confused, Max thought, but he himself felt affirmed.

The house stirred. How could it not, with the ghost of his father occupying some of its space? Max propped himself up on his elbows and listened, looked for Bastian in his room. The movement pressed on his bladder. He needed to use the bathroom.

He crept lightly from his bed, fearing he'd wake the dead. His mother would be long asleep. The woman was famous for her ability to sleep through anything. Fights with his father, breakfasts before school, important events … she slept.

The bathroom was six paces ahead. He'd counted it many times as he snuck from one place to another in his home. Max never wanted to disturb his family. After a while it seemed like they'd mostly forgotten he existed. It suited all three of them best.

Soft moans came from his mother's room. Was she having a nightmare? A place in his heart broke a little, for her pain and his, their shared emotion on this night. He moved with careful steps to her door. Should he wake her from the dream? Should he reassure her that he was there? Perhaps this was something his father had done. He had no way of knowing. Max stayed out of their intimate relationship. Anything that happened behind their closed door was a mystery—and he'd liked it that way.

Max was two steps away when the moans formed into words.

"Harald, Harald."

Max raised his hand to knock when the moans changed in cadence and sound.

"Bastian. Yes, please. Help me. Help me." The mix of pleasure and pain in her voice left no question. If he'd had one, what happened next expelled it.

Bastian's voice. "I will. I will," followed by hard, quiet grunts.

Max turned from the door and ran into the bathroom, almost tripping on the way. He threw the lid of the toilet backwards and vomited into the bowl. But even the sound of his retching could not block the clear voices in his head; they invaded every space until he was shaking and knew that, like the ghost of his father, they would never leave him.

***

Bastian rolled off of Francesca and buried his face in a pillow. He was crying. When was the last time he'd allowed himself this? She was quiet next to him and he muffled his sobs from her. It was not her fault, only his. He thought the shame he'd felt for sleeping with Max could be washed away. As if one action could erase another.

Bastian was in love with Max. Had been for weeks, he knew. So why had he gone and done this? If Max found out, he'd never forgive him. Bastian didn't think he'd be able to forgive himself anyway. Was it the thought of his father, of the disgust he'd have worn on his face if he'd ever known how Bastian felt about boys, that drove him to step forward into Francesca's embrace?

He felt her hand on his shoulder. "Harald."

He turned to face her and she climbed toward him. Bastian pushed her away. "No," he said, his face buried in his hands. He grabbed his clothes, his black shorts from camp, and slipped them on.

Francesca sat up in bed, not bothering to draw the sheet to her bare chest. She watched the man leave. That was not Harald. That was the boy. The boy Max had brought home. She reached for the pill bottle on her nightstand and unscrewed the cap. She took three. How many did that make today? She'd lost count. Her husband had died. She should be afforded extra allowances, extra pills.

Francesca remembered her doctor handing her that first bottle, years before. At first, she'd refused it.

"I don't need these," she'd said, sitting up on his couch and pushing the glass cylinder away.

"I think you do, Francesca. Your hysteria, your longing for Christina—"

"Do not say her name," she said, lying back down.

"I am only saying that these things will not go away. What you have cannot be cured. I want to help you numb it only. Not forever. Just until some of these feelings fade a little."

Francesca sat up again and reached for the bottle.

"You only need one or two a day, no more. Then you can come and see me in a month and let me know how you are coping."

She'd barely seen Dr. James after that, only to refill her prescription every six to eight weeks. He'd been right. She could not be cured.

***

Bastian lay on the couch. He could not bring himself to go back into Max's room. In school, they'd learned that every action required an equal and opposite reaction. That's what he'd done, created an equal and opposite reaction. So why did he feel worse?

Tears began to fall down his face, chafing his cheeks, until he felt arid and empty. Even after the fire, he hadn't cried like this. Because of the drinking, of his father's misery, Bastian had lost the man long before the factory caught on fire. The lie burned inside of him, the lie he told anyone who didn't actually know him. That his father was dead.

It was true that the last piece of Herr Fisher's humanity *had* died in the flames. How else could Bastian explain how his father had sat there in court, half of his face melted away, and told the jurors it was not his fault all those people had died? Bastian had watched some of them plummet to their demise. He had heard the screams. It was his father's fault, along with the owners, that the conditions at the factory were so degraded and unsafe and the fire had wreaked so much havoc. If the doors had not automatically locked in the stairwells, if the fire hoses and extinguishers had been properly maintained, if the wiring had been upgraded as to not set the flame in the first place, those people would not have died. His father had sunk every penny he made back into that hellhole and still it had not been enough. The pride he'd felt in owning something, even in part, clouded his morality.

Bastian was borne of a man who had a hand in killing over a hundred people, and had not been punished. Sure, the factory had closed, but was that really a punishment? The man stayed at home all day, drinking and beating his only son whenever he got the chance.

Bastian was a part of that, had come from that. No one could understand other than Ilsa. She also told people her father was dead, also never brought any friends home.

For Bastian to tell people that he, a strong, witty, young man with a temper and a fist to back it up, would ever allow anyone to treat him the way his father did, was impossible to explain.

The pieces of himself, the dirty, mean ones, the ones that came directly from his father, those were what drove him into Francesca's bed, what made him violent and careless, what would be the end of him. If no one else cared for him, why should he care for himself?

Max cared for him. *Had*, was more like it once he found out what Bastian had done.

Bastian knew he was wallowing, allowing himself to feel bad about his situation, his life. He knew what he had to do. He had to go home tomorrow. To say good-bye to his sister, for now. To say good-bye to Max, forever.

CHAPTER 10

THE THREE SAT AT THE KITCHEN TABLE together without speaking. Max had risen from bed early, never falling back to sleep after his middle-of-the-night revelation. He made oatmeal, enough for all three of them, in a momentary lapse of judgment when he managed to think of his dead father for a second and not mother's and Bastian's betrayal. He couldn't blame his mother, he reasoned. The woman was heartbroken and not in her right mind. Bastian, on the other hand, seemed to know exactly what he was doing.

"Mother," Max began, unsure of what would come out of his mouth next.

She looked up from her bowl. "Hmmm?"

"I want to go. To Italy. Like Uncle Franco suggested."

At this, Bastian raised his eyes to Max. He looked confused. But with one glance from Max at Francesca and back at Bastian, Max cleared any question Bastian may have had.

"Yes, dear. I think that is for the best," she answered without really looking at him. "Soon I can join you, once everything is settled here."

"It's decided then," Max said, echoing his uncle.

"I can telephone Franco and tell him." She spooned oatmeal into her mouth. "On second thought, why don't you take care of that? I need to go and lie down."

She stood from the table, leaving her bowl. When she leaned down to kiss Max's forehead, it was all he could do not to recoil from her. Francesca didn't seem to notice. They listened as her slippered feet padded down the hallway.

"Max," Bastian began.

For the first time that morning Max looked at Bastian straight on. This boy had broken his heart, something Max could not have thought possible twelve hours before.

"Max," he said again, pulling his eyes away. "I should go. Don't you think? Do you think I should go?"

Max looked at his friend's downcast eyes and said nothing. It was all the answer Bastian needed. The chair legs squeaked against the hard wood floors when he stood from the table. The sound of his footsteps were hollow, like a man walking in a vast empty hall. After a moment, Max followed him into the bedroom and stood in the doorway. For the last few days Bastian had been wearing a combination of Max and Herr Amsel's clothing and now he began to gather what lay in various places in the room. He folded two pairs of slacks, a black pair and a khaki pair, both Herr Amsel's. On top of them he placed three shirts. He carefully hung the suit he'd worn to the funeral. Max watched him smooth out the sleeve of the jacket, wondered if it was something his mother had taught him.

Bastian turned toward Max and opened his mouth, parting his lips. He said nothing. Instead, he began to shed the clothes from his body. First his shirt, one of Max's.

Max stayed in the doorway, watching, and Bastian did not turn from him. They looked intently at one another, each telling a story they were unable to speak. Bastian's stomach was taut and brown, only faded slightly from a few days indoors. Max remembered the first time he'd seen Bastian, almost two months before, though it felt like much longer than that.

When Bastian took his pants off, he stepped a half-turn away from Max, who saw he wore no underwear. Had he been without them the night before? Max imagined the white undergarment lying on his parents' bedroom floor, or under his own bed, to be discovered by a maid in the weeks to come as she cleaned out Max's abandoned room. By the time Max came out of his illusion, Bastian was dressed again in his own black shorts and white tee shirt he'd worn when they'd fled camp.

"Do you have everything?" Max asked, knowing the answer. Bastian bent down and removed something from under the mattress and placed it in his pocket.

"Yes," Bastian said. "I guess I'll go then."

"I'll walk you home," Max said.

"You don't have to."

"Well, I don't want it to end like this," Max said, surprising himself.

"Have it your way."

Bastian brushed past him in the doorway and Max held his breath.

Francesca was in her bedroom and the house was quiet. They stood in the living room for a minute, not meeting one another's eyes. Neither really ready to leave, for similar reasons and different reasons. Bastian was the first to step forward. He pushed the button to the elevator. When Max joined him, their shoulders brushed against one another. It felt natural again, for them to be side by side, like it had always been that way. Max squeezed tears from his eyes and reached for Bastian's hand, grasping it for a moment until the elevator door opened. Uncle Franco's face greeted them from the other side. They stepped apart, creating space between them.

"Uncle Franco," Max said and reached his hand out to greet the man. "What are you doing here?"

"I'm here to follow up on our conversation," his uncle replied.

"Yes, well, I am walking Bastian home just now. Can we talk when I get back?"

"Where is your mother?" Franco asked.

"Lying down." Max glanced at Bastian. "She had a long night."

"I should go," Bastian said. "Max, take care of your business and we'll talk another day, okay?" He stepped toward the elevator.

It was Max's opinion that pivotal moments often proved hard to identify while they were taking place. In every movie he'd ever watched, the moments were obvious to him. He'd urge the characters on the screen to reach out and grasp the other person in the room, to watch out before they fell, to acknowledge love when love was present. It had been one of Max's goals in life to not let his own moments pass him by.

"No, Bastian. Uncle Franco, it's important to me to do this. I will see you when I return."

"It's fine, it's fine," he said, waving them away. "I'll see you when you return, Maxwell." The boys boarded the elevator together and watched as Uncle Franco disappeared beyond the closing doors.

***

The sun hurt Bastian's eyes when he stepped onto the busy sidewalk. Men and women strolled or hurried along in front of them. Bastian pointed to the left and said, "This way." Max followed and they did not say anything for several blocks as the world went on around them.

"How far is it?" Max asked.

"You don't have to walk with me. I don't want to take the train." Bastian sounded mad, as if Max had been the one to offend.

"That's not why I was asking. I'd just like to know is all." Max said.

When Bastian spoke, some of the edge from his voice was gone. "From here I'd say about a half-hour walk."

"Great, I could use the fresh air. I feel like we've been inside since we got back to the city." Max could feel Bastian looking at him. "It seems like a long time since we left the camp, even longer since we met."

Bastian grunted in answer. Every piece of Max wanted to ask about last night. About what had happened between the two of them, about what it meant. And about what had transpired in his parents' bedroom— how it had happened, who was to blame.

"Are you really going to Italy?" Bastian asked him.

"I think I have to."

"Why?" The edge was back in Bastian's voice.

"Because," Max said louder than he wanted to. He stopped and grabbed Bastian's arm. "I don't want to spend the rest of my life taking care of my mother. It's selfish, I know—and obviously not the choice you made. But maybe you're a better person than me."

"Don't antagonize me. You know damn well what kind of person I am."

Around them people streamed past on either side. The smell of fried potatoes drifted through the air, which was thick with exhaust, smoke, and haze.

"Bastian, I don't know *anything* about you besides the fact your dad is dead. Something is obviously happening at your house and you won't let me know. Won't tell me. Even though I have let you into every inch of my life. Why won't you *talk* to me?"

"You don't want to be that close to my life." Bastian began walking again and Max had to hurry to catch up. "Besides, you're way too fragile to get that close. You would implode if you knew what my life was really like, what I have to face every day."

Max's face flushed red. It made his ears burn. "How could you possibly know that? How?"

Bastian took a sharp turn at the corner. "Look," he said, stopping. "We're almost there. We should just part here."

"No," Max said. "You don't get to decide everything."

Bastian shook his head in exasperation and kept walking, Max by his side. The nearer they drew to his house, the more Bastian's stomach turned. Trash littered the street and everything lay in grime and dirt. This life was very different from the one he'd been living the last few days. He would not let Max up to the apartment; that he knew. There was too much risk.

He would never do that to Max, his only friend.

The last several weeks were like a dream Bastian was about to wake from. Despite the rivalry with Hans, the beating he'd taken, being leaned on so heavily by Max, all these things were better than what lie eight floors up in his parents' apartment.

When they were a few buildings from his own, Bastian stopped again. He could not meet Max's eyes. None of it seemed real until now.

"We're here." Then, "When will you leave for Italy?" he asked Max.

"I don't know. End of summer maybe. It will take me a few weeks to get everything together." He paused and then asked, "Will I be able to see you again?"

Bastian reached out and ruffled Max's hair. "Sure kid, why not?"

"Funny," Max said. He fought back tears again. Something in him knew this was it, the last time he would see Bastian. It was as if his life was a movie and he was seeing the ending.

Bastian pulled Max into a side alley and then brought him into his chest. He liked how Max fit under his chin, how they fit together. "We will meet again, I promise. No matter what."

"How could you know that?" His voice was muffled and defeated in Bastian's white tee.

Bastian wished he believed what he'd said. Then again, he wished many things. That he had not gone into the bedroom with Francesca, that he had made smarter decisions in life, that he and Max could be together, really together as he had never been with someone before. He squeezed Max tighter but did not answer. He didn't like to lie to him.

They stepped back from one another. "Do you want me to come up?" Max asked.

"No, that isn't a good idea. Another time, okay?"

Max smiled at him and looked up toward the sun. "I guess this is good-bye then."

"For now." Bastian gave Max's shoulder a long squeeze. It felt insincere. "I've got to go and face my fate."

Max screwed his face up in question.

"Don't worry. Everything is fine. Go home and take care of your mother," said Bastian. As soon as he'd said it, he wanted to take it back.

Max turned from him. He didn't want to leave it at that, but belaboring the good-bye made them both feel hollow. Bastian walked away first. Max looked back at him, only once, and then strode in the opposite direction.

***

Max walked unhurriedly, not paying attention to where he was and going blocks out of the way. He did not want to go home. To his mother. To his father's absence. To the bedroom he'd shared with Bastian the last four days. Everything back at the apartment was coated in reality. How was he to plan for a trip to Italy? What would happen once he was there? To think about all of the questions ahead exhausted him, let alone the path he would need to take to arrive at the answers. Sooner than he hoped, Max stood in front of the door to his building.

"Good afternoon, Mr. Amsel," the doorman said.

He wanted to correct him and say that Mr. Amsel was his father. But he supposed he wore the man's name now. "Do you know if my Uncle Franco has left?"

The doorman said no, Uncle Franco was still there. Perhaps it was a good thing. Max could ask him some of the questions on his mind and then he would feel better. Together they would make a plan of how to proceed over the next couple of months.

"Max," his Uncle greeted him as the doors opened.

"What took you so long? Never mind, never mind." He pulled Max from the elevator and sat him on a chair.

"Where's Mom?" Max asked.

"Oh," Franco said, lowering his voice. "She's sleeping, poor thing. Yesterday really took it out of her. But I was able to speak with her earlier and it seems like it's all settled."

"Yes, I've decided to go to Italy like you suggested. But I have a lot of questions." Max was desperate to know the details, as if knowing would give him some control in the situation.

Uncle Franco pulled Max out of his chair. "Well, you can ask me while you pack—but not too many because I need to get home to your Aunt Viola."

"Why do I have to pack now?" Max asked, confused.

"Didn't your mother tell you? The ship leaves tomorrow. There won't be another for months. I know it's rushed, but we both thought it best if you took this one."

Max felt the color drain from his face. Uncle Franco saw his reaction and steadied him, both hands on his shoulders.

"Uncle Franco, I can't leave tomorrow. There is no way."

"There is no other option. I've already purchased your ticket. I am sending a wire to my sister and brother-in-law in Rome. They will be waiting for you and will get you set up with school and housing. You will stay with them until you get a job. Okay?"

Max felt powerless. And he felt guilty. Everything was being decided for him again and he was taking it.

It was not okay.

CHAPTER 11

BASTIAN ASCENDED THE STAIRS to his apartment, feeling like he was walking toward his death; a steady drum played when he planted each foot in front of him. Or was that his heartbeat? The tight hallway was hot and the air around him hung still, no movement to be found. He wanted a cigarette, had almost forgotten about his habit the last few days, but now craved one like it would give him breath. He'd still not decided what he'd do, go inside or run away, when he found himself at the front door. No sounds came from inside. He knew they were home though; where else would they be?

He slid the key in the door and found it already unlocked. A sudden yearning for Max overtook him. Bastian was turning to go back down the stairs when the door opened. On the other side stood his little sister, a quizzical look on her face. At thirteen, she was equal parts beautiful and awkward. He reached out and ruffled her hair and then rested his palm on her cheek.

The last time he'd seen her, they'd sat on his bed, talking in muted tones. Ilsa was just beginning to look like a woman. He was glad for it. It meant her time in their house was limited and she too could escape soon.

"You're not really going back again to that camp, are you?" she'd asked him, glancing at the door nervously.

Bastian stretched out on his bed and she pushed his feet from her nose.

"I don't have much choice, Ils. I can't spend the whole summer here." He wiggled his toes near her face once more. "Besides, you'll get my room for the summer again. Wouldn't you rather that than the couch? You could have some privacy."

"My privacy isn't worth what they're filling your head with. I've seen the pamphlets."

Bastian sat up, offended. "You don't think I know my own mind? I've gone three years in a row. It would raise more suspicion if I didn't go. Anyway, you know he and I cannot be in the same house. At least during the school year I'm hardly here."

"Yes, but that means you're leaving me alone."

He reached for Ilsa's hand. "You will be fine. You're always fine. You're the strongest, most gangly teenager I know."

She smiled at him in a forced way. "So … you'll take care of you and I'll take care of me, I guess?"

"Please don't say it like that. I'd never leave you here if I didn't know you could handle it. It's worse when I'm here. It incenses him." He ruffled her hair and she pushed his hand away.

"I'm getting too old for that, you know."

***

In the seven or so weeks he'd been gone, Ilsa had grown another inch.

"We wondered where you were," she whispered to him, keeping the door tight against her. She was a taller, slighter version of his mother with piercing blue eyes and round cheeks.

"What do you mean?" Bastian asked.

A hand reached around the partially opened door and the older, stonier version of Ilsa stood behind her.

"Mother," Bastian said, nodding.

Frau Fisher said nothing aloud. In her head, though, she asked why on earth her son had chosen to come home after all. She extended her hand to the room and invited him in. It was best to accept their fate and get it over with.

Bastian felt like she was giving him permission to return to his own house, and in a way, she was. The way they'd left things, he'd been unsure if the door would be opened to him again. He entered their tiny two-bedroom apartment and sat in a chair. His mother and Ilsa sat across from him on the couch. It was the couch Ilsa called her bed when he lived there too. Bastian told her that as soon as he moved out, his room was hers.

He remembered the first time he'd held Ilsa, on the very same couch. She'd reached her fingers out, so small and fragile, to his and he held them delicately. He was almost four years old, still he felt the weight of the world upon him. She was his to protect. He sang her a German lullaby he remembered his mother had sung to him. If he could have articulated it, Bastain would have told her how grand her life would be. He would have said: "You will be lucky, because you will be beautiful. The world is nicer to you if you're beautiful. And you will be smart, I can tell. And not just smart for a girl, but as smart as a boy. Smarter even. And I promise I will be here for you, because you're going to need me. We'll need each other. You'll grow up and I bet you'll become a famous actress and everyone you meet will fall in love with you. If anyone at school pulls on your hair, I will punch them."

Baby Ilsa smiled up at him. He believed she knew what he was thinking. "Because you're smart, you are so smart, you'll help us both escape."

He cradled her head as if it would roll off her shoulders if he let it go. The memory of feeling desperate for her safety, as he looked down at her tiny body, was still palpable. Better than anyone, he knew what she'd been born into, the chaos that surrounded them, the fear that engulfed him.

He'd been wrong, though.

His life would not be hers. She'd be a witness to the pain inflicted by his father, but not a recipient of the same hands, nor the belt. If he had to guess why, and he often tried, it was because she looked so much like his mother. The man could not bear to lift his hand to either of them. So, Bastian took the aggression meant for his mother and sister. Because of this, Ilsa was a model daughter. She did everything she was told and more. She always tried to blend into the flowered wallpaper, and did so well she disappeared, even for Bastian at times. He sometimes forgot about the promises he made to her.

***

Now, two sets of the same eyes stared across at him.

"Maybe you should just go," Ilsa said. "Maybe he hasn't realized—"

Frau Fisher put up a hand and said with a tremor in her voice. "He knows. We will just have to deal with the consequences."

Bastian said nothing, only settled deeper into the chair, testing his constitution. They waited another whole minute before Herr Fisher appeared out of the bedroom, a belt in one hand, a piece of paper in the other. After all of the years of seeing his father's disfigured body, Bastian never got used to it. The fire had made a mean man meaner and he wore it on his face, his neck, and his right hand—the hand he used to wield the belt.

Herr Fisher had not always used a belt. At first he'd been able to control his son with words alone. It made Herr Fisher ashamed how easily the boy had cowered as he launched insults at him, jagged weapons that stung. A few years into this control tactic however, Bastian seemed numb to the words. They no longer touched him as they had. So, Herr Fisher had graduated the control, first using his hands and then, as Bastian grew more resilient, the belt. This was the way to raise a strong German man. Dedrik Fisher knew this first hand, had been taught by his own father; strict discipline had been a tradition for generations. When a man understood how to exercise his control and power, Dedrik believed, he understood how to truly be a man.

How else could he have gone from a simple janitor, sweeping up the scraps people left behind at the factory, to a line worker, to a machinist? Every night, Herr Fisher had stayed later than everyone else, figuring out on his own how the gears and mechanics all went together. Only a strong German man would go from that to foreman. Then, when he was presented with an opportunity to become owner, he took it with his own hands.

The previous owners, a pair of Italian brothers, had been brought to court for embezzling. Herr Fisher had stepped in, saving the factory, saving the six hundred and two jobs. Six hundred and two lives that depended on him to make everything run smoothly. He'd gone to the bank for a loan.

He was a strong German man and he took care of those people, those workers. It was the fire that ruined him, the fire that killed all of those people and shut down the factory. It was not his fault. How could it be?

When Herr Fisher returned from the hospital, his son was thirteen and had grown almost as tall as his father. He saw how the boy looked at him—with no regard, no admiration. With disgust. The man would not stand for it. It was his home and he deserved respect. The first time Herr Fisher beat Bastian with the belt, they both bled. His hand had not healed from the fire and the deformed skin ripped and shredded as he brought the belt down on his son, whip after whip.

Herr Fisher had taught Bastian to be a man. And now this? He glared at his son, sitting there on the chair, and waived a letter in his hand.

"You were kicked out? You hit a supervising officer?"

As his father came toward him with the belt, Bastian looked at Ilsa and smiled at her. He remembered the words he had heard over and over again, from Herr Fisher's mouth to Bastian's ear. *When a man understands how to exercise his control and power, he understands how to truly be a man.*

Bastian allowed his father to strike him once, whipping his thigh, before he launched himself forward. His fist felt good against the man's flesh, years of resentment and hatred converging into a solid punch to the jaw.

Herr Fisher was so surprised, he was unable to react. He stared, stunned, at his son before Bastian threw another punch, this one landing on his right eye, the taut, marred skin stretching under impact. The hit threw him backward. His body twisted and bounced off the coffee table, his face and arm making contact with the dark cherry wood.

Bastian's whole body shook as he stood over his father, who lay still.

"What have you done?" his mother wailed.

Ilsa put her hand on Bastian's and pulled him into another room. "You need to go," she said. "Now. You need to go now."

The room came into focus. This was his room. The room in which he'd spent the past seventeen years and where he would likely never return. Ilsa rummaged under the bed, half of her thin body pushed beneath the frame.

"Yes, I have to go." He was in a daze and spoke slowly.

"Hold on," Ilsa said. She panted, as if she'd just run a very long race. And she supposed she had. The next part of her life was about to start and she'd come to it out of breath.

She found what she was looking for, a piggy bank stuffed with bills and coins, hidden away. "I've been picking up side work when I can. And saving. I figured one of us would need it eventually. It looks like it's you."

Ilsa took the pink pig, a symbol of what a childhood was meant to be, and smashed it against the nightstand. Coins and paper money spilled onto the floor. Bastian could not help. He could not move. She collected each piece of money and placed it in a small bag.

"Here. Take this."

"I can't," Bastian told her.

"You have to and you will. You can't come back."

"What about you? I can't leave you."

"Bastian, I have been fine all of this time. I will be fine again. In a couple of years, I won't even be here." Ilsa caught his hand and pulled him into her. "Promise me you will write," she whispered. "So I will always know where you are. So I can find you."

He could feel tears rimming his eyes. Bastian held her for a second longer until he heard a voice from the living room. Or voices? Ilsa pushed him away and he shoved the bag into his pocket. There he found his lucky penny. He pulled it out and gave it to her. "For luck." He kissed her cheek, ruffled her hair, and was gone.

Ilsa watched him leave, listening for sounds from the front of the apartment. She placed the penny between her thumb and forefinger and rubbed. No genie appeared, no one to save her. She would save herself.

***

Bastian strode down the street. Sweat pooled on his forehead. He had nowhere to go. Hatred for his father bubbled inside him, propelling him farther and farther from home. If the man harmed his sister in any way, Bastian would kill him. There would be no second thought.

But before he could ever be an asset to Ilsa, he would need to find a way to survive on his own. He could get a job in some factory. No, that wouldn't do. If he ended up there, every day he would think of his father walking the factory floor. Food and shelter would not just appear out of nowhere, though.

Or, he thought, looking up at the sign above his head, maybe it would.

Bastian stopped in front of a door that read, *American Armed Forces*. Two uniformed men sat behind handsome wooden desks. One looked up from his paperwork and waved. What would anger his father more than anything in the world? If he joined the fight against the Nazis.

He opened the door and walked into the air-conditioned room. Pamphlets lined two long tables opposite the officers and he browsed through them. A proud looking uniformed man stood on one cover, holding an American flag by his side. In bold red letters, the pamphlet read, *Men are needed now!* Then, *Join the Armed Forces. Protect your country. Make your government proud!*

"Can I help you?" asked a voice from behind him.

"Yes," Bastian said, turning to face one of the officers. He held out his hand. "I would like to join up."

The man stood a head taller than Bastian and beamed a bright, toothy smile. He gestured toward the desk and they both took a seat. The room was decorated modestly with propaganda posters framed in black stained wood. The man's desk was tidy. He pulled papers out of a drawer and then looked at Bastian.

"Where do I sign?" Bastian asked, and then added, "Sir."

"Officer Kent," the man said and smiled. "Son, you know we may be about to embark on a war in the near future, right?"

Bastian felt like he knew even better than the officer. "Yes, I've heard of such."

"How old are you?"

Bastian gave the man one of his break-your-heart smiles and said, "Just turned nineteen last week. Not going to school, don't have a girl, so I figured I'd fight for my country. Maybe that will win me some nice girl to come home to."

Officer Kent nodded. "Yes, maybe." He didn't think the boy in front of him was more than sixteen or seventeen, but the army needed men, and this kid wanted to join. Who was he to say no? With a wife and three kids at home, the more men who joined, the less of a chance he'd have to move from recruitment to the field.

Kent brought the papers to the center of the desk, read the discretionary paragraph, and said, "Sign here, son."

CHAPTER 12

I T TOOK MAX LESS TIME to pack than he expected. There was not much he needed that he could not replace when he arrived in Rome. The new city would have clothes, movie posters to put on his walls, and day-to-day essentials. He did pack his father's nicest suit. Yesterday, the woman who laundered their clothes came to the house to drop off the latest load. In it were two of his father's shirts, one suit, several pairs of socks, and underwear. There was nothing of his mother's. Max thanked the woman and took the garments. Along with the suit, he took one of the nicer tailored shirts and three undershirts from his parents' closet. He folded each item with care, hoping he would grow into them someday.

Along with his father's clothes, and a few of his own favorite shirts, he packed the photo of Christina and his grandfather's pocket watch. Finally, he started loading in his favorite books. Afraid that they would not carry English language books, Max crammed as many texts into his bag as he could. Part-way through the task of shoving novels into the nooks and crannies of his suitcase, his mother came into the room. She sat on the edge of his bed, a cigarette in hand. She said nothing. Max studied her through quick glances. She looked smaller to him.

"Mom," Max said.

"Hmmm," she flicked embers into the ashtray on her lap.

"Are you sure I should be leaving? Don't you need me?"

She looked at him and smiled. For a moment, Max felt like he had his mother back. Then she faded away turning her face from him. "I'll be fine, darling. Uncle Franco promises to take care of me."

He gathered his courage and sat next to her on the edge of the bed. "Why can't I take care of you?"

"You're just a boy, dear."

"If I were just a boy, you wouldn't be shipping me off. Alone."

She looked at him again. The truth was, Francesca was exhausted. Sending Max to Italy was the simplest solution. There was no way she could take care of her son. She could barely drag herself out of bed anymore. No, that was not a burden she wished to place on him. Franco would care for her until she was back on her feet and the rest of her family would care for Max. It was for the best.

"Mom?"

She was doing it again, going to her far-off place and not letting him in.

"Max. Have you packed everything you need?"

"Sure, Mom. I guess so."

She returned to her cigarette but did not move from the bed. He packed three more books into his case and then looked around the room for anything he may have missed. Max had grown up in this house, had dreams and nightmares in this bed, had fallen in love with Bastian in this room. In the beforetime, before the market had crashed and before Christina was born and died, they had been happy. Max thought he even remembered feeling loved. By both of them.

On his sixth birthday, they had tucked him into bed with his new stuffed bear, one parent on either side of him. They each kissed him goodnight and then, in a rare instance of affection, they kissed one another. They were happy, in love, still excited to be parents in anticipation of what their son could turn out to be. The city stretched out in front of them and they would conquer it.

"Mom."

A flick of her ashes. "Hmmm?"

"Do you remember when—"

"No memories right now, darling." She stood.

Max felt rage bubble inside of him. She always did this, always shut him down. His face flared red and he stood, ready to burst. But Uncle Franco appeared in the doorway of his bedroom with a smile and a wave and Max felt his body deflate. This was not the way to leave his mother, in anger.

"Uncle," Max said. "Welcome."

Franco kissed Francesca's cheek before she left the room, then he pulled a watch from his pocket and flicked it twice. "It's time to go."

He was taking Max to the pier in Chelsea to board the SS *Conte di Savoia*. It felt like the man did not trust Max, that if he did not take him all the way and see him onto the ship, Max would make a last-minute escape. To where, Franco did not know. He did know it was important for Max to get on board, for him not to be around for what was to come. Franco had already discussed it with his wife—if Francesca did not recover, they would have to send her away for care.

PART TWO
ITALY, 1943-1944

CHAPTER 1
ROME, ITALY; JUNE 1943

THE SWEET RED WINE tasted like strawberries. Max ran his finger along the rim of the glass, a habit he'd picked up the same time he'd started drinking. Or rather, when he'd moved to Rome.

The small café was crowded but he didn't see anyone he knew. It was just as well. The funeral had taken it out of him. More than he'd expected. His Nonna was the reason he'd survived the last five years—thrived, even. From the moment Max landed in this strange, old city, she'd guided him, scolded him when needed, and pushed him forward into his new life. Now she was gone.

He should have been with the rest of his family, mourning, but three days in the packed house was bringing back too many memories of his father's funeral. Max thought he'd shed his grief for his father when he moved to Rome, like stepping from one skin to another. In many ways, he'd mourned the loss of both his parents, having left them both behind, feeling more with each passing month, the war swelling around him like a boil about to pop, that he may never see his mother again.

When Max first moved to Italy, he'd written his mother each week, convinced they would be reunited. She never responded as rapidly as he wrote, still, there had been one to two letters a month from her in the beginning. Then it was a letter every six weeks. Less than a year after Max moved, the letters all but ceased. Francesca had met a man, a businessman, and married him the same month Max graduated high school. It was then that he'd stopped entertaining the idea that his mother would come to Italy, or that she would ask him to come home. She'd abandoned him, erased him from her life and started a new family.

Uncle Franco wrote to say the wedding was lovely, and that Max was not to worry about his mother anymore. Was someone to worry about him? At eighteen, he'd had the world in front of him and no idea what to do with it.

It was Nonna who'd told him to go to film school.

"Every day and every night, where do you disappear to? The cinema. Every chance you get, right?" Nonna said.

"Right, but …."

"Right, *and*—not but, Max." She'd leaned in close to him and rested her wrinkled forehead on his own. "This world is scary and unknown. Best to do what you love while you can."

Nonna had taught him so much in the time they'd spent together. To go after his dream when he'd found it, to always be kind, to love his family, to be himself. That last bit was the hardest for Max. After Bastian, he'd worked hard to deny who he was. He'd never told his Nonna, and she never asked why he didn't find a girl like the rest of his family had. Max believed she knew, somehow, and even though they never discussed it, she gave him her blessing. Nonna wanted Max to be happy, above all. She often told him he'd made the last years of her life extraordinarily happy.

"To have a brilliant, kind, great-grandchild. What else could a Nonna want?"

The rest of the family had embraced Max, loved him when he arrived. But the only person who made Italy feel like home to him was Nonna.

***

A young couple pushed their way to the bar and ordered drinks. Max recognized them. Luca and Angie were among his closest friends. He shut them out by shifting so that his back was facing the bar. He didn't want to socialize, wanted only to think of his Nonna.

He remembered sitting down to his first meal with his great-grandmother and his three cousins. Nonna had placed a full glass of red wine in front of his bowl of fresh gnocchi. Max drank it down, too fast, and asked for another. The cousins had laughed at him when he became silly and giggled at everything they were saying. Although his mother had taught him some Italian, that first night he could not follow anyone's words. The more he drank, the more he laughed. No matter what was said, Max laughed. He was giddy with relief, which he'd not expected. To be freed from his mother, her burden, his burden, made him feel light. He could have floated away. That was until he went to bed, head spinning, and found himself missing home, his parents, Bastian. He was heartbroken. It took the better part of the first year to repair some of the fragments. Max also came to understand that certain shards of his broken life would never be mended, would never be put back together.

The part of himself where he carried Bastian was locked up so tightly, there was no chance he could reach into that dark, indescribable place. He ached to extricate

Bastian from his being. If he succeeded though, what would take refuge in his place?

Once in a while he'd get through days without thinking of him. Not often.

***

The friends Max had been avoiding met his eyes and waved. They came over and he smiled. He liked Angelica and Luca, after all.

"Maxwell, so nice to see you." Angelica kissed his cheeks.

"We never see you here in the afternoon," Luca said, slapping him on the back. "Are you drinking away your sorrows?"

"My Nonna died, actually," Max said.

They both scrunched up their faces in a sympathetic way. Angie hugged him. She felt warm. Max did not remember the last time he'd been touched by someone other than a family member. Her embrace almost brought him to tears; he pulled away.

"So sorry, friend," Luca said, patting him on the back again, gentler this time.

"And so soon after graduation," Angelica said.

"Yes, but she was able to come. I was really happy about that because it was her idea for me to go to film school."

"Really?" Luca asked. "How did I not know that?"

Angie playfully hit him. "Probably because you never ask questions," she said. "Four years of film school together and I bet you can't name five things you know about Max."

"I can," he protested. "Let's see ... he's a Yank."

"You could know that by just talking to him," she said.

Max wasn't sure if he should be offended by the comment. He'd worked hard on his Italian.

"I also know that he came here after his Dad died. Right, Max?"

Max gave them a pained look.

"You're an idiot sometimes, you know that?" Angie was actually mad at Luca now. How was she to marry a man who always said the wrong thing? She turned to Max. "I am so sorry about your Nonna, and that my fiancé never learned about time and place."

"It's okay," Max said. "So, now what? Have you found a job, Luca? You're not going to be able to support Angie working at a restaurant. I've seen how she likes to shop." He winked at Angelica. "That's a beautiful jacket by the way."

Luca's father owned a café and Luca had helped pay for his own schooling by working there. Everyone knew the man did not approve of his son going to film school. Max was lucky in that way. Whatever Nonna said, went. And she wanted him to go to school to study film.

"I've been looking, but it's a terrible time to get a job. With the war ..." he faltered. They all shared the belief that if they didn't talk of the war, it would not be as real.

When America had entered the war in 1941, Max had tried to leave Italy and go back to New York. He didn't know why, but the idea of being back in the States felt safer. He could live with his mother and her new husband, finish school in New York. It never happened. His mother would not answer his pleas and his Nonna thought it best he stay. Max obeyed and waited for the war to come to Italy. Italian men in the armed forces were off in North Africa and who knew where else. Rome, though, remained safe for the most part. Max heard of terrible, terrible events taking place in other countries, so awful were the stories that he did not entertain their truth. No human could be so cruel to another human.

Max had graduated from college a few weeks previously and now there was an expectation from his family that life should move forward. War or no war, he was meant to get a job.

"I've had no leads," Luca told him. "I guess I'll keep working at the café until I find something. I'm sure my father will be thrilled. He can rub in my face every day that I chose the wrong career path. How about you?"

"No leads either. I've been asking around. No one is making a film here. Maybe I should go to Florence or something, but with the war—I don't want to leave home right now," Max said, sighing.

"Maybe we should make our own film, like we did in school for our senior thesis," said Luca.

"Yes," Max said. "Except then we had financial backing from the college. How would we come up with the money now?"

"Great question," Luca said. "And I have no idea."

Angie kissed her fiancé on the cheek. "My little dreamer. You'll figure it out. You both will," she told them. "Max, I'm sorry again about your great-grandmother. She loved you very much. Let's have dinner soon, okay?"

They all kissed and hugged good-bye and Angelica and Luca were on their way. Max ordered another glass of wine and settled into a stool in the corner, wishing to blend into the background.

As he often did after a few glasses of wine, he thought of Bastian. Several months after moving to Italy, Max had written him a letter. It was impersonal, revealing nothing except that he'd arrived and had settled into his family's home in Rome. That way, if Bastian wanted to contact him, he'd now have Max's address. A month later a letter came for him. It was not from Bastian, but his sister, Ilsa. Max read the note a dozen times before it sank in. Bastian was gone.

Her letter was short and formal:

Max,

I don't know who you are, but I am looking for my brother, just as you appear to be. He has been gone since August. If you hear from him, please beg of him to write his sister. If you would like me to do the same, please reply and I will be sure to inform him of your letter.

Max agonized over writing to her again. He and Bastian only shared seven weeks together. A flash in a lifetime. Why would he try so hard to find the boy who was probably not looking for him either?

Four years later, Max had come across Ilsa's letter. He drank a bottle of wine and drafted a reply. Had she ever heard from Bastian? Was he okay? Max never sent it. In the sober morning light his questions didn't matter anymore.

He could not stop himself from dreaming of Bastian, wondering where he was, thinking of him any time he found himself attracted to another man.

Max looked up from his empty glass, lightheaded. The bar was filling up now and outside it was dark. His family would wonder where he was. They thought he was only going out for a quick errand. He dragged himself from his stool and entered into the warm summer air. The city buzzed around him—cars, bicyclists, couples holding hands, and friends laughing into the night. Max could not make another appearance at his Nonna's home where the mourners were. Tomorrow he'd return. For now, he would walk the three blocks to his small flat and sleep.

CHAPTER 2
SEPTEMBER 6, 1943

MAX SMOOTHED THE PRESSED white tablecloth in front of him. His professor was late, a man who was not known for lateness. Max heard stories, more every day. Another bomb? A random disappearance? Since the Americans had landed in Sicily in July, he'd been living in fear. Now, if someone was late, he expected the worst. Only nine days after the Allies invaded Italy, Rome was bombed. The news said more than 4,000 from the San Lorenzo district had died. Max lay awake at night wondering which of his schoolmates were there that day. He tried to locate as many as possible, but it was too difficult to find them all. At least Angie and Luca were safe thus far. Their wedding was scheduled for October, despite the war.

Samuel Rita, Max's favorite professor, entered the restaurant looking frazzled. Max stood to greet him.

"Max," he said, taking the boy's palm firmly in his own and shaking it. "I'm sorry for my lateness. I had to—to take care of something."

Max motioned his hand to the table, "No problem. Please sit, Professor."

"Please, call me Samuel. No formalities here. I am no longer grading you." He smiled at Max. When the two men had run into each other on the street three days prior, Professor Rita had chosen the restaurant. He told Max he wanted to catch up, to see how his former student was doing.

Samuel looked disheveled, as if he'd slept in his clothes. It disarmed Max that someone who'd always appeared well-kept looked so unraveled. "I've never been here before," Max told him, looking around the empty restaurant.

"Ah, it's one of my favorite places in Rome. It's been here for many years, though few seem to know about it. My family alone could have occupied this place before ...."

"Before what, Professor? Sorry, Samuel."

"Oh, nothing, nothing. Tell me, what have you been doing? It's been several months since you graduated. Have you had any luck finding a film job?"

"No. With the war, no one seems to be making movies." By now, Max talked openly of the war. It had come to Italy, to him. There was no denying its existence any longer. "I'm working for a couple who owns a print shop. I found the job in June."

"Oh, yes, I think I did hear something of that from another student. What do you print?"

"A small local newspaper twice a week. I'm first to read the news. Which of course is not always welcome. The week after Mussolini was ousted from power, we sold more papers than ever before."

Samuel looked around the restaurant before responding, "They say he did not even fight it when the Grand Council voted him out. Il Duce says the war is lost. Mussolini let them arrest him with no fight."

"I know," Max said, smiling. "I helped to print that story."

The waiter brought them a bottle of wine at their request and bread with olive oil. The bread tasted like it just came from the oven, warm and soft. After they ordered, Samuel lifted his glass to Max.

"To whatever is next."

Max tipped his glass to Samuel's. "I don't know if I want to toast to that."

"I myself felt relief when Mussolini was arrested," he said quietly, looking around the still empty room again. "The remaining question is whether Italy will continue to fight with Germany or surrender to the Allies."

Max had heard talk of surrender and thought it was the best plan, though he didn't dare say it. One never knew whose side someone was on.

"Well, whatever decision is made, when it is printed, you will be the first to know, Max." Samuel took a sip of his wine and sighed. "It is time for this terrible war to end. For terrible things to stop happening."

Max agreed. Since his Nonna died, the world had deteriorated. Italy in particular. She would have worried herself sick.

"Did you read this morning's paper? About the fighting in Salerno?" Max asked him. Three days ago, the Americans and British had invaded the Italian town. They were less than 300 miles from Rome—a short distance for men to travel when armed with guns and bombs.

"Terrible. 'Hitler's Europe' they call it. It is not my Europe." Samuel said this louder than he intended and darted his eyes around the room, though there were still no other diners. He wanted to talk to Max, to confide in him, to warn him, and to ask him a favor.

The waiter brought their food and they ate quietly for a while, taking large bites of their creamy pasta and drinking down their bottle of wine. Max poured a third glass for each of them. Samuel took a sip and leaned in close to him.

"Can I tell you something?" he asked.

Max nodded in response and bent toward him. He noticed his professor looked older than he had three months prior at graduation. Something was bothering him. Max did not know if it was the war in general, or something more.

"My wife," Samuel began, "is Catholic."

"Okay," Max said.

"I am now also Catholic. But," he looked around once more before he said, "I was born Jewish."

Max had to tell himself not to lean backward, away from the man. Samuel was the same person he had admired, listened to in class, emulated even. But now, he was dangerous. Max heard his Nonna's voice in his head. *Be kind and be yourself.* He was not one to turn his back on a man because he was Jewish. Max adjusted his face, hoping his smile appeared kind and not as a grimace.

"I'm sorry you now have to carry this knowledge."

"Don't be silly," Max told him. "You are no different. How? When—when did you convert, I mean?"

"In 1938. After the radical laws were enacted. My sister, she moved from Italy to Poland in 1932 and she married a Jewish man there. In '35 she came home with her husband and two children. Italy was the only country that did not require a visa to enter in the '30s. Did you know that?"

Max thought he'd heard of this and nodded his head in affirmation.

"Well, in 1940 her husband was sent to one of the detainment camps," Samuel continued, "the one in Campagna, along with several of my other relatives who were born outside of Italy but emigrated when the trouble began." He took a deep breath. "To be honest that is why I was late tonight. Campagna is very close to Salerno. I was afraid the fighting had reached the camp and that my brother-in-law would be in danger. I was trying to get word from relatives who live closer to the fighting."

"And did you? Do you know what is happening?"

Samuel shook his head, no. "We have not been able to find out." He paused and then said, "You know, if I were still Jewish, I would not have been your professor, not after 1938 anyway. I've heard such terrible things about the war, about what the Nazis have been doing, but it feels like only now that the terror is truly coming to us."

In class, Samuel had chosen his words carefully, pausing midsentence to pluck the correct phrase from memory. But now he talked in rapid succession as if the words would be stolen from him if not spoken quickly enough. And why was he choosing to share this information with Max? They'd both been drinking, had loose tongues. His secret sharing seemed bigger than a tipsy confession though. Max suspected his old professor had another motivation in telling him.

"Enough about the war. Tell me more about your work," Samuel said.

"There is not much to say. When we are not printing the paper, we run greeting cards, posters of Mussolini's face. Well, we used to do that, anyway. To be honest, it's a bit lonely and boring."

"How so?"

"The couple that own the place, the woman has a sick daughter she takes care of most of the time, so she is hardly ever around. And her husband—my boss—is older. He takes a lot of breaks during the day, and goes home often. I am by myself more than with him."

"I see," Samuel said, taking a sip of his wine.

"It's okay, really. I read books when there is nothing to be done. I can't complain about being paid to read."

"Not in this state of the world," Samuel gave Max a weak smile. The comment sounded bitter. And it was. Why were his people being persecuted? Why did he live in constant fear for himself and his family? Why had God abandoned them? He looked around the room again. "Max, can we walk and talk?"

Max agreed, paying the bill and then helping the professor from his chair. The man seemed to have aged in the hour they'd spent together.

The area the restaurant occupied was on a side street, minimally populated, but Samuel led him toward the city center where crowds of people still were. They skirted the area near the Trevi fountain. There was safety in numbers. It was easier to have a secret conversation with many people around; it appeared less suspicious.

Once they joined a main street with couples and friends strolling down the sidewalks, Samuel spoke again. "I think that Italy is going to ally with the Americans and British."

This did not surprise Max. It was what he'd been hearing, too.

"But Germany will not give up without a fight. In Salerno, they are killing and being killed as we speak. They are coming toward us. Once Germany is our enemy, I am afraid no one will be safe."

"Professor, I say this with much respect: I'm not sure that I have anything to worry about. I am not Jewish."

Samuel turned from him and looked out into the city. He did not know how to explain to Max that the Nazis were hunting more than Jews.

"I know you think you don't have anything to worry about, but you are not like everyone else." He said this quietly, almost in a whisper.

"What do you mean?" Max asked.

"Do you remember a young man from your class, Gavino?"

The name caused Max to stumble and stop. How did his professor know?

Samuel looked at Max with a slight furrowing of his brow. "I saw the two of you together."

"How? When?" Max felt exposed. Like he'd finally been found out. How could Samuel know? They'd been so careful. Not even really talking in class, keeping their distance in the halls. Gavino was the only person since Bastian. After Gavino graduated from university, they'd moved, he and his family, deep into the countryside where it was supposed to be safer.

"I could tell by the way you looked at each other. You did nothing to reveal yourself except appear to be in love. Don't worry, no one else knew. People talk, so if they'd suspected, I would have heard about it." He placed a hand on Max's shoulder. Samuel knew Max's father had died shortly before Max came to Rome. He'd had Max as a student all four years at school and took a paternal stance with him, more so than with any other student. Samuel felt a connection with Max, and when he discovered his secret, he was happy to keep it for him.

Max was stunned. They kept moving, not wanting to draw attention.

"I only tell you all of this because if Germany does occupy Italy, I do not believe you will be safe. I have heard of lists of names in other countries and I'm sure Italy has a list of its own."

"What should I do?" Max asked him.

"Find somewhere safe. That's what many people who'd do best to stay out of the Nazis path are doing. My family is going into the mountains to hide soon. They say there are people who will keep us safe."

Max realized he was sweating. "How do you know?"

"I don't, but I must have faith," said Samuel.

"What about the other kids from class, the ones who are Jewish?"

Samuel gave a half shrug. It pained him too much to think about all of those people. He'd grown up in Campo di Fiori, or as it had been known, the Jewish Ghetto. He'd been born a few years after 1882, when the walls that surrounded the ghetto had been torn down. Over 13,000 Italian Jews still lived there. He urged his family to abandon their homes, to go into hiding. Since he'd converted and lived as a Catholic, Samuel was savvy to more news than what was available to his Jewish family. People did not hold their tongues around him; they spoke freely and he was able to pick up information. Most in the ghetto still did not see the danger. He could not help them all; perhaps, though, with Max he could help some.

"Max, there is one other thing."

Max was trembling. He felt like someone was pounding a hammer on his chest from inside his body.

Samuel looked at him. He pulled Max to his chest and held on until the shaking subsided.

"I am sorry to lay all of this on you." He took hold of Max's shoulders and looked at him closely. "I know something about you that you don't realize."

"What's that?" Max asked.

"You are stronger than you think you are."

Max shook his head no.

"Yes, you are. I have seen it. And that is why I must ask you a favor." Samuel took one step back but kept his hands on Max's shoulders. "The printing press you work for. You are in a valuable position to help."

A crowd of people walked toward them and Samuel dropped his hands. They bowed their heads and walked forward, to the Trevi fountain where throngs of people gathered.

"How can I help?" Max asked.

"You can print documents for me. Documents that will help my friends and family become different people. I had a connection at the university press but that person is no longer there. There is no one else who I can trust." Samuel spoke at rapid speed and then trailed off.

Max nodded.

"Do you understand what I am asking of you?" Samuel asked.

"Yes."

Once Max agreed to help, Professor Rita found a crowded café where they discussed the details. They would need to bring in a third party, a man who was with the government and could help create the correct documents. Max wanted to know how they could trust this person.

"Because he is the one who helped me get my papers in line when I converted. He has kept my secret all of these years."

"This is a different time than five years ago. How do you know you can still trust him?"

"I don't. But you have to have faith in situations like these." Samuel said.

"Faith in what?"

"In the good in people."

Max scoffed. If even half of the stories about the war he'd heard were true, he saw no reason to trust in the good in people.

Samuel said, "People are helping. Not all people. But enough of them. Please, Max, I need you for this."

***

Max realized as he walked home that it was not happenstance that he'd run into Samuel on the street several days before. It was calculated. Max considered what Samuel had said, that he was stronger than he thought he was. Hadn't Bastian tried to show him the same thing? Even after agreeing to help Samuel, Max was not sure he could.

As he drifted off to sleep that night, he thought of Camp Siegfried, dreamt of it. He was stepping into the boxing ring, standing up for Bastian. He was taking a beating for a cause, for something he believed in. He was being stronger than he thought he was.

CHAPTER 3
OCTOBER 16, 1943

THE LIGHT DRIZZLE MADE THE NIGHT feel colder than it was. Max found almost no one on the streets as he made his way toward the Campo di Fiori neighborhood, which merged into the Jewish Ghetto. Walking the Eternal City, he'd never before found himself alone. The streets of Rome now held a new reality, one of curfews and SS officers checking papers and taking people away. Much had changed in the six weeks since he'd shared a meal with Samuel.

Max felt for his identification in the pocket of his jacket. The ID contained a photograph of him, his address, his ethnicity—his safety. The paper protected him. It was a right he was granted that others were not. It was one of the reasons he'd decided to help Samuel, the unfairness of one people being picked out against another. What if half-breed Italian-Germans were next?

In the bag slung over his shoulder were twenty packets of forged documents. It had taken him and Samuel almost a month to secure all of the information needed to print them accurately. Then Max did his work at night, printing a few sets at a time, hiding them away as he compiled twenty.

It was Samuels's idea to come in the middle of the night.

"Won't it look more suspicious?" Max asked him.

"The SS are not patrolling as much at night because people are keeping to the curfew. Have an open bottle of wine in your hand. If someone stops you, blubber about your girlfriend leaving," Samuel told him.

Max drank one full glass from the bottle before leaving home to give him courage and confirm his story.

The Portico d'Ottavia loomed in front of him in the dark night; ancient and crumbling, it represented the entrance to the Jewish Ghetto. Samuel had told him to walk through the structure and he would find the street where the house was located. Covertly, he removed a scrap of paper from his pocket and looked at the address yet again: *23 Via del Portico d'Ottavia.* It was the home of Samuel's sister. Max's feet teetered on the cobblestone street as he walked through the archway. He took a swig from the bottle and looked around, trying to locate a street sign. Based on Samuels's directions, he should be close to the house.

Over the past month, he and his professor had only contacted each other as much as was needed to get the job done. Samuel was sensitive to watchful SS eyes. It was only two days after their dinner that Italy signed an armistice with the Allies and Germany occupied Italy, flooding the streets with Nazi soldiers. The city had been quieter than Max expected. No bombs were dropped. Not since San Lorenzo in July, anyway. But there were often sounds of gunshots, somehow always in the distance from Max. He saw the German SS on the streets clad in their familiar uniforms and he kept his head down. This was the stance each Italian took when walking through the streets. After Mussolini was forced from power, the alliance with the Americans, and the occupation by Germany, lines and sides had become blurred. Not many seemed to know what they believed in anymore.

Max's mind drifted back to the camp in New York, to the raising of the flag, the blood on his palm. He'd been one of them, or at least he'd walked among them.

***

There was talk of rounding up a great amount of gold from the Jews. A couple of weeks before, Max had overheard his boss, Mr. Cavallo, talking about it in whispers with another man. They were in the back office, the door partway open. Max stood outside, hardly breathing.

"I heard two SS officers talking. They said the Jews are to gather fifty kilograms of gold. If they come up with the sum, they will not deport them."

"Do you think it's true?" Mr. Cavallo asked.

"I have no idea. But they are trying. I heard from someone in my neighborhood that their church sent out a call to the congregation to help. People are bringing their gold forward."

Cavallo made the sign of the cross. "May God have mercy," he said.

Max did not ask around to see if this was true. He did not know who to ask, who to trust. If they only had to gather gold, perhaps there was no need for the documents. Could gold be all the Germans wanted from them? The Nazis were losing ground to the Allies. It could be their effort to focus on securing weapons instead of killing Jews.

Max could not say for sure, so he continued to print the documents until all twenty packets were finished;

new identities for those who didn't want them, who would stay the same if there were a choice.

He used to think the war—the Nazis—were at the end of a long road in the distance, one he could clearly see and avoid. But, somehow, he found himself continually turning onto that road, when he'd rather be anywhere else.

***

The wine was warm from his grip on the bottle, but he took one more swig anyway. Max found the address that matched the one in his pocket. Knocking quietly, he took a step back from the door when it opened. Rain dripped into his eyes. It was hard to see Samuel in the darkness, but he was there.

"Come in, Max, you must be freezing."

The narrow stone house was attached to a larger structure, making up over a dozen homes, all housing Italian Jews. After the Ghetto walls came down, some moved across the river to Trastevere. Most stayed. They'd lived there for many generations, year after year, calling the four-block radius home.

"The children are sleeping, so we'll need to be quiet. My cousins are awake and waiting for you in the kitchen."

"How many are here total?" Max asked.

"Normally only my sister and her two children. Right now, we've been joined by my two cousins and their families. Together we're eleven—thirteen if you count you and me."

Since the war began, Max found he wanted all information available. It made no difference if they were two or twenty, but the knowledge gave him comfort. He took another drink from the bottle.

Samuel patted his arm. "Don't worry, you are safe. We'll get you out of here soon."

Max nodded.

"You have done an incredible, brave thing. You will save lives with these documents," Samuel continued.

"I did very little."

"The lives of my family are not little," Samuel said.

He led Max into the kitchen where Aaron and Ethan sat around the table with their wives Dalia and Rivka, their heads close together, talking. Three candles and an oil lamp lit the room. When Max came in, they stood.

"You must be Max," Rivka said. "Would you like some tea? I'm Rivka. This is my husband Ethan," she pointed to a man with curly dark hair and circles under his eyes. "And Dalia and Aaron." The couple was young. They held hands. It looked like Dalia had been crying.

"Tea?" Rivka asked again.

"Yes, please." Max said.

Ethan stood. "It looks like he has a better idea with the wine." He took the bottle from Max's hand and poured himself a glass. "You don't mind, do you?"

Max said nothing. Samuel stepped forward. "Don't mind Ethan," he said quietly to Max, "he just received word his parents may have been injured in an attack in Naples."

"The Allies are killing just as many of us as the Germans at this point," Ethan said bitterly.

"Hush," Rivka told him. "You don't know what you're talking about. Why don't you and Aaron check on the children?"

The men obeyed, leaving the room.

"All five of the children are in one room together. We told them it was a sleepover," Rivka said.

"Are you Samuel's sister?" Max asked.

"No, Sarah went to bed hours ago," Samuel said. "Since her husband was taken, she's been nervous. Doesn't want to know more than she has to."

Max made a note to think carefully before he spoke. He knew from Samuel that his brother-in-law had been taken to the internment camp in Campagna.

Rivka handed Max his tea and the four of them sat at the table together. In the quiet moment, Max looked around the humble kitchen. It was clean and organized, though worn. He wondered how many generations of their family had lived in this house. He was going to ask, when Aaron and Ethan joined them.

"The children are fine," Aaron said, kissing his wife's head.

They must be newlyweds, Max thought.

Ethan sat next to Max. "How will this work?"

"What do you mean?" Max said.

"What do you want from us?" Ethan added, sounding annoyed, as if Max were missing a point.

Max did not understand. Samuel came forward and put his hand on Max's shoulder. "He wants nothing but to help."

Max extracted the documents from his bag. "Here they are. Twenty new identities."

The group looked through the packets. "Who do you want to be?" Rivka teased Dalia. "I've always fancied myself a Sophia."

Max sipped his tea and watched the family. Despite the war raging around them, they were together. It made him long for his own parents. He doubted his mother would recognize him if they ran into one another on the street. He'd grown another three inches since he'd moved away and his skin was a shade darker from the Italian sun. In truth, Francesca had stopped seeing who Max was years before he moved away. He would now be a distant memory to her, part of a former life she used to live. His Italian family meant well, but only Nonna knew him, understood him. After she'd died, he felt just as adrift as he always had with his parents. Maybe he was just incapable of connecting to most people.

Samuel and his family spread out the documents, finding the correct dates for the intended recipient. They all leaned into each other. The image created a beautiful family portrait. They could be doing anything in that moment in time. If it had been captured in oil and canvas, no one would have suspected what was spread out in front of them. Samuel told Max they planned to use the documents to go into hiding. The papers would allow them to travel and find a safe place. If they were stopped, they would present them and hope for the best. Both Samuel and Max had heard that some Nazis arrested people indiscriminately, papers or not, Jewish or not.

Loud noises came from the street, the sound of trucks and shouting brought them from their family scene.

"Was that gunfire?" Ethan said.

A small girl with green eyes ran into the kitchen and jumped into Dalia's lap. "Mama, what was that sound? I'm scared."

"Hilda, darling. It will be okay." Dalia looked around the room. Her hands shook as she took her daughter into her arms.

At once everyone was up from the table. The women rushed from the room, the men to the window.

"Max," Samuel said. "They have come. We must hide."

Max felt like he was swallowing a boulder. "No."

"Yes, now! Ethan, Aaron—gather the children and my sister. We have five closets in the house. It is our best chance. The papers will not work for us. They came to our neighborhood knowing who would be here. Quickly and quietly. Don't panic anyone."

Ethan and Aaron ran from the room. Samuel turned back to Max. "We should hide under the beds, there is room for both of us in my sister's room."

"No," Max said again. "I will go to the door. Make up a story. I am the only one they might believe."

Samuel looked like he may argue with him. A fist pounded the door. Both men jumped. Max pushed Samuel into the hallway and made his way to the front of the house.

When Max opened the door the early morning sunrise was just breaking through the clouds. A tall man grabbed his shirt and pulled him outside. Max wiped at the rain falling in his eyes and read the sheet of paper the officer had shoved into hands: *You are being transferred. Take along food for eight days, blankets, money, and jewelry. Close the apartment and bring the key. The sick cannot stay behind. There is a hospital in the camp. You have twenty minutes to get ready.*

"How many are here?" The man said in a thick accent with an edgy voice.

"Kann ich Dir helfen?" Max answered in a cordial, steady voice. *How can I help you?* All of those years being yelled at in German by his father had paid off.

The officer faltered. "Sie sind ein Deutsch?" *You are a German?*

"Hälfte," Max answered. *Half.* "My father was German. I am here to collect money from my tenants. I just arrived and searched the house. The dirty Jews are late on the rent. I found no one."

The officer nodded in sympathy.

"I think they've left," Max said, hiding the quaver in his voice by clearing his throat.

"Where is your ID?"

Max pulled his wallet from his pocket and presented his ID.

"Amsel. I have a cousin named Amsel. Good man."

Behind them more shots were fired. On either side, Nazis dragged people from their homes. The officer extended his hand, indicating the chaos that arose. "Feel free to watch."

There was nothing Max wanted to do less, but he watched all the same, protecting the front door from prying eyes. He became a reluctant witness to the horror. The old and the young were marched along the streets. They pulled whole families from the homes and herded them into tight crowds. Max saw a little girl with green eyes cling to her mother. For a second he thought it was Hilda. No. He was standing guard at the door. No one would come in or out from Samuel's home.

Hundreds of families flooded the street. They were jostled and pushed. He saw one SS officer spit at a young man and his wife. *How could so many people be packed into these tiny homes?* Max wondered. Large trucks surrounded the area, blocking them all in. Some of the people were in their nightclothes, having been pulled from bed. Those who bothered to gather supplies carried suitcases and bags. Many were clothed in suits and dresses and hats. Children were bundled in coats. The rain continued to fall.

The officers pushed and directed families to the street in front of the Theatre of Marcellus. The theater loomed in the gray morning light; massive, ancient, and blind to the crime being committed. An old bearded man tripped, falling onto the cobblestone street. Three women helped him up before he could be trampled. Children clung to their parents and grandparents, wailing, red-faced. Some of the officers smiled. Some looked tired. One or two looked sick to the stomach like Max. Across the street, three SS men threw themselves against a door. Something must be blocking it. Or someone. After several more attempts, they gave up and steered more families toward the theatre. One by one the people were loaded into the backs of trucks.

Others, Italians who lived on the surrounding streets and were not Jewish, or who worked in the area, passed by the commotion. Some openly witnessed the scene while others walked quickly, their heads bowed.

A shrill scream. A woman on the street pointed to a baby on the truck being held by another woman. "That is my baby. Give me my baby. I am a Catholic."

They checked the woman's papers and sneered.

Max watched, astonished, as the woman on the truck handed the baby to the officer who shoved the infant into the hands of the crying woman on the ground. Max knew this woman. Her daughter lived in the same neighborhood as his family. It was not her child, but she saved him anyway. The woman who gave up the baby fell against a teenage boy and he wrapped his arms around her. Never had Max seen such devastation.

Hundreds of eyes from the trucks searched the misty scene, looking for help. None came. Max could do nothing other than what he was already doing. If he left the front of the house, one of the officers would go in and find Samuel and his family. If he tried to save someone, he risked the lives of those he was already protecting.

As the sun rose over the city, the people were driven away. On the streets, he saw a child's doll and items of clothing that had fallen off or been torn from bodies as they were shoved against one another. A few broken dishes lay amongst the cobblestones.

After a long while Max went back inside, locking the door against the now still morning. "You're safe," he called quietly. "They have gone."

Slowly, the members of the family emerged from various rooms. Max saw little Hilda with Dalia and Aaron. From another room came Ethan and a teenaged boy and then Rivka and two young girls, their hair in curlers. Finally, Samuel came out with his sister Sarah and her two young children. The boy looked like he'd skinned his knee somehow and the girl, his twin maybe, was still crying.

"Max," Samuel said in a whisper. "You have now truly saved our lives." He pulled him into a hug and Max melted into the man who had shown him more love in his life than his own father. Max cried, for what he had seen, for what may happen to the people in the trucks, and for the triumph of what he'd done.

He pulled himself away from the embrace, only to be taken into another one by Rivka and Ethan and then by Dalia and Aaron, and finally by Sarah, who held him the longest of all. Looking at the family, Max understood for the first time that he had a duty not only to Samuel and his family, but also to anyone he could help. He would not go into hiding. *Amsel.* The name would protect him and he would use it to protect others. Max felt his father's spirit rumble, somewhere just beyond his reach. He would counterbalance his father's use of the name with his own. It was his responsibility to fight.

MAX DIDN'T WANT TO LEAVE his apartment. The unseasonably cold weather did not help, though the weather had nothing to do with his self-imposed exile. The last six weeks had been some of the hardest of his life. Leaving Samuel's he'd felt purpose, drive, like he could make a difference in the world.

That was gone.

When he'd arrived home that morning, after some of the most heartbreaking and exhilarating moments of his life, there was a telegram taped to his door.

His mother was dead.

He'd thought of his mother over the past five years of course, but not every day; still, her death left an unexpected and gaping hole inside of him. He was an orphan. He belonged to no one. When he'd said good-bye to his mother, he never considered that he wouldn't see her again. As flawed as she was, Francesca was the only mother he'd ever have.

Max called Uncle Franco after he'd received the telegram.

"What happened?" Max asked.

"A terrible accident. I was not there but, Anthony, her husband, was. She walked out onto the street without looking. She was struck by a car. They were going very fast."

"Did she do it on purpose?" Max asked.

"Now why would you ask that?" Uncle Franco replied.

"You know perfectly well why I ask that."

His uncle sighed into the phone. He seemed very far away. Max wondered if the operator who connected them could hear their conversation. "I don't know Max. She seemed to be better these last few years. But she still had ... spells."

"Okay," was all Max could say.

"As soon as this terrible war is over I will come see you. I've been wanting to come for years. It feels like you took the last boat to Italy."

"Good for me," Max mumbled.

"What, son?" Uncle Franco said.

The name, son, caught him off guard. He was no one's son now. "I need to go to work, Uncle Franco."

"Okay, okay. I am so sorry, Maxwell. Please write to me if you need anything."

Max almost asked him if he'd seen Bastian since he'd left, if he'd ever come around the house again. "I will try, Uncle. Good-bye."

***

The loss of his mother brought back his most recent loss of his Nonna and then, like an avalanche, the death of his father, the wake and funeral, his night with Bastian. His broken heart. It left him feeling breathless and isolated. He was angry with his mother—inconceivably angry—for sleeping with Bastian, for sending Max away, for abandoning him and starting over. For never getting better. For never being the mother he'd needed. Within the deeply embedded anger was a sadness so raw and grisly he could not allow himself to sit with it. The anger was easier.

When he walked to work in the morning, went to the movies in the evening before curfew, sat in the darkened theater, he carried his parents with him. With both of them gone, he felt their presence in his life heavier than he ever had while they were alive. He spoke to no one, interacted with Mr. Cavallo only when he needed to. The old man offered him time off but Max could not go back to America. The press gave him something to do, to occupy his mind. Along with his mother disappearing from one world to another, Samuel and his family had also vanished. Max hoped they were in a safe place; he understood why they could not contact him. What he'd done that morning lived inside of him, hidden away now as they were. Max was too afraid to tell anyone else what happened. With this fear and the death of his mother, he hibernated; when he was not working, he lay for hours on end in bed in the dark, or sat in blackened movie theaters, shutting out the world as it deteriorated around him.

On the occasions when he thought of someone other than himself, he was racked with such guilt that his body felt too heavy to lift. The day after the trucks pulled away with hundreds of Jews shoved into the backs of them, Max saw an Italian resistance newspaper, *L'Italia libera*, and picked it up. *The Germans during the night and all day long went around Rome seizing Italians for their furnaces.* He read and re-read the line. He'd stared into their faces; he saw their fears. Not unfounded. He'd done nothing. He could have saved more.

Someone knocked on Max's apartment door. He didn't move from the couch. He heard another knock.

"Max, it's Luca. Come on, open up."

He peeled himself from the couch to open the door.

"You look like shit," Luca said.

Max lay down again without saying anything.

Luca shifted Max's feet to the floor and took the spot they'd occupied.

"I'm not in the mood," Max told him.

"I'm sorry about your mother."

At this, Max sat up. "How do you know about that?"

"I stopped by your work since you haven't been answering my calls. Mr. Cavallo told me."

"Well, now you see why I don't want to talk." Max turned onto his side.

"Christ, Max. I thought for a second that you'd been taken or something, that you were sitting in some basement, beaten half to death or had been shipped out to one of those wretched camps." Luca looked at his friend, studying the deep bags under his eyes and the yellow tinge of his skin. "What's going on with you, Max?"

"Didn't you just answer your own question?"

"No, you've been weird since before your mom. And I haven't seen you since the wedding."

"I don't want to talk about it. Did you come over just to ask me questions?"

Luca looked wounded. He stood up and walked the length of the room, away from Max.

"I'm sorry, Luca. I'm being a jerk," Max said.

"Yes, you are. And no, I didn't come over to ask you questions. I came to check on you and to tell you some news."

"What news?" Max asked.

"A movie. A movie being made here in Rome."

Max sat up and looked at Luca straight on. "Really?"

Luca smiled. "I knew you'd be excited."

"I wouldn't go that far." He melted back into the couch. How could he take part in something so frivolous when the world was falling apart around him?

"Come on, this could be an opportunity for us. Work, money, something to do. Plus, it gets me out of the restaurant," said Luca.

"Who in their right mind would shoot a movie right now with Nazis roaming the streets?" Max asked.

Luca looked around the room as if Max was hiding someone who would overhear them.

"That's the best part. It's being made by De Sica."

At this Max opened his mouth, part wonder, part disbelief. De Sica had come to their school sophomore year and talked about his movies. He was a rising star.

"Okay, even if De Sica is doing the film, do you really think the Nazis are going to let us shoot on the streets of Rome?" Max asked.

"They will if the Pope says so," Luca said with a smile.

"What? Just lay it all out for me. What do you know?"

"Okay," Luca paced. "De Sica is directing the film. It's called *The Gate of Heaven*. I've heard that Pope Pius XII commissioned the film himself and that he's allowing De Sica to shoot it inside a Vatican-controlled church."

"They are allowing it to be filmed *inside* the Vatican?"

Luca stopped in front of Max. "Not exactly. At the Basilica of St. Paulo Outside the Walls. It's not in Vatican City. In fact, it's the only church outside the walls. But it means the film has the protection of the Pope. Not even Hitler will go up against him. And the leading lady is Maria Mercader. She's been in a ton of movies. They are saying Massimo Girotti has signed on too. This thing is going to be huge!" Luca felt giddy. This was their chance to start their film careers.

Max had other ideas.

He stood and took Luca by the shoulders. "I need to tell you something."

"That you're in?"

"Yes, but … no—rather, *yes, and …*" Max said. His mind was moving fast. A film as big as this was bound to need more people. Actors, crewmen, extras. "Do you remember October sixteenth, the round up?"

"I heard about it, if that's what you mean. You know what they're saying, right? Where they took them?"

"Yes, I read about it," Max said.

"Why are you asking me this?"

Max led his friend to the couch and they sat. "I was there that morning."

"In the ghetto?" Luca asked in disbelief.

"Yes, I'd gone to help. You can't tell anyone this next part."

Luca looked weary. He was tired, didn't want to keep anyone's secrets. He'd only married five weeks before and the day after the wedding, Angie had gone to stay with relatives in the hills, where they heard it would be safe. They weren't Jewish, but like many of Rome's citizens, they wanted to steer clear of the Nazis completely. She'd begged Luca to go with her, to wait for the Allies in a distant place that seemed untouchable. Luca could not go. He had a duty to stay with his family in Rome. Angie tried to stay with him, but he in turn begged as well; for her safety, she needed to go to the mountains. She'd been gone the length of their marriage. Luca was afraid he'd never see her again. That he would forget what she looked like.

"What did you do, Max?" Luca asked cautiously.

"I helped make documents. Fake papers for some Jewish people so they could travel, find a place hidden in the city or in the mountains."

Luca stood. "Do you realize what could have happened if you'd been caught with those papers? Did Mr. Cavallo know?"

"No. And he can't," Max said sternly. "There's more. I saw the Germans that morning. Saw them herd the people into trucks like cattle. Whole families. Young. Old. Everyone in a several block radius who didn't hide or manage to escape." Max breathed deeply, gaining clarity. "I think all of those people were driven to their deaths. That is what they call the places. Death camps."

"That's awful. I'm sorry you had to see it," said Luca.

"See it? They are *living* it. Don't you understand? We must help."

"You mean print more papers?"

"No, we can do something much bigger," Max said. His apartment felt suddenly small, as if it could not hold the idea itself. He raked his fingers through his hair, looking at his friend. Luca had people who loved and counted on him. He had a wife. Max had no one like that. He turned away. "Or maybe not."

"Maybe not something bigger?" Luca asked.

"Maybe not *we*."

Luca and Max had been friends for many years. What did that amount to? Was it Max's right to possibly put him in danger?

Luca flopped onto the couch. "Enough with the big reveal. This isn't a movie, for Christ's sake. Just tell me already."

So, Max did. He told him of his idea: they would get hired onto the movie, they would speak to De Sica, together they would convince him to bring on Jews as actors, crew, and extras to shelter them from the Nazis. They would have the protection of the church. The Vatican even. Max could help to rescue many more than twenty.

"I don't know. What if De Sica says no and we lose the job?" Luca asked.

"The lives of hundreds of Italian Jews are worth that risk."

Luca gazed out the window. "You're crazy, you know that?"

"We can do this. I know we can."

With that, they plotted their plan. For a long time after, they sat in silence, the night turning in around them as the light faded from the room.

CHAPTER 5
SALERNO, ITALY;
SEPTEMBER 15, 1943

THE MORNING LIGHT REFLECTED off the sand and streamed through Bastian's makeshift tent. It gave him a headache. Next to him the men began to stir, their bodies fighting against the oncoming light. In the distance, there was gunfire. Always.

Salerno was supposed to be simple. Instead, they'd now been pushing back against the Germans on the shoreline for six days. He had no idea how many they'd lost. The numbers seemed insurmountable.

Tanks and equipment littered the landscape. They'd been fighting a literal uphill battle, the Germans maintaining the higher ground as they fought their way up the beach. The troops were dispersed, Americans and British, at three key points along the coastline. Bastian wondered how the other two units were holding up. It felt like they were at a tipping point; at any moment, they would either mount the hill, defeating the oncoming Germans, or be driven into the water, back onto the ships and made to retreat.

***

Lieutenant General Clark came into the tent. He towered over them, his tall frame not fitting into the space. He looked irritated for so early in the morning.

"Up, men. We're meeting on the ship at 0700 to discuss our plan of attack for the day. I'm tired of fighting these damn Nazis on this damn beach."

The men all nodded in agreement. Bastian had thought, before he joined the Army, that he knew what tired was. He'd had no idea. The last year and a half of his enlistment had taken him partway across the world. He'd seen things he never thought he would. Bodies stretched for a half-mile at Henderson's Field. They'd burned or buried as many of the 1,500 dead as they could. The bombed-out city of London had taken him by surprise. The destruction appeared endless. Then in Tunisia, tanks had rolled through previously pristine beaches with enough artillery to wipe a town off the map. He'd spent sleepless nights holding a gun against his chest; hours standing still and silent, waiting; days longing for something familiar. And now he was finally in Italy, the place he'd been aiming for the last several years, just hoping Max was still there.

The soldiers dressed and made their way to the ship. Sleepy as the men were, when they stepped onto the beach, they were ready for the day. The chaos of the last week was reflected in the sand; the stray bullets, the equipment, the bloodied shore. They trudged together up the steep ramp and into the belly of the ship.

***

"Today, we will take a double-pronged approach to push these sons a'bitches back so we can finally gain ground," Clark said as the men gathered around him. "We'll utilize heavy naval gunfire and aerial bombardment. Once some of the path is clear, troops will go on foot." The men received the rest of the instructions. Often as they gathered together, Bastian would look around the group, wondering who would come back. General Clark looked directly at him. His chest felt tight.

"Staff Sergeants Bastian Fisher, Charles Miller, and James Bell, stay behind while the troops disperse."

Bastian and the two men glanced at each other while the others streamed out. A few looked back. Clark never gave anything away. Bastian used to love being singled out, asked to prove himself. He was always able to rise to the occasion. Now, being asked to prove himself was likely to result in death. That only bothered him sometimes.

"I have a special job for Bastian and James. Charles, you will be in charge of your unit today as well as Fisher's and Bell's."

Charles Miller saluted Clark and cast his eyes to Bastian and James. He didn't know if he should want to trade places with them or not.

"You're dismissed, Miller."

They watched him walk away. Bastian had been part of a special intelligence unit with Bell and a few others for the past year. Perhaps they were being assigned a new mission?

The two men followed Clark into his office. Bastian had only been in there one time before. Since he'd risen in the ranks, taking on the position of staff sergeant and assigned intelligence jobs, Bastian had been pulled to do special operations only twice. The first time was in London. He'd been sent to a bar with Bell, dressed in civilian clothes and put behind the counter to serve drinks. The bar was a suspected hangout of Nazi sympathizers and they were sent to gather intelligence. That night, he and Bell learned important information as they got four men drunk enough to loosen their tongues.

The second time, he'd been pulled with four other men to ambush a house where they suspected a high-ranking Nazi officer was staying. When they arrived, heavily armed and naïve, the house appeared empty. It wasn't until a bomb exploded, killing two of their men, that they realized it was a set up. Bastian and two other soldiers were in another part of the house when the explosion went off. They found pieces of the men, nothing discernible. They'd been reduced to dust.

***

"Bell, Fisher," Clark addressed them, pointing to two chairs in his office, indicating for them to sit. "We've received intelligence that the Germans are storing some pretty heavy artillery a few miles from here, in town. We need you to confirm the location of the building."

"General," Bastian said, "how will we do this without being caught?"

"You're going to pretend like you belong there," Clark said. The other two men waited for him to enlighten them further. "You both speak German, correct?" Clark asked.

"Yes sir," the two men said in unison.

"We're going to send you into town. You'll go to the building, act like you belong there, and see what you find."

"What do we do with the arms?" James asked.

"You leave them exactly where you find them, Bell," the General said.

"But …" Bell began.

"Then you'll bomb out the building, right sir?" Bastian asked.

Clark smiled at Bastian. "Smart. Yes, that's exactly what we'll do." Clark stood and walked over to a cabinet, opened it and removed a pile of clothing. He handed each man a stack. Bastian held his up, the final piece of the puzzle. Two grey-green uniforms, much like the ones they wore themselves, except these had different collars and they bore the insignia of the German officers. Bastian saw the familiar lightning bolt shapes he had donned on his camp uniform many years ago.

"Once you've passed the beach, you will put these on. Speak only in German when you get to town and only speak when you have to. If anyone hears you, they may recognize your accents."

Bastian felt his heartbeat pulsating through his body. A familiar exhilaration took over. It was something he'd felt at camp more than once, felt with Max more than once, and felt in war many times. James looked white. His leg was shaking up and down next to Bastian's. The General eyed him with suspicion.

"Are you two up for this?"

Bastian stood and saluted. "Yes, sir!"

"Bell?" Clark said.

Bell rose, unsure, but repeated Bastian's words. "Yes, sir."

***

They moved through the woods with less trouble than they'd anticipated. Around them, they heard the sounds of guns, of tanks moving, of airplanes overhead. Once they were clear of the woods and at the edge of town, they stripped off their clothes, hiding them. They dressed in silence. After so many years in camp and then the army, Bastian was used to seeing half naked, or in some cases, fully naked men. He was vigilant to not linger with his gaze. Since joining up, Bastian had been with a few men, when he was able. Publicly, he was with women whenever it seemed necessary.

They each buttoned their jackets. Bastian's fingers lingered over the SS Eagle with the circled swastika at its base. He could have easily lived a totally different life. Sometimes he wondered if he'd chosen the correct one.

***

They arrived in town, walking with their heads held high. The place was mostly intact, with a few buildings showing damage from one of their bomb raids. They'd only hit the town once, without much success. Bastian heard they'd killed more Italian civilians than German soldiers, which was part of the reason Clark was being so careful about their next attack. Sometimes Bastian thought the American Army made choices based on appearances, instead of intelligent tactical planning. But they were the good guys—they needed to maintain that image.

"What if our own planes hit us while we're in town? Do you think Clark told them we were here?" Bell asked in a low voice.

"German only," Bastian reminded Bell before he continued. "He needs us to come back to tell him what we learned. I'm sure he won't do anything to risk our lives." Bastian only half believed his own words. He knew Clark was smart. If there were an opportunity they could gain battleground, he would risk what he needed. "We should stop for lunch," Bastian said.

Bell stopped walking and started again, only missing a step. "Do you really think that's a good idea?"

"We're supposed to blend in. If we go skulking through town, straight to their armory, they'll notice. Besides, I feel like I haven't had real food in a long time. Isn't Italy known for its cuisine?"

"There probably isn't even a restaurant open."

Before Bell could make his case, the pair came upon a small café with an open door. The man behind the counter shrank away when they walked in. Usually they received a warm greeting—the Allies coming to save them! But this man would not know that; now they were Nazis.

"Can I help you, gentlemen?" the man asked in a broken English accent.

"We'd like lunch," Bastian answered in German, only half managing the accent.

The man screwed his mouth up in confusion then decided against whatever he was going to say.

They sat hunched over their food at a corner table near the window. Bastian watched the people hurry along the street. No one looked like they wished to be far from home. Two German officers strolled passed the café window. Bastian and Bell held their breath and smiled curtly. In return they received two nods, one from each man.

"We should finish up and get over there," Bell said quietly. He wiped his mouth with the cloth napkin.

"At least the food was good," Bastian said. "Last meal material if you ask me."

"Funny," Bell said, shaking his head.

When they walked out, the streets were mostly deserted. Bastian took the address and small hand-drawn map from his pocket to check it once more. "I think it's down this street, past that church and then around the corner."

They went along the cobblestone road, each thinking of the task at hand. The day was sun-kissed and warm. The breeze swept softly along the street, a light caress against their skin. None of it matched the mood or the mission. Bastian supposed that God, if there were one, didn't care about their undertaking when designing the day. Or, perhaps, it was His last gift to them.

"Bastian," James said, stopping in front of the church. Only when they peered up at it together did Bastian realize it'd been bombed. "Can we stop here? Just for a moment?"

"You're not turning religious on me are you, Bell?"

"I'm not turning anything," he answered snidely. "I've been Catholic since the day I was born."

Bastian avoided getting to know his fellow soldiers, who their families were and who they'd left behind, their political views, what they liked to do for fun, and yes, what they believed in.

"Sure, Bell. Let's go in."

Bell walked ahead of him toward the altar, his Nazi boots clicking on the stone floor. Bastian watched him make the sign of the cross and stare up at the damaged building. He realized Bell may take a while and sat in the pew, three rows from the front. Behind an adorned archway, where the statuary was, part of the church had been blown away. Bell stood on the rubble. There was a broken beauty to it, Bastian thought. This is what churches should look like, to accurately mirror those who need them the most. Not the gilded, detailed, perfection that composed a cathedral. This broken mess was what he longed for others to see. On the outside Bastian was sculpted perfection, cheekbones just so, a strong jaw and twinkling smile; the physical characteristics hid what he looked like inside.

Bastian reached into his pocket and pulled out a letter that he'd transferred into his new uniform, along with his wallet, the address and map. The handwriting on the envelope was well known to him. That of his best friend, his sister, Ilsa. It arrived the week before as they were docking at Salerno. He'd read and re-read the letter, having mixed feelings about its content. Bastian felt constant guilt that his little sister was in the bombed-out city of London. She'd followed him there, only for him to be shipped to Africa before she arrived. Now she was asking to be transferred again.

August 8ᵗʰ, 1943

My dearest brother,

London is as gray as ever. I don't know how the people are still holding up. The other nurses tell me they cannot remember a day without rations. By the time this terrible war is over, I wonder if all the men will be gone. Walking down the streets continues to be bizarre. Women, children, a few elders—hardly ever a man among them. Poor England will go extinct at this rate. You were here not long after the Blitz so you know what it's like. Everything is collapsing.

Clara— you remember me talking about her, right? She's the woman who convinced the Red Cross to take me, even though I was technically too young to join. I had top marks at school, though, as you know, having graduated high school early and joining the accelerated nursing program. And they desperately needed nurses to travel overseas, so I don't think they needed that much convincing. Anyway, Clara read in the paper that you all are gaining ground there. First Sicily, where next? It won't be long until you get to Rome and can take the city. Perhaps by the New Year?

Everything here is as expected. The men who come back come in pieces. Even if their bodies are unharmed, their minds are fractured. I only hope that you, dear brother, are holding up better than them. I know you tell me that you are strong, and I believe you, but it does not take much for a stream to become a river, for a crack to make a foundation structurally unsound.

Do you know what today is? Today is the fifth anniversary of the last time we saw each other. I don't know what made me remember the date, then or now. Five years seems like half my life. In truth, it's more like a fourth of my life. But that is still a long time. And you, from training to war: to the Solomon Islands, to London (before I could arrive, of course), to who knows where in Africa, and now to Italy. You're a world traveler who refuses to take a break. I know it's not your fault that you were shipped to North Africa before I could arrive in England, but I'm still sore about it. Blame the Army, right? Just not out loud.

You said in your last letter that you feel like a lifetime has passed since we saw each other, since you joined up, and I agree. Which is why (and don't get mad, I know you will) I've put in a request to be transferred to Italy, where I am more needed. There is an influx of British and American nurses here now. I can be used there. And Clara said she would go with me. She's like

a mother to me. She'll protect me. Speaking of mothers ....
Once I know more, like if they will send my unit to
Italy and when I will be sent, I will let you know. Please
just promise me not to rush off to another country before
I can get to you? Okay?

Sending all my love,
Ilsa

P.S. Seriously about mother, she misses you. I think he
misses you too, though he wouldn't say it. Each time I
write to them, I tell them you are well. They'd really love
to hear from you, though.

P.P.S. Please write me soon!

***

When Bastian looked up from the letter, Bell was standing next to his pew. He folded it back into its envelope and shoved it into his pocket. "Ready?" Bastian asked.

"I guess so," Bell answered, a slight shake in his voice.

They walked the half-block toward the suspected armory. At a corner building that looked onto the front of it, they leaned their black boots against the brick and took up watch.

"How should we do this?" Bell asked.

"We'll watch for a bit, see who goes in and out. Then, we sneak in, take a quick look around for the weapons, and get out of there. Simple."

"Yeah, nothing is simple with you, Fisher."

Bastian smirked. "Give me a cigarette, will ya?"

Bell obliged. They smoked and watched in silence. After two cigarettes each, Bastian leaned forward and said, "It's time." The street had been quiet, but who knew how long it would last. Bastian had moved forward two steps when he felt Bell tug on his sleeve.

Bastian planted himself against the building again and asked for another cigarette. When he was halfway through it Bell said, "I don't think I can do this."

"Yes, you can. We'll be fine."

"Did I tell you Emily is pregnant?"

"No shit," Bastian said, hitting him on the back in congratulations. The man looked white. "It's yours, right?"

"Of course it is. Asshole. I just—I was thinking when we were in that church, what if I never get to meet my son or daughter?"

"Okay," Bastian said, snubbing out the butt of his cigarette on the cobblestone street.

"Okay, what?" he asked.

"That's a valid fear and I get it. I'll be right back."

"Wait," Bell half shouted as Bastian moved forward. This time when Bell grabbed his sleeve, Bastian did not miss a step.

Bell stayed put while Bastian marched forward and watched as he opened the front door and walked inside. Act like we belong, Bell thought. That's what he was doing. Five minutes passed. Then ten. He was on his third cigarette when a decorated Nazi officer came walking down the street. The man stopped in front of the armory, looked around, and walked inside. Moments later, Bell heard a gun. A single shot echoed through the street, disturbing the sky-blue day like a fish leaping from still water. The noise rippled through his body. He waited for Bastian to reappear.

BELL PACED IN THE General's small office. When they'd been in there the day before (had it really only been yesterday?) he'd noticed nothing about the space. His eyes focused on the painting hanging on the wall: George Washington crossing the Delaware. The desk was tidy. A small pile of papers to the right. The General must be right-handed. A fountain pen laid in a way that looked purposefully artistic, though Bell doubted General Clark considered such a thing. His left eye twitched. He paced faster. In the small space, it took him three strides to cross from one side to the other.

The door opened and General Clark strode in. Bell could not read his face. That was part of what made the General a good military man.

"Bell and Fisher, I have good news," he said.

While Bell paced, Bastian had sat. Calm. Contemplative. Both of them saluted when the General entered.

"Sit down, sit down." He looked up at Bell. "You too, have a seat."

The two young men took their place in front of Clark's desk. Bell was on edge, shaking his leg until Bastian placed a hand on his knee.

"The Germans have evacuated Salerno. After we took out their armory, they had little going for them.

Between that, the air assault from the beach, and what we were able to do on the ground, we drove them out. Good job, boys."

"What's next?" Bastian asked, eager.

"Next," Clark said, looking directly at Bastian, "you're going to tell me exactly what the hell happened yesterday."

"What do you mean?" Bell asked, his leg shaking again.

Bastian nudged him discreetly but the gesture was apparent to Clark. Bell was the weaker link, he would tell Clark what happened.

The General continued. "What I mean is, after we hit the armory, we went in by foot. There were only a few people in the building, mostly in pieces. There was one person near the front door, furthest away from the weaponries, dead, but not from the blast."

"How was he killed?" Bell asked.

Bastian rolled his eyes. There was no way around it.

"It seems he was shot."

Bell looked at Bastian, his eyes wide. If Clark had not known what happened, he now had most of the pieces to figure it out.

"You were supposed to go in and out, unseen."

Bastian locked eyes with Clark. "Who was it? Someone important, right?"

"His name was Fedor von Bock. He was a field marshal. He played a decisive role in the defeat of Poland and France. And now he is dead. Either of you care to explain how that happened? When you reported back yesterday, there was no mention of a dead field marshal."

"I can explain," Bastian began.

Clark interrupted him. "No, you did all the talking yesterday, Fisher. I'd like Bell to explain."

Bastian nodded slightly at Bell, who spoke with a quiver in his voice. "Okay, sir. We were not completely honest with you yesterday. Bastian didn't think you needed all of the details, and I agreed. Sir."

"I'm waiting," Clark said.

"We were set to go in together. And … did I tell you my wife is pregnant? I'm hoping for a boy." Clark looked at him, unblinking. "Bastian was trying to do me a favor. I was going to go in. But I chickened out. He went in alone."

Clark stood. He stared down at them. "So, you allowed your comrade to go into a dangerous situation alone. With no backup?"

"Sir," Bastian said. "It was me who was in the wrong. When he said he didn't think he could do it I should have stayed put until he changed his mind."

"Damn right you should have," Clark shouted.

"But," Bastian flashed his biggest smile, boldly, "all's well that ends well, right? The man I killed sounds like a bad guy, and the Germans have pushed back. We can move forward now, right? Toward Rome?"

Clark's face was red. He sat in his chair and wiped his brow with a handkerchief.

"Fisher, you ever pull something like that again I will have you stripped of your rank. And Bell, you ever allow a man to go in on his own, to you, I will do much worse than relieve you of your position."

Both men nodded at the General. Clark could not punish Bastian for his effort. It was a critical step and he had helped them make it. They could not move on to Naples and keep pushing forward toward Rome without it. He was not going to openly admit it to them, though he suspected Fisher knew as much. Eisenhower was feeling the impetus from Churchill to take Rome by year's end. If that were to happen, Clark would need to be lenient about some things.

"Bell, you are dismissed."

Bell stood, glanced at Bastian once, and hurried out.

Clark contemplated the boy in front of him. He looked no more than a boy. Despite his height, his angular face, Bastian had a childlike quality about him. It was likely what made him so impish in his actions. It was also what would help him in this next mission. He looked too young to be up to something of substance. Even after Clark had decided on it, he wasn't sure it was the right move. Bastian was smart, savvy. He could hold his own. He wasn't the highest-ranking sergeant on his unit (perhaps that was for the best); still, he was shrewd and able. Clark would not send him unless he was sure. The General realized he was trying to talk himself into something. In the end, it would be Bastian's decision.

"Sir?" Bastian said. They'd been sitting in silence for almost two minutes. Bastian watched the seconds tick away on the clock by Washington's head.

"Yes. Sorry, son. I have a mission for you. After the stunt you pulled, I wasn't sure you were the right fit for it. If you elect to take the mission, I will support you and if you decide not to, I will understand."

Bastian moved to the end of his chair. This was it.

"Once, you gathered intelligence in London. You did a good job. Is that something you'd do again?"

"Yes, sir," Bastian nodded. He was good at blending in when need be, at getting the right information from the right people. It was his charm. Or his smile. Likely both.

"We need someone to go to the Eternal City to listen, to discover, to report back."

"You're sending me to Rome?" He was sure Clark could see his heart beating in his chest. This. This was the plan, the point. The motivation.

Clark's eyebrows twitched upwards, for a second only. "If you accept. Yes. We hope to be there in the next month. Your information could be critical in starting us off on the right foot. We need to push past Naples and then who knows what else we may encounter on the way. We need someone on the ground floor and you are our man."

Bastian jumped from his chair. "Yes, yes, of course. I'm your man."

Clark stood. "Have you ever been to Rome?"

"No, sir. But I'll be able to find my way."

"Know anyone there?" The flicker of the eyebrows again, imperceptible if Bastian's eyes were not trained on them.

He didn't misstep. "No, sir. No one."

Clark nodded. As Bastian listened to the rest of the instructions, his mind raced. At once he was back in New York, at Camp Siegfried, under his father's belt, in Max's arms.

***

The train was jarring. It jerked back and forth as if they were running over cavernous furrows in the track. Without interruptions, it should take around nine hours to get from Salerno to Rome. Bastian knew in war there were always interruptions. He was hopeful despite this.

An hour or so in he settled deeper into his seat and pulled his cap down over his eyes. Above him, his bag contained several pairs of slacks, shirts, two sweaters and a tie. At Clark's suggestion, he'd left his uniform. When the army entered the open city, Clark would return it to him. He'd worn civilian clothes since joining up, though not a lot. He felt at once like his old self and like no one he knew at all.

He pulled his tweed coat tighter around his shoulders. It made him look a bit like his father, before the fire, when he was handsome and smooth-skinned. Bastian didn't want to, but he thought of his father often. He would be in a foxhole and have a flash of his father's deep brown eyes, or of the belt coming down on him, or, on rare occasion, of his father's smile. He'd been imprinted by the man; Herr Fisher drove deep ruts into Bastian, like a well-traveled path, nothing could fill the space.

Bastian did not know why he chose to do the things he did. Did he really join the army just to spite his father, to prove he was not a Nazi? Did he have an ideology or was he simply fighting against the one bestowed on him? The convictions he held were not as much convictions, as happenstance. If the recruiters' office had not been on that corner, what path would he have chosen? Clark was wrong to trust him. If it came down to life or death, Bastian was sure he'd choose life over allegiance.

In the army, he did not need to question if he was a good person. He killed in order to not be killed. The rules of civilized life did not apply. *That* may have been the driving factor in opening the recruiting office door. Not to anger his father, but to live beyond the rules of society. As he lay in bed at night, counting the number of men he'd killed since the start of the conflict, he felt like he'd been made for war. Or war had been made for him. It was order and chaos all at once.

Or, had he joined because he hated himself so much, down to the core of who he was, that he hoped another would take his life, so he would not have to do the job himself? Bastian felt the best and the worst when he was with a man; he was at once completely fulfilled and completely hateful. It was a dichotomy that split him in half, caused him consistent pain. Did Max have this argument with himself? That night, Max had seemed at home with Bastian, as if he had no question of his motives, of his place. Bastian watched him sleep and he could have been dead, that's how at peace, how unconflicted he appeared. Why then did Bastian feel like someone was driving an axe through him when he thought of Max? Sometimes at night he was convinced his heart was breaking apart. His chest heavy, he'd roll over and silently sob, wondering if the pieces of his heart would lodge themselves in his veins, stopping his blood from pumping and killing him. More often than not, he hoped for death.

Yet, he'd always pulled the trigger first.

***

Bastian awoke to frantic voices. He reached for his gun then remembered it was tucked safely in his bag. Unlike his uniform, he'd refused to leave without it. The train had stopped and passengers were being called off. They could not have arrived already. He stood and followed a woman from the train car to the platform outside. The passengers were ushered into the train station. The signs read *Naples*. Bastian spotted four SS men and was sure there'd be more.

People whispered, a child cried, the officers shouted commands in German. "Inside. Everyone inside. Take out your papers. They will be inspected. Take out your papers for inspection. Inside." The orders were bellowed over one another as they herded the people inside from the platform.

Clark had given him fake papers. He was an Italian student, a threat to no one. The crowd cowered in clumps and corners inside the train station, waiting for the officers to inspect their identification. Many wrung their hands, wiped at their brows. Were there Jews among them? Did the people have something to worry about?

To Bastian's right was a family huddled together. To his left were two young women, they looked like sisters, and a little boy. One of their sons maybe? Or a little brother? No parents. The SS made their rounds. Bastian heard the family next to him speaking.

"Nothing to worry about ...."

"How can you say that?" The woman asked the man.

"We have our papers."

"When has that mattered?" she hissed. "You know what happened to the Riccis!"

"There was more to it than that."

"Papa," the little boy said, taking hold of his sister's hand and squeezing,

"I will be brave. Just like you told me."

An image of Ilsa flashed into Bastian's mind. She'd said that exact phrase to him as they huddled under his bed together, his father pulling him out by his ankles.

He removed the papers from his pocket. He'd been given a new name. Bernardo Lombardi. Born in Rome, he was heading home to be with his family. He was single and not Jewish. This was the information that stared up at him, along with a photo of his freshly shaven face.

The little boy held tightly to his sister as the officer inspected the family's papers. Silent tears streamed down the girl's face. The man looked at each document carefully, taking his time. He barked a question at them in German. The father looked around in desperation. The Nazis thrived on fear and the people in the train station were feeding them heaps of it. Again, the officer barked a question in German at them.

Bastian stepped forward, masking his American accent with a broken English Italian one he said, "He wants to know if there are any more of you. It says you have three children and there are only two."

In Italian, the man explained that his youngest son had died of pneumonia last spring. There were only two of them now. The officer looked to Bastian for an explanation he could understand. The uniformed man had a hand on each of the children's shoulders. The boy held onto the girl more tightly. Bastian spoke in German, explained what the man had said. The Nazi dropped his hands from the kids and took a step toward Bastian.

Bastian presented his papers, he did not meet the man's eyes, which were directly in line with his own. "Why do you speak German?"

Bastian looked at him. "I am a student. I studied the language in school."

The officer looked over his papers and nodded. "Where are you going?"

"To Rome. To visit my family."

"People are leaving Rome, not going to Rome."

"Only if they mean to hide," Bastian said. "I have no need for that."

The officer said nothing. He moved on to the young women and the little boy to Bastian's left. Before he could ask for the papers, all of their attention was drawn to the other side of the room. A woman was screaming while a Nazi held his gun pointed at her and the man beside her. Bastian instinctively reached for his own weapon. He thought the officer noticed the gesture, but then the man walked away, toward the commotion.

The room fell still. Only the woman, the gun pointed at her husband's head, whimpered.

Bastian watched and listened, unsure of what he would do, if anything.

"My name is Maria. This is David. We are married. He is my husband. We are not Jews," Maria said to the circle of officers and the crowd.

The one with the gun said to the others, "This man looks like a Jew. Do you all agree? Some have fake papers. He could be one of them."

The couple looked on, terrified, not understanding most of what was said by the officer. But they knew the word for Jew in German, *Jude*, had heard and seen it a million times. Maria shook her head again. "No, no, no. No Jude." Her husband stayed still.

Bastian guessed the man had been Jewish until he converted, marrying outside of the faith. He did look Jewish. The officers spoke together in low tones. A moment later the one with the gun lowered it, looked at his mates, laughed and then shot the man in the chest.

Maria wailed. The room took a collective inhale and forgot to breath out. David died quickly and without much sound. Maria threw herself at the officer who shot him, begging to be sent to the grave with her husband. As a final cruel joke, the man with the gun did not oblige. Instead, he walked away.

The officers checked the rest of the papers, making the crowd of people wait another hour before they were loaded onto the train to proceed to their destinations.

Most would not go the whole way to Rome. The Eternal City was not safe.

The crowd thinned around Maria and David as the people walked to the train, their heads bowed in silence. She would not leave him. The SS did not seem concerned with what did or did not happen with the body of a suspected Jew.

Bastian bent down and placed his hand on her shoulder. She twitched, but would not move from David's body.

"I will help you," he told her. "Where are you heading?"

Maria looked up at him for the first time. With his blond hair and sharp features, Bastian looked much like the man who shot her husband. She drew back.

"I can help. Let me help," he said in Italian.

"We live here. We were here to board the train when we were pushed in with the rest of the crowd." She lowered her voice, "We were headed toward the mountains."

Bastian knew that those who wanted to hide went to the mountains.

"I can carry him for you. Just tell me where."

Maria sat back on her heels and placed her hands in her lap. How was she to decide where to take her dead husband? Home, where her mother and father were? To Rome, where his own parents lived? David's lips were turned up in a smile. She adored his smile. His last gift to her.

Bastian carried the dead man half a mile to Maria's parent's home. She trailed behind him and cried the length of the journey. He said nothing. There was nothing to say when one experienced a great loss such as this.

He waited two hours for another train. This one passed through without incident. Sometimes he felt the actions of the Nazis were random, other times they were precise. A random act will kill a man.

***

An hour from Rome, Bastian pulled an envelope from his bag. This time he was not staring at his sister's familiar writing. It was a foreign hand; he had never seen Max write in the short time they'd spent together. Ilsa had sent him the letter after Bastian wrote to her for the first time. When he'd joined the army, he was afraid she'd be angry with him. He'd waited almost a year before writing, before deciding she'd be angrier having not heard from him. With her own terse letter, she'd sent along a note from Max, still in the envelope. The Rome address stared up at him, alien and strange. *Via Cavour, 63, 00184 Rome, Italy.* It had been four years now. Was there a chance Max could be in the same place? Would he even still be in Rome? The Nazi at the train station was right—no one was going to Rome; people were leaving it.

Bastian thought of the first time he'd seen Max at the bottom of that hill. From the back of his narrow shoulders and bowed head, Bastian had made assumptions about Max, most of which were untrue. He thought of the first time feelings began to bubble up inside of him. A flash of love and appreciation when Max stepped into the boxing ring to save him from Hans. He thought of the first time he'd held Max, on the train. Of their first kiss, the tenderness of it. Of how it filled him up. He thought of the last time he'd seen him, standing outside his parents' apartment building.

Despite his most practiced denial, he was in love with Max.

Max was the reason he was in Rome, had volunteered to go first to the Solomon Islands in hopes the military-road would eventually lead him here. Now, with this mission, he had the freedom to find him.

Bastian stopped himself from thinking of Francesca, of what he'd done with her. His feelings for Max, what they *meant*, were clear to him on that day, but too late. He'd made a stupid mistake, with dire consequences. It was only a night, barely more than a moment with her. Then, it only took a moment for Bastian to realize his love for Max.

A moment with Francesca could not dispel his love for Max, or the weight it all carried.

CHAPTER 7
ROME, ITALY;
NOVEMBER 1943

B ASTIAN SAT OUTSIDE a small, almost deserted, café sipping coffee. The drink could only be found at restaurants. With the rations, citizens could not buy it at the grocery.

Since arriving in Rome he'd kept a pattern, for his own sanity and as a way to measure the possibility of gathering information. It'd taken him a few weeks to figure out the best spots, where the officers preferred their lunches, where they took their victims, where people whispered the loudest.

He'd discovered almost nothing of merit and was beginning to worry that Clark would pull him if he didn't come up with something soon. When he wasn't on patrol, he was uncovering Rome's secrets. Bastian often walked the San Lorenzo district, looking at the destruction. He had not been on the mission that dropped countless bombs on the region. Entire buildings were reduced to almost nothing. Churches stood open and barren. Few people walked the streets. In a radius of several blocks, there was nothing inhabitable. One small café stayed open among the wreckage. He'd stopped several times, giving his patronage. It was the least he could do after his country dropped bombs on the neighboring buildings.

***

Bastian drank his coffee. It was rich and lay on his tongue like a blanket.

"Pardon me," a beautiful woman approached him, an unlit cigarette dangling from her fingers. All the women in Rome were beautiful, even to him. "Do you have a light?" she asked in Italian.

Bastian pulled a pack of matches from his pocket and offered them to her. In response, she placed the cigarette to her lips and sat in the chair next to him, leaning forward, smiling. He lit it for her.

"Do you have another?" he asked. He had half a pack in his pocket, but guarded them. One never knew when the supply would run out. Perhaps the war effort would stop if cigarettes were no longer available.

The woman slid one from her pack. He took it and lit it. She stayed beside him, blowing the smoke out the right side of her mouth, away from him. She smiled and he smiled back.

"Where are you from?" she asked, noting his American accent.

"America." He did not ask her the same question. He could tell by her accent and her look she was from here.

She offered her hand. "I am Isabella."

He shook it. "Bernardo."

"An Italian name, but not an Italian. This is strange, yes?"

"My mother was Italian," he lied.

She eyed him with suspicion. "No, I don't think so. You look like a German." She smiled at him again.

He was disarmed. He was in Rome to gather information. How did he know she wasn't here to do the same thing? Everyone was a spy, or a double agent, a member of the resistance movement, a Nazi or former Italian officer, a Jew, a terrified family member. Everyone played a role and no one was without motive. For many it was simply to survive, for some it was to find justice— others told people they were just doing their job.

She touched his arm lightly. "Do not worry. I don't care where you are from, or your name, or who you are."

Whether this was true or not, it was comforting.

They smoked together silently.

The day stretched out in front of him, more of the same. He would finish his drink and begin his rounds. He would walk to Via Tasso 145, now one of the most feared addresses in Rome. It was a nondescript yellow apartment building that happened to double as the place where the Gestapo tortured their prisoners. Bastian woke from nightmares in which he was tied to a chair, beaten and watching others being beaten. It was a risk to go there almost daily, but it was one of his best chances of gathering intelligence. He saw who went in, who did not come out. There were two SS officers, Field Marshall Albert Kesselring and Obergruppenführer Karl Wolff, general of the Waffen-SS, that he now knew by name. Wolff often came out with blood on his uniform. Never his own, Bastian was sure. A few times he'd followed the two men, together and separately, from Via Tasso. There was nothing to learn except that they were both miserable bastards who drank too much, had too many women, and tortured anyone they suspected of being a Jew, anyone who looked different. Bastian, with his blond hair and square face, was safer here than most places. He looked like the men who did the torturing, not those who were tortured.

When Bastian looked up, the woman was gone. She'd lost concern or patience. If someone was interested in you in Rome, they had a reason. He put lira on the table, stood, and left.

Sometimes the charged tension of Rome proved too much, reminded Bastian too much of his helplessness as a child. On these days, he stayed indoors. He looked out his window that peered onto the street. There were gunshots, some farther away, some closer, every day. He noticed them more when he was in the apartment. Staying in one place allowed him to observe and listen to the whispered cacophony of the city. He watched German soldiers march down deserted streets and families huddle in alleyways. Pope Pius XII stayed inside the Vatican Walls. Bastian never saw him once. If he'd had faith in God, the last few years would have been enough to make him lose it.

He lived on rations, just like everyone else. The apartment was all but empty of food and furniture, but he was better off than most because he had the support and therefore money of the army behind him. Along with his rations, he received funds deposited every week into a secret bank account. This allowed him to travel the city, to eat and drink at cafes, to be among the people who braved or ruled the streets.

Everyone in the city was hungry, scared, and desperate enough to do or try almost anything. The SS were smug, but Bastian recognized deep-rooted fear in them as well. The charged feeling in the city made it feel as if it would explode at any moment.

After taking similar routes for weeks, Bastian had begun to recognize some people, like the hunched over shopkeeper, the siblings playing close to home, the mourning widows gathered together. He varied his routine, but included several places each day: Via Tasso, the Jewish Quarter, and the address on Max's envelope. He was there the day the Gestapo rounded up more than a thousand Jews from the Ghetto and took them away in trucks. Bastian watched the huddled masses climb onto the huge lorries, some in coats and hats, some still in pajamas. Many of them carried suitcases. He suspected that where they were being taken, they would need nothing. He'd heard stories of people being stripped of their belongings, their families, their dignities. Soldiers doing their jobs, some willingly, some because they felt they had no choice. Was he a better man than those in the SS? Bastian had shot and killed just like them. He knew from history that the victor told the story of who was right and who was wrong. Was he on the correct side?

As he watched the Jews being rounded up, he placed his hand on his gun. It would accomplish nothing to kill a Nazi in that moment, except to kill one or two men and sign his own death warrant. Strategy had to be applied with intelligence for either side to win.

The Ghetto had been quiet since the October roundup. Any who had escaped the capture had fled.

***

At the end of the day, Bastian found himself in front of a small apartment building on Via Cavour. In all the times he'd stood near the building, he'd never caught sight of Max. It made no sense to risk his identity to ask about his friend. Above all, he had to protect himself. Still, he watched and hoped, almost daily. The fruitless visits resulted in mounting frustration and feelings of helplessness. Max may not even live in Rome anymore. With the war and the occupation, people were wise to head to the hills of Italy. It was too much work for the Nazi forces to invade each village; there was more safety there.

Listless, Bastian made one final stop to send a telegram to Clark. *Still cloudy. Hoping for sun soon.* The pair had developed code words before Bastian departed. Most of his telegrams read this same way. Nothing he gleaned from the whispers, the occasional pamphlet lost in the wind, the mocking SS, amounted to news that would help the American Army take Rome. He often wondered, as he sent each telegram, if there were other men, all over the city, sending similar messages. Winning the war was not on Bastian's shoulders alone, he knew that. Still, he had no idea if there were others gathering intelligence in Rome at this very moment. How much responsibility had he taken on?

He walked home before dark, before curfew. After hours, fewer questions were asked and more guns were drawn.

Bastian did not appreciate feeling helpless. More than that, it made his insides vibrate with an energy that scared him. He climbed the four flights to his apartment, exhausted from no activity. War invigorated him, filled him. This was not war. It was waiting.

Most nights he ate pasta and tonight was no exception, only he could not eat more than a few bites. He looked around his barren apartment. The walls were white, no longer crisp, a backdrop for the small table and an armchair. There were basic cooking supplies in the sparse kitchen. In the single small bedroom, there was a mattress on an iron frame. He liked the emptiness of the rooms. They mirrored his insides.

On his counter were two bottles of wine. They'd been procured with some effort. Like coffee, most of the alcohol was scarcely available in shops. Bastian had been walking down a quiet street when he saw a man standing in a doorway with a glass of wine in his hand. He ventured to ask if the man had more.

"For a price, anything can be arranged," the man told him. Over the last few months the man had sold most of the contents of his wine cellar. He'd known all the way back in July when Mussolini was ousted that trouble would head their way. The title of Open City was a myth. At any moment, the Americans could bomb them again. As long as the Germans stayed, no one in Rome was safe.

Bastian worked out a favorable price with the man and bought two bottles. He knew little about wine, but the seller assured him they were both good choices. When Bastian had purchased them, it was with the plan to save the alcohol for a victory. That was six weeks ago when he was foolish enough to think that the American Army would have arrived by now. Bastian had fantasized, on the train and in his first days in Rome, that he would take down the Gestapo, and find Max, bringing the war to an end and a victory to himself. Those thoughts were irrational and stupid. He knew it then and now.

He went to the counter and picked up one of the bottles. The cork popped with a pleasurable sound. If Bastian waited for victory, he might never have the chance to open the wine. He drank deeply, not bothering with a glass, and plopped down on the armchair with the bottle. He read Ilsa's last letter again. *First Sicily—where next …. It won't be long until you get to Rome and can take the Open City back. Perhaps by the New Year? … I've put in a request to be transferred to Italy. I can be used in Italy … I only hope that you, dear brother, are holding up better than them…it does not take much for a stream to become a river, for a crack to make a foundation structurally unsound ….* He read it four times and finished half the bottle.

He set Ilsa's letter down on the counter and picked up an envelope next to it. Max's letter was so worn and creased it looked like a relic. His tone in the letter was not how Bastian remembered him. Despite his better self telling him not to, he opened the sheet of paper and read. The words were perfunctory, revealing nothing of how Max may feel about him. The most useful piece of information was not the letter, but the envelope bearing the address. Reading and rereading it did nothing to encourage Bastian, but it carried weight for him that Max had bothered to write at all after their parting. If Max had been done with Bastian, he would not have wasted the stamp.

His finger traced the outline of each word. And he drank. The contents of the bottle seemed to disappear, though the feeling pulsating through his body told another story—he'd absorbed each drop. Bastian stood and went to the window. The street was empty. A light drizzle and a fog hung heavy. It would be helpful cover.

He pulled his shoes back on and flung his tweed jacket over his arms. Even in war there was sex and desire. Most occupiers of bars after curfew were SS men and Italian officers who had joined the Nazis. But he knew of one little space, hidden away, where Italian men still went.

The weather and his drunkenness carried him from the apartment; both ever changeable and therefore unwise companions. Bastian had learned the city well enough to get where he was going without traveling on the main roads. The haze drifting from his knees to above his head gave him unearned comfort. He found the nondescript building with ease. Inside, the room was smoky, dark, and filled with men. Bastian had come to the bar once or twice during the day and found a tamer but similar atmosphere, single men or small groups keeping to themselves. When the darkness fell and the curfew came on, only those with devilish motives came into the city.

He opted to sit at the bar. There was an older man to his right and no one to his left. After a few minutes, the man stood and left, teetering slightly.

"I'll have a glass of your house red," Bastian told the bartender.

The crowd kept to itself and drank. Perhaps he'd had the wrong impression? Or perhaps the people were cautious. They did not know Bastian, and he did not know them. He downed his first glass with ease; his intoxication had not worn off. He liked adding to the feeling. It revved him up, like a thermometer rising to 110. He'd had three glasses when a man around his age sat next to him. He was handsome and wore black-rimmed glasses. The man smiled at Bastian and ordered himself a glass of wine. Bastian eased his body, inch by inch, toward the man, in what he hoped was an indiscernible manner. They made eye contact. With the boldness only two bottles of wine will give, Bastian slid his hand onto the man's leg.

Faster than he could comprehend, the man stood and Bastian was surrounded by him and two others. One pushed Bastian from his stool and he fell to the ground.

"Okay, okay. I'm going. I'm sorry," he mumbled. His elbow had struck the ground when he fell and it throbbed.

"You bet you are," said one.

They pulled him to his feet and out the door. Outside the drizzle had become rain; within moments his tweed jacket was damp. One of the men pushed him to a brick wall. Bastian slid down to the wet cobblestone street, aware that he was laughing. He spoke through his intoxication, words he didn't wish to say, to the three backs that were walking away.

"Fuck you." Bastian laughed harder.

"What did you say, you fucking homo?" the tallest of the three said.

"Sodomite piece of shit," said another.

The tall one pulled him from the ground by the front of his shirt and punched him in the face. Bastian's head ricocheted off the brick wall, thumping like a heartbeat. Another man (was it the one whom he'd touched?) moved forward and punched him in the stomach. Bastian doubled over. Another hit to his face, his angular cheekbone taking the brunt of it. The man spit at his feet.

"Fucking homo," the tall one said again, taking a gun from his jacket.

Bastian slumped to the ground, wet and in pain, and pulled his own gun discretely from his belt.

Kill or be killed.

The man with the gun laughed, looking back at his friends.

Bastian raised his own weapon. It felt heavier in his hand than it usually did. He aimed at the man closest to him, the one with the gun, and pulled the trigger. His body fell to the ground. *Thud.* The sound satisfied Bastian. A trail of blood flowed from the man's head toward Bastian's outstretched foot, which he moved to avoid the stream. He wiped at his face bringing away sweat, tears, blood. His own? On Bastian's patterned jacket splotches of the man's blood bloomed, opening like a morning glory to the sun.

When he looked up, the other two men were gone.

Bastian stood with the help of the wall. He did not look at the dead man. The alley was quiet and slick. He moved with considerable speed, holding onto his aching stomach where he'd been hit. As the adrenaline faded, his intoxication returned. It was not enough. He walked down an empty street and spotted a café. Lined up along its back wall, behind the counter, were several bottles of wine. Bastian tried the door. Locked. With the pain he was in, another bruised elbow would not be much bother. In one movement, he broke the glass. Getting in after that was easy. He slipped his hand inside and unlocked the door. At first he removed two bottles from the shelf, then, thinking better of it, returned one to its place. He removed the cork right there and took a long, satisfying drink. Alcohol had to beget alcohol on a night like this.

He left the shop, sticking to narrow alleyways and paths as he made his way home. When he'd consumed half the bottle, he heard footsteps. Bastian went toward the sound. A man walked swiftly down the street away from him. Bastian observed him; his narrow shoulders, his curly hair, his small frame. He looked like a slightly taller and older version of Max. Bastian followed him, trying to get a glimpse of the man's face. The wine sloshed from the bottle onto his hand as they both picked up speed. The stranger turned to look behind him. Bastian gasped. It had to be him.

They both ran faster, one chasing the other, hearts racing quicker than their feet.

Bastian tripped on the uneven cobblestone. He landed face first, his already-injured cheekbone slamming onto the road. When he looked up the man was gone. So fast. Had he been there at all? Had Bastian been chasing a ghost? He sat up, the stones hard under him. The wine made some of the pain dissipate.

Bastian looked around. He had no idea where he was.

***

In the morning, Bastian found himself in the most unexpected place—his bed. The night came to him in flashes he didn't believe. He was still wearing his coat, spattered with blood, and not his own. His face ached. In the chamber of his gun, he had one less bullet.

Bastian got up, groaning, and went to the window. The haze had cleared and the sun peeked through the cloud cover. People hurried along the streets, heads low, coats wrapped around them tightly. In the distance, gunshots.

CHAPTER 8
NAPLES, ITALY;
OCTOBER 2, 1943

ILSA HATED FLYING. She rubbed Bastian's lucky penny between her thumb and forefinger as the small plane skipped up and down. The penny hung from a chain on her neck. At nineteen, having spent the last nine months in a war-torn country, while finding the love of her life and coming out alive, she counted herself indeed lucky. She'd always been a romantic at heart and a part of her believed that the penny, the piece of her brother she carried with her at all times, *had* brought her luck.

Ilsa thought of her last encounter with Bastian. It felt like so long ago. Maybe that was because she'd had a lifetime of growth since they'd said good-bye.

Promise me you will write. So I will always know where you are. So I can find you.

He had finally written, close to a year after disappearing. Those months while he was nowhere to be found were among the most painful and anxious of her life. Thinking about it now, her face reddened and she clenched her jaw until her teeth hurt. Ilsa was so angry at him for making her wait to know that he was okay. He was the only person in her life then who helped her to keep going. She'd thought she was over it.

She felt a hand on her arm. "You okay, honey?" Clara asked.

"Oh, yes. I'm fine. I don't like flying is all."

"Me neither!"

"Clara, thank you so much for coming with me. It means the world. Really." Clara had the option to stay with the other half of the nursing unit in London. Instead, she'd agreed to join Ilsa and six other nurses on a journey to Naples. The small plane was thick with women's voices, talking about what was to come, who they'd left behind in London, what may befall them in this new country.

Clara leaned into her. "I've gotten you this far. Not about to abandon you now."

She loved Clara's southern accent. It soothed her, like a trickling stream in the woods. For the past few years, Clara had been like a mother to her. She was the sweetest woman Ilsa knew. Over her lifetime, Clara had experienced great loss: both of her parents and a brother in a fire a week after she'd turned eighteen; her daughter, at age five, from pneumonia (that's when she became a nurse); her husband in the Great War.

Clara had suffered and yet there wasn't a day since Ilsa had known her that the woman didn't smile. Ilsa's loss was minimal compared to hers. She reminded herself of that often; anytime she felt badly about her childhood, felt lonely or missed Bastian, Clara would flash her brilliant toothy smile and Ilsa knew it would be okay.

Ilsa's own mother had tried, she knew that. But not everyone was fit to be a parent. Frau Fisher never stood up to Ilsa's father, not once; she never stood up for her children. Ilsa supposed that wouldn't be a problem anymore. The miserable man had drunk himself to death a few weeks ago. She'd only found out four days before, by way of a letter. She expected she would cry. So far, she hadn't.

"Did you have a nice good-bye with that man of yours?" Clara asked.

"Yes. It was something," she laughed. Eliot Lock had reported back to duty with the First Infantry Division the day before. He would be halfway to North Africa by now. Before he departed, he gave Ilsa one of the most brilliant nights of her life. She didn't remember ever laughing or crying so hard.

"Do you think he's happy to go back to Africa?" Clara asked.

"No, I know he isn't. In my opinion, he's barely healed from the last round. But the infantry needs him. That's what he says. Damn him and his honor."

"You don't mean that. You want a man of honor. Every woman does."

Ilsa didn't answer. Clara was mostly right. When Ilsa thought of her father, she thought of the opposite of an honorable man. Anyone different from him was a good fit for her. She still had nightmares about the factory fire. They hadn't lived far from it and both she and Bastian heard the sirens. She was so small that he carried her most of the way. Not too small to remember though; the young women jumping from the building and landing with an excruciating thump on the pavement, the screams from the families below, the smoke and the crowds. And her father, nowhere to be found. He would have been better off if he'd died in that fire. They all would have. It was his fault Bastian had joined the army to fight a war. It was because of her father that her mother never smiled.

Ilsa placed her hand on Clara's. "You're right," she told her. "As usual."

"It's on account of my age and wisdom."

Clara was almost fifty. Older than anyone else in the nursing unit. She'd been sent to supervise more than anything else. Not many people of her age and experience volunteered to go overseas. Ilsa knew Clara had come for her. After Ilsa had told Clara about her father, the fire, her desperation, Clara said, "Don't you worry, honey, Clara is here for you now. I'll protect you." Anytime there were gunshots, Ilsa thought about those words. Clara continually put her life in danger for her.

"Do you think Bastian will be excited to see me? To find out I'm in love?" Ilsa asked.

"From everything you've told me, he only wants what is best for you. I'm betting he'll be pleased as punch."

"I've always hated that phrase. You know where it comes from right?" Ilsa said.

"You and your convictions. Always need to be up in arms about something, don't you?" They were both quiet. Ilsa's *convictions*, as Clara called them, had gotten her into some trouble. After doing nothing to stop her father for so much of her childhood, she needed to stand for something now. It was the reason she'd pushed herself to graduate high school two years early, and study to be a nurse—her conviction that she could make the world a better place.

She wondered if her brother had killed anyone in the last five years. He must have. She was not naïve. She knew in war it was kill or be killed. Still, she didn't want to imagine it. In her mind Bastian was her tall, strong, handsome brother who took all the blows so she never would have to experience them. Not a killer.

"Anyway," Clara said. "He loves you so he will be happy for you. I know it."

"I should have told him about Eliot in my last letter. But my love feels so insignificant compared to what he must be going through."

"Love is never insignificant. Love is the reason we're here."

Ilsa didn't know if her brother believed in love.

The plane shook and Ilsa grabbed Clara's arm. "We must be close, right?" she asked.

"I hope so!" Clara said.

Ilsa rubbed the penny between her fingers and looked out the window. Outside she saw Rome. The other women pointed at the towering Coliseum, the crumbling ancient buildings. Ilsa wondered if she'd get the chance to visit Rome, or if she'd spend her time in Naples only. She wondered if there were people on the streets, living life like they were not in the midst of a war, as they had in London. She'd read that the government had declared Rome an Open City. According to the papers, an Open City was one that was undefended, thereby making it free from enemy attack. But Ilsa knew there were German soldiers on the ground, their tanks and their guns terrorizing the city. She imagined the people hurrying along the street with their eyes cast downward.

Clara settled deeper into her seat and closed her eyes, tired from the day. Ilsa had more she wanted to say, more nerves to unravel, but she kept quiet and let Clara fall asleep as they began the final leg of their journey. They would land on a beach in Naples, instead of at the airport. The new Naples Airdrome had not been finished yet.

Ilsa's thoughts bounced from her mother, to Eliot, to Bastian. She could barely form one thought before another intruded and took over. She pondered how different Bastian and Eliot were, at least to her best recollection of her brother. Bastian liked to brood, to be in charge, to keep secrets. Eliot was open and sincere. He'd told Ilsa he liked her the first day they'd met. He didn't attempt to manipulate her, or worry what it would mean if she didn't feel the same way. When Eliot had a thought, he said it out loud. That was how they came to be engaged on her nineteenth birthday. They were lying in the grass together at a park. He'd picked flowers for her earlier in the day and he was braiding them into her long blond hair.

"I could lie here like this every day for the rest of my life," he'd told her.

"Could you now? We wouldn't get much done this way."

"There is not much more that needs to be done in life," Eliot said.

"Only to work, and cook, and clean, and garden," Ilsa replied.

"We could do all of that too. I would be happy to do anything for the rest of my life if you were next to me." He sat up and looked at her. As she lay, her hair cascaded over her shoulders and onto the grass like a golden fountain. "I'm serious, Ilsa."

She sat up too. "Serious about what?"

"About spending the rest of my life with you. The war, it's made me realize things. We only have here and now. I want to be with you."

Ilsa smiled. "Are you asking me to marry you?"

Eliot unwound a flower from her hair and fashioned it into a circle. He slipped it onto her finger. "Would you? If I asked?"

She was flustered. They'd only met the month before, when he'd been sent back for an injury to his right leg. Ilsa was his nurse. What if they were just caught up in this war story? Could one find true love under such circumstances?

"Ilsa?" He placed his hand on her cheek.

"Yes."

He kissed her and enveloped her face in his hands.

"You've made me a very happy man." He smiled.

***

She'd kept the flower ring, carried it now in her bag, pressed between the pages of a book—Shakespeare's sonnets. Eliot promised her he would buy her a real ring when he came back from North Africa. *And they would live happily ever after.* He'd actually said that to her. Ilsa knew too much about life to find truth in this. Her mother had not been allowed happiness, so why should she expect it? Herr Fisher was not cold and mean when he'd met his future wife; she would not have married him in that case. He may have been just like Eliot.

Her poor mother. She was so alone. Both children overseas, a husband dead, no other real family to speak of in the States. It had been Herr Fisher's idea to move to America, to leave everything they knew and everyone they loved. She bent to his will, as she always did.

Ilsa removed a piece of paper, a pen, and a book from her bag.

Dear Mother,

I received your letter. I am sorry for any pain you may be in. I hope you are able to find comfort in someone or something. He gave you two beautiful children who love you deeply. That I can say. I am not sure what else would ring true in this moment.

I am on my way to Naples to see Bastian for the first time in more than five years. They say in the papers his unit is gaining ground. They want to take Rome by the New Year. Are you following the war as well? I don't know if they cover it as well over there as they do here. If you're seeing the photos of the destruction, I can only imagine what you must be thinking. You must be worried sick with two children in the war. The most important thing is that we are both fine! The war cannot go on forever and then your children will come home to you.

Again, I am sorry about the loss of Father. I wish you peace and much love.

Love,
Ilsa

She addressed the envelope and tucked it into her bag. Moments later, the plane began to descend. The six other young women chattered, nervous and excited for their next adventure, always aware it may be their last. It was dusk and the late day sun reflected off the water, making the ocean shimmer. Ilsa saw the beach from the window and two trucks waiting nearby to take them into town. This was where she would find her brother and reunite with him after all of these years. She rubbed the penny between her fingers and woke Clara as the plane came to a stop.

LSA COULDN'T SLEEP. There was too much running through her mind, too much uncertainty. She turned from her side, to her back, to her stomach, over and over again on the thin mattress. A British soldier had shown them to the building where they would sleep, a block from the hospital. She'd asked him about Bastian.

"Don't know 'im, sorry."

"His unit is supposed to be stationed here."

"Lots of units here from several branches of the military. Just don't know 'im. Sorry." He looked at Ilsa, took her in. "What unit is he in?"

"The Fifth Division Army," she said, looking at him.

He sucked on his lip, thinking. "Those are General Clark's boys, I think. He'll know where to find your brother."

"Thank you so much." She hugged the man, surprising herself with the action.

"You fancy a drink?" He asked her as they turned the corner toward their building.

Ilsa thought of Eliot, of the flower ring pressed against the sonnets. Just picturing him made her smile. "No, thank you. But thank you for the information. Really."

Ilsa and the rest of her unit spent the next morning getting to know the immediate requirements of the wounded, who was in the most critical condition, how they could help. The city desperately needed them. There was only a handful of medical staff left in Naples after the fighting. More English and American nurses needed to be flown in.

By mid-afternoon, Ilsa and Clara took a break. Exhausted already from caring for the wounded and knowing they only had a short time to find Bastian before they needed to be back, Ilsa and Clara went looking for General Clark. They found him in a tavern, nursing a beer. Several soldiers surrounded him; none were Bastian. They all looked so tired. Ilsa wondered if she looked the same.

"General Clark," she said.

He stood and shook her hand. "And you are?"

"My name is Ilsa. I am looking for my brother."

He looked her up and down. She was pretty, taller than most women. Her eyes were so pale they looked like they held mist in them. "Is he one of mine?" Clark asked.

"That's what I've been told, yes."

Clara interjected more information. "We are both nurses with the US Army. Ilsa and I are working at the hospital—just got in yesterday. She asked to be transferred so she could be reunited with her brother. We were told he would be here."

Clark sat down and offered them two empty chairs. "Nurses. I'm glad you're here. We sure as hell need you. A lot of severe injuries, our men and civilians."

"I know, sir," Ilsa said. "We spent the morning at the hospital. But right now, I am here to ask about my brother."

Clark nodded. "What's his name?"

"Bastian. Bastian Fisher." Ilsa noticed the general's eye twitch. She'd spent much of her childhood learning how to read faces, to minimize her father's outbursts. "You know him, right? Where can I find him?"

Clark shook his head. "I can't help you."

Ilsa slammed her hand onto the table. The action took Clark and Clara by surprise. Both jumped a little. She'd been on this journey for too long to have this man lie to her.

"I know you know him. Please, just tell me where he is."

"I can't. I'm sorry," he said sincerely.

"Why not?" Clara asked.

"Because it would compromise an ongoing mission."

Ilsa was crying now. She didn't want to. "General, please."

He stood from the table. In truth, he didn't know exactly where Bastian was. In Rome, yes. It was a big city and for both of their protection his exact address had not been revealed. Clark thought tactically. If he didn't say something helpful, the girl looked like she might run off to find Bastian herself and he and his men needed her here. "All I can tell you right now is that he is somewhere gathering intelligence for us. I don't know where exactly." He paused, looked at her. Her eyes searched him for more. "Stay here, help in the hospital, and I promise I will tell him you're here next time he reaches out."

In truth, Clark could not do that. The telegram system they'd set up was a one-way street. Bastian contacted him, not the other way around. Still, he had other men on the ground there, as did the British, so he may be able to contact someone to help find Bastian if need be.

Ilsa looked at him. He didn't seem to be lying.

"That is the best I can offer you," he said.

"No, thank you," Ilsa said. "I am going to find him myself."

"No, you're not," Clark said, a growl to his voice. "You cannot leave. We need you here. If you leave, you will be AWOL."

Clara drew back at the word and clutched onto Ilsa's arm. "Honey, you are closer than ever," she said. "Don't do anything stupid. You'll find him once his mission is over."

Ilsa looked at Clark. She thought of the men and women lying in the hospital beds.

Clara leaned in close to her. "Ilsa, look at me." They made eye contact. "You just have to hold on a little longer."

Ilsa nodded her head yes.

***

Back at the hospital, Ilsa felt deflated as she looked around the room. So many injured. The beds lined the walls, some even in the hallways. Too many people, not enough space.

"This is the right thing," Clara said.

Ilsa had spoken very little since their meeting with Clark. "I know."

"Our duty comes first."

Ilsa wanted to tell her that her first duty was to her brother. He needed her. She couldn't explain how she knew it, but she did. It had been too many years. She held onto the penny. "Okay," she answered.

Clara handed her a pair of gloves. "Let's get to work."

***

Tears stung Ilsa's face as she lay in her bed for the second night in Naples. She'd imagined the day unfolding so differently in her mind. She strained her ears for outside sounds. The fallen city did not stir. No gunfire, no tanks rolling through the street. Where was her brother? He had to be in Rome, where else would he be gathering intelligence?

Ilsa sat up, swiped at the tears. She went to the window and looked out. It was so dark. She could leave right now, find the train and take it to Rome. And then? She didn't even know for sure her brother was there.

She sat back down onto the bed and lit a candle, careful not to wake anyone else. To pass the time, she wrote a letter to Eliot, telling him of her latest setback in finding Bastian, how much she missed them both. She told him not to worry, that she loved him. It would all work out. Sometimes, life has to work out.

CHAPTER 10
MID-OCTOBER, 1943

"ILSA, I NEED YOU HERE," Clara shouted from across the hospital room.

Ilsa ran to Clara's side. They stood over a young man, hardly older than Ilsa, his leg black, bloody, and necrotic. He had fair hair and skin. He was sleeping somehow, through the noise of the room, a faint grimace on his face.

"It wasn't like this yesterday," Clara whispered to Ilsa. "Do you think …?"

Clara nodded. They would have to take his leg.

The last two weeks had been frenzied. Short staffed as they were, Clara, Ilsa and the other six nurses from their unit were doing most of the work, pulling twelve-hour shifts, seven days a week. If there were twenty more of them, they maybe could have kept up with the patients.

Clark walked around livid most of the time while one-by-one his men and people from the town died. More help was on the way—that's what the American and British commanders kept saying. But when?

Ilsa had only been in the operating room for six amputations, always with a doctor by her side. Clara had lost count of how many limbs she'd seen sawed off.

"We need to do it now," Clara said. "Tell the other girls they will have control of the floor while we operate on Matthew."

"We can't wait for a doctor?" Ilsa asked.

"Oh, honey," Clara faltered. "This morning they told me that Dr. Abruzzese is sick. A high fever and all. They don't know when he'll be able to come back in. We're going to have to do this ourselves. No, it can't wait."

***

The operating room was quiet, unnerving.

"Ready?" Clara asked.

Ilsa stood by her side, ready to hand her the medical tools and watch that the soldier stayed under anesthesia. Clara had only used this sedation method twice before, both times with a doctor. What if they didn't give him enough and he woke up?

"Yes," Ilsa answered, handing her a scalpel.

She watched as Clara put blade to skin. That first cut, when the blood flowed from the wound, was always the hardest to watch. Ilsa knew from her training that the limb needed to go. The inflection would spread, killing him. They would take the leg above the knee, sawing through skin, muscle, tendon and bone.

Ilsa repeated the steps she'd learned in training aloud: "Apply a tourniquet above the amputation line, make a circular incision, cutting down to the deep fascia, cut through the muscle and then the periosteum. Switch to a saw and go cleanly through the bone—"

"Shhh. I know what I'm doing."

The prescribed method gave Ilsa comfort. She continued silently to herself. *The nerves will be severed cleanly. Extreme care should be taken not to include large amounts of muscle in the ligation of small vessels; precise hemostasis of the stump is essential. Remove the tourniquet, inspect the field. Cover the stump with a mesh gauze.*

Why, after sitting through six other amputations, did Matthew make her feel ill-equipped? His face, his smile. Ilsa held onto his hand and squeezed. There was something of Bastian in him. It was her brother's face she saw when she gazed down. Bastian's face she saw as she watched Clara cut through the final layer of muscle and skin, detaching the leg from its owner.

After Clara applied the gauze and the surgery was done, Ilsa excused herself.

"What's wrong?" Clara asked, grabbing onto Ilsa's arm.

"Nothing, I'm sorry. Just tired. I need a break. Away from the hospital."

"I don't like you going out to town on your own. Why don't you wait for me to get cleaned up? I'll go with you," Clara said.

"No, thank you. Really, I just need a couple of hours alone."

Clara nodded and smiled at Ilsa. The smile usually worked. It didn't faze her this time.

***

Ilsa walked the few blocks to the same bar where she'd met Clark the first time. Outside, the air was chilled and the street was quiet. When she approached the building, she heard voices coming from inside. The large room was half-full, some townspeople, and some soldiers in uniform. She went to the bar and ordered a glass of wine, keeping her head down. She didn't want to speak to anyone, wanted to be alone, surrounded by people.

There were two empty tables to the far left of the room. She sat and closed her eyes, her palm around her glass.

"The two of you look just the same, you know."

Ilsa opened her eyes. A man with wide shoulders and a serious brow stood next to her.

"Who?"

"You and your brother. You're Ilsa, right?"

At this she sat straighter in her chair and offered the man a seat. He bent down and offered his right hand. It was slick with sweat. In his left hand was a tall glass of beer.

"James Bell." He sat down.

"You knew my brother—*know* my brother," she corrected herself. It was not time to start referring to him in the past tense.

"Yes, we ran intelligence together. We did a mission the day before he left to—" he stopped.

"To where?" Ilsa asked, leaning into him.

"I don't know, I guess," Bell said, taking a drink, the light amber liquid rushing from the glass to his wide lips.

Ilsa knew she was pretty, beautiful even. She leaned further toward James Bell, sweeping his hair from his forehead. "Tell me about yourself," she said.

"Not much to tell. Graduated school, married, joined the army," he said, taking a sip of his beer and avoiding her eye.

"You're married?" Ilsa said, drawing back. He wasn't wearing a ring.

James saw her eyes glance at his finger. He pulled his identification tags from beneath his shirt. Along with two silver squares with his name, social security number, blood type, and a "C" for Catholic embossed onto them, the chain held a ring. "It kept slipping off. I didn't want to lose it."

"What's your wife's name?"

"Katherine. Are you married?"

Ilsa pressed her lips together and shook her head. "No. I'm engaged. His name is Eliot."

"Where is he?"

"In North Africa, with the war effort. I miss him deeply." Ilsa's voice waivered. She told herself Eliot was fine, but his letters were intermittent and she knew he faced danger daily.

James sighed. What was the harm in telling her what he knew? Rome was a big city and he'd heard Clark wasn't releasing her from duty anyway. "I may know where Bastian is."

Ilsa wiped away a tear. "Really?"

Bell had stood outside of Clark's office that day, after he'd been dismissed, his ear pressed tightly to the door. He'd been afraid he was in trouble and wanted to know what Clark was saying. He didn't hear everything but gathered that the General was sending Bastian on a mission, to Rome. "I think he's in Rome."

"Rome?" Ilsa repeated. "Alone?"

"Alone enough. There are likely more men undercover there, though he may not know of them."

"Are you sure? Where in Rome?" she asked.

He arched his back and took a long drink of his beer. "Honestly, I'm not sure. I was listening to a conversation that was not meant for me. I think I heard the word 'Rome' and then that same night Bastian packed a bag and went. Don't go on my word alone."

His word was all Ilsa had. Bastian was not in Naples. It made sense that Clark would send him to Rome, their next intended target. And James had said he and Bastian gathered intelligence together. She touched his hand. "Thank you. And good luck. I hope you make it back to your wife."

He raised his glass to her and finished his drink. Standing, he said, "Nice meeting you." He turned to go, then looked back at her. "He talked a lot about you, and he didn't really talk about anything."

Ilsa smiled at him, her throat tight.

**

She walked home, her heart jumping excitedly with each step. Clark had not released her to go, and more than that, the men and women in the hospital needed her. Still, she was closer to finding Bastian. Ilsa came to the street where the hospital was located. If she turned right, she'd be there in less than five minutes. If she turned left, it was a ten-minute walk to the train station, a several-hour trip to Rome. She stood there for a long moment, contemplating.

Ilsa made a right, toward the hospital.

She was tired, her neck tight and her feet aching from standing on them all day. She would check on Matthew to see how he was recovering from surgery, and then go to bed.

There was a cacophony of voices as she climbed the steps to the main ward. Who was making so much noise this late at night? She quickened her pace, running the last flight of stairs. The sight in the room made her stop short. In front of her were new nurses, at least twenty or so, chatting with Clara and the other six girls from her unit. Finally, they'd come. Ilsa slumped onto an empty bed and allowed the tears to stream down her face. She would sleep tonight, for the first time in weeks.

***

Ilsa heard Clark's heavy footsteps before she saw his tall body appear in the doorway.

"They finally came," he said, referring to the thirty-two new nurses and two doctors who'd been flown in the week before. "And now the troops and I are leaving. We're pushing forward. We'll take a dozen of the nurses and one doctor. You all should still be well-equipped with those who are left."

Ilsa smiled and nodded.

Clark gazed at her. She reminded him of his own two girls, both tall and too pretty for their own good. Isabelle and Lauren, they were everything to one another. He tried to imagine the lengths they'd go for each other.

"You still want to find your brother?" he asked her.

"Yes of course," Ilsa said, walking toward him.

"I can't tell you where he is." He hesitated. "But I can let you go, if you'd like. The staff has it handled here. You've done good work. I am releasing you of your duties."

"Really?"

"Just promise me that once you find him, you will report back for duty, wherever you are." He'd seen her talking to Bell in the bar the week before and had a suspicion that both James Bell and now Ilsa knew Bastian was in Rome. "Good luck," he said, putting a hand on her shoulder.

Moments later, Clara came into the room. She looked over her shoulder at Clark, disappearing down the hallway. "What did he want?"

"Clara," Ilsa said, taking her friend's hand. "I'm going to Rome."

CHAPTER 11
ROME, ITALY;
DECEMBER 3, 1943

THE CONSEQUENCE OF THE CURFEW and the cold weather was that Ilsa slept a lot. More than seven weeks of searching and no sign of her brother. The first day she arrived in Rome, Ilsa had withdrawn all of the money from her account. It did not amount to much. As each lira dwindled, she became more desperate.

Her nights were restless, many sleepless. In the mirror, she did not know herself. Nine months of war-torn London and looking for her brother would be her demise. Ilsa never had been good at being alone. One morning, as she fixed her hair, clumps of long blond tresses came out with the comb.

Ilsa spent most of her days sitting outside, huddled against the wind on a bench or stone wall, watching, looking. It was a big city, there was no denying that. Had she been so naïve to believe she would have found him by now? Often she saw a blonde SS guard who looked like her brother and each time she entertained the idea that he'd switched sides. Bastian believed in the good in people; somewhere in her soul she knew that. He was also the king of self-preservation. Ilsa had watched it growing up; he had to look out for himself. To survive.

She covered her hair with a scarf each day. Partly to shield herself from the wind, but also to be anonymous. There were not many blond-haired, tall women walking around. It was imperative she not be noticed, not be drawn into anything. She ate alone. She talked to no one but the woman who'd rented her a room, and then only when absolutely necessary. When Ilsa was younger, she had an imaginary friend named Freundin—simply, 'friend' in German. Ilsa called upon Freundin when she was alone. A few times when the beatings became too much, Bastian had left for a few days while their father calmed. She especially needed Freundin during these times.

Instead of summoning her old friend, now she initiated conversations with Eliot. He was a soothing presence. She told him about her day, expressed her mounting frustration. He would answer in calming tones, sweeping the hair from her face. Ilsa imagined him so clearly, at times it felt like he was really there. To a stranger watching, she must have looked like a crazy woman.

When Ilsa was not looking for Bastian, or talking to someone who was not there, she was writing letters. She was desperate to connect with someone who knew her. She'd been writing to Eliot for weeks with no answer. Each day she waited for a letter that did not come. Clara, on the other hand, wrote her twice a week. She encouraged Ilsa to keep going, keep looking. Clara had been with her from her first day of nursing school and knew more about Ilsa than her own mother. Clara was the only one who knew that she and Eliot were engaged to be married.

Writing to Clara, Eliot, and even her mother was soothing, but it was an inferior replacement for what she longed for—her brother. Ilsa felt more desperate than she had growing up, as if her circumstances would never change. She was so close, sharing the city with someone she could not find.

Two weeks ago, she'd made a decision. If she did not find Bastian by December first, she would go to London and stay with Eliot's family, work at the hospitals there, rejoin the unit she'd left behind when she went to Rome. Eventually, Eliot would come home from North Africa. Together, they would find her brother. And Bastian would stand next to her at the wedding.

Now, December third, it was two days past her self-imposed expiration date. She decided today would be her last day of searching.

Ilsa went to the San Lorenzo district. The destruction of war did not faze her anymore. One more crumpled block, one more deserted area. She saw a child's doll lying next to rubble. Clothing that bore the resemblance of a lived life. She did not see her brother.

Ilsa sat at a small café outside of San Lorenzo. Very few people were on the street. She took her scarf from her head and drank her coffee. A delicacy these days.

"Ma'am," said the café owner, standing over her. "Would you like another?"

Ilsa looked in her purse and shook her head.

The owner thought she looked so sad. Her light blue eyes rimmed with tears while she sipped her coffee. Everyone in Rome had lost someone. Who had she lost? She was very pretty. With her angular jaw and her height, she reminded him of another young person who came to the café sometimes. The young man stuck out because he was one of the only blonde men not wearing a German uniform. But his eyes were different than hers. His were a liquid brown, almost like coffee with a touch of cream.

He brought the woman another drink. It was only a matter of time before he ran out of coffee. Why not give this sad girl a gift?

"Thank you, sir."

"Are you American?" he asked.

She nodded her head.

"How long will you stay in Rome?"

She looked up at him, solemn. "I am going back to London in a few days' time."

"Travel safely, signora. It is a dangerous world we are living in."

Her world had always been a dangerous one. A gun instead of a fist, a war instead of an irate father, her present didn't feel so different from her past. She tried to offer him a smile, a thank you for the coffee. She felt tears run down her cheeks.

He left her to her coffee and her sadness. He had enough sadness of his own.

***

When Ilsa decided she'd go back to London, she'd written to Molly, Eliot's sister. She wanted to know if Molly had heard from him and if she could wait out the war with their family. It was only Molly and her mother left. Like so many men, Mr. Lock had died in the Great War more than twenty years before, when Eliot was an infant. It broke Mrs. Lock's heart for her son to go off to war, too. Molly was a spinster, almost thirty-five years old, and never left home. Ilsa considered this a small blessing, for Mrs. Lock anyway.

Ilsa worried her request had come across as an imposition. She and Eliot had not known one another that long and Ilsa didn't know if Molly and Mrs. Lock liked her.

She stopped at the post office on her way home from the cafe, but there was no word. She planned to leave in two days. If she didn't hear from Molly by then, she'd risk it and go anyway. Nothing in Rome was changing for the better; the American Army didn't seem any closer to capturing the city.

Ilsa entered her room in the dark and lit a candle. It was almost burnt down to the wick, but she didn't want to buy another just two days before she departed. With her, she carried a bowl of pasta made by her landlady. Many of the girls in the house had become friends and ate dinner together, but Ilsa could not bear to let someone else in, to hear another person's sad story. Most nights she took her meal in her room.

"You think I should go back, right?" she asked the dim room. "Your family will welcome me. After all, I will be Molly's sister. Your mother's second daughter. Oh Eliot, please come home. Come home. I will be waiting for you."

A knock at her door. A messenger boy, no older than twelve, stood in the hallway. He handed her a telegram and stuck out his palm.

"I have nothing for you, little boy. I'm sorry," she said.

He turned and left without a word. Who would send her a telegram? Perhaps it was Bastian? Or Clark? But neither of them knew where she was. It was either her mother, Clara, or the Locks. Her mother had not even sent a telegram when Herr Fisher died. Eliot wouldn't send her a telegram, would he? She read:

DEEPLY REGRET TO INFORM YOU THAT ELIOT LOCK IS MISSING. PRESUMED KILLED IN FIELD NOVEMBER 26. LETTER FOLLOWS.

MOLLY LOCK

Ilsa dropped the paper to the floor. Doubled over with nausea, she stumbled to the edge of her thin mattress. She couldn't breathe. She huffed air into her lungs. The tears felt sharp on her raw cheeks. One single person was not meant to hold so many tears.

She would not be going back to London; she would not be going anywhere. In one fluid motion, Ilsa slid from the bed to the floor. She was liquid, meant to pass from one state to another, but here she was—stuck, frozen.

MAX WATCHED IN AWED fascination as Vittorio De Sica directed his actors to stand beyond the statue of Saint Paul so that the famous sculpture was not in his shot. It was the first official day of filming and an electric buzz seemed to radiate through the church yard, so different from the feeling of the last few months. The grass in the courtyard looked like any other patch of pale green and De Sica set that as his backdrop. Next to Max, Luca was grinning. They were making history—rather, De Sica, the writers, and actors were. Max was thrilled to be a part of it. In the excitement, he almost forgot he was in the midst of a war.

"What do you think of that?" Luca said excitedly. Max didn't answer him. Luca wasn't really asking a question, only accompanying Max in his wonder. Their job title on the film was a little vague. De Sica had called them runners, which meant they were to fetch actors when they were needed, make sure the stars were comfortable, and get anything De Sica may ask for. Max suspected he and Luca were brought on more because of the idea they had proposed to De Sica, to use those who were in danger from the Nazis as extras in the film. After they approached the famous director at a café, De Sica had agreed to go to the Pope and let the boys know the result. A little more than two months later, they were standing on the set of *La Porta del Cielo*. Neither was completely sure what the film, "The Gates of Heaven," was about, but all that mattered to Max was that the Pope had sanctioned the hiring of the extras and they were under his protection, for whatever that was worth.

Around them hundreds of people roamed in and out of the Basilica of San Paulo. The building would be their home for the duration of the film and, unbeknownst to them, the duration of the Nazi occupation of Rome. There were 400 or so Jews, dissidents, and resistance fighters taking shelter in the church, eating, sleeping, working, playing, fighting, and loving in several thousand square feet.

Last Max had heard, the Americans were still in Anzio, only thirty miles from Rome. Still, they had not come. The surprise landing of the Allies in Anzio had created a temporary euphoria among those who were fighting back against the Germans. For a moment, they thought they had the advantage, that they were in not as much danger. They paid for this relaxed vigilance with their lives. Max heard that some of the resistance members' most important leaders were captured, tortured, killed. There were two men who'd been taking refuge in the church. They were gone now, dead in the basement of Via Tasso 145.

"Amsel," De Sica yelled. "Come here."

Max rushed to the director. "Yes, sir?"

"Get Marina, will you? It seems she's already mad at me and I think she likes you. I need her in this shot now."

Max walked through the marble columns and the massive carved doors into the Central Nave of the church to find Marina. He'd been there a few days, but his eyes still darted left and right, up and down, as he took in the detailed artwork. Along the length of the church were mosaic portraits of each Pope, ending with the current Pope Pius. A dozen Corinthian columns on either side of the Central Nave lined the church, leading to the sanctuary. The golden mosaic dome stretched toward the delicate stained glass on the ceiling and reflected the afternoon sun, casting a saintly glow on the pews and patterned marble floor. A few people knelt or sat on the long benches, praying or just allowing themselves a moment of peace. The detail—the time it must have taken to construct such beautiful pieces of art—represented centuries of work, endurance, pain, and skill. The painted, gilded ceiling seemed to stretch for miles, lengthening the church in such a way that though they were many people (over four hundred in all), the cast and crew appeared to be few.

Max's steps echoed against the marble walls as he hurried toward the tomb. That was the last place he'd seen Marina before they started filming for the day. The actress, an up and coming star according to Luca, had taken a liking to Max. She was several years younger than him, but to Max, it felt like she was much older, possibly because she'd already made seven movies and it was his first time on a set. Of course, the circumstances of this movie and this set were beyond the ordinary, beyond anything she would have experienced.

The tomb of Saint Paul stood several feet below the altar. Max descended the few stairs and found Marina kneeling at a pew and staring through the protective glass, into the excavated hole that held the body of the saint.

"Did you know him?" Max said, indicating the tomb and attempting levity.

Marina turned to him. Her face was solemn. It was a stupid joke.

"You helped do this, you know," she said, patting the pew and inviting Max to sit.

"De Sica is asking for you—" he began.

"Just sit for a moment. De Sica will wait."

Max obeyed and sat next to her. She had a long straight nose and sad eyes. Her eyes made her appear worldly, like she knew things. He thought she was beautiful. It was no mystery why, at barely twenty, she was a rising star. Her face was perfectly symmetrical. From forehead to chin, Max could have drawn a straight line. He remembered something from one of his art books, symmetry equaled beauty. The eye was drawn to it, wanted to see it.

Not for the first time, Max wished he liked women.

"All of these people," she gestured upward, out of the tomb, "are here because of you. These are lives you saved."

"I only played a small role."

"That's not how I heard it. I heard you were the first person to go to De Sica and suggest hiring Jews and dissidents to be extras in the film."

"My friend Luca and I went to him. But De Sica and Zavattini agreed right away to go and see the Pope. They were at a nearby cafe the day of the round up. That's why they agreed to help. I only brought them the suggestion."

She turned to face him. "You are too humble. You will not get far in the film industry being so humble."

Max smiled. The people who were a part of the film world were special; Max never thought of himself that way. He'd seen Marina in five of her seven movies. Never would he have believed he'd be sitting next to her today.

"De Sica ...."

"Coming, coming," she said and stood.

***

They filmed outside for several more hours until they lost their light. They moved briefly to the back courtyard, set everything up, only to discover the shot would not work there. At the end of the day, the cast and crew were exhausted. Max was not sure if it was because of what led up to this day—their first day of shooting—or if working on a movie really was this wearing. Throughout the day Max had watched the actors cry, scream, kiss passionately for the camera, a nonstop flurry of emotions and he'd taken them all in.

"Protect these with your life," a voice said, breaking through his thoughts. A few members of the crew were circulating papers throughout the church. "Take one only. This special pass will help you through Rome when you absolutely must go out. It equals security for you, identifying you as someone who is working on this film, by order of the Pope. It identifies you as someone who is needed."

De Sica stepped beside the man who was speaking. "Well said, Diego. Thank you for securing these for our cast and crew." De Sica turned to the crowd. "Most of you should not leave. Many have already set themselves up with sleeping quarters in the basement. If you have not done this, I suggest you do it tonight."

A woman with a child on her hip called over the crowd. "How long will the movie take to film?" Max knew her as one of the Italian Jews who was playing an extra and taking shelter in the church. He'd gone to the Jewish quarter with one of De Sica's assistants the month before and she was one of the people they'd recruited.

"We will film until the Nazis have left our city. As long as there are Germans threatening to take away Italian citizens, we will film. And we will stay here while we do it. Safely," said De Sica.

One of the actors, a middle-aged man, spoke. He had a sharp chin and graying hair. "Do we *need* to stay? Are we being held prisoner?"

De Sica chuckled. "Of course not, Marcell, but you know as well as I do that some people's lives would be at risk if they left the basilica. You are free to go whenever you please. But you should know there is a chance you will not return. No one is safe right now."

Marcell stepped forward. "I am not a Jew." He sneered and everyone in the room understood his meaning. "Jew" was a bad word to him and he wanted to separate himself from the extras. "I have nothing to fear."

De Sica cleared his throat. "No, nothing to fear. Only that you now find yourself without a job or a paycheck. Thank you and good day."

The man pushed through the crowd to the front door. The church echoed from his movement. Max held his breath.

De Sica continued. "Let everyone in the room understand something. Our first job is to save our fellow Italians. Jews, Catholics, dissidents and the lot. Our second job is to make this film." He winked at Max. "Now everyone, get some rest, it's been a long day and we have many more ahead of us. You will find food in the downstairs kitchen."

The initial day of filming *La Porta del Cielo* was complete. As Max made up his bed on the floor, he felt satisfied for the first time in a long while. Blankets and bodies lined the surface of the lengthy room. In the two smaller rooms to the right it was the same. More still ate in the kitchen, talking in quiet, swift voices. Max looked at his special pass. He was in less danger than most of the people in the building. The Pope had wielded his power and agreed that Mass would not be held while the film was being made. Between that and the passes, Max felt like the man was trying to make up for something. Perhaps for the roundup and for not using his power when it could have saved a thousand lives or more. Ever since the trucks full of men, women, and children had left, Max yearned to hear them rolling back into the city, down the cobblestone streets. He so badly wanted the stories in the papers to not be true. It was a tragic flaw of his to concentrate on what could have been done, instead of what was being done.

***

Luca came in from the kitchen and plopped down next to his friend. When Max had proposed this whole thing, Luca had been doubtful. He still was doubtful, but he was beginning to find faith in Max. Anything that kept him safe while he waited for the war to conclude and for Angie to come back to the city felt like a good idea. Especially if he could make some money while doing so.

"That was amazing today, Max," said Luca.

"Sure was."

"Four years of school and here we are. Working on an actual film."

Max grinned at him. "Pretty amazing." He paused. "Have you heard from Angie?"

Luca felt his shoulders tense and he lay down on his blanket. "No. I haven't been able to get to a phone. Maybe there's one somewhere in here?"

"You could write her," Max suggested.

"I wouldn't know what to say. Besides, the Germans are intercepting some of the letters. That's what I hear anyway." Luca didn't know what any SS Officer would do with a letter of his, but he'd rather not write one to find out.

"Do you miss her?"

"Like crazy. I lucked out with her." Luca peered at Max who was also lying down. He'd never known Max to have a girl of his own. Luca wondered about that, but didn't like to wonder too hard. It was Max's prerogative, whatever that was, to like and date whom he wanted. Luca knew of a person or two in school who were rumored to be homosexual and he didn't know how he felt about the whole thing. As long as Max didn't like him in that way, he supposed it didn't matter. In war, fewer things mattered than used to. And the things that did matter, mattered more.

"I'm going to sleep." Luca rolled over. "Good night," he said through a smile. He thought of Angie while he drifted off. Luca slept and dreamt of jungles and mountains, of guns and battle, of churches larger than the sky.

Max listened to the sound of Luca snoring next to him. He was finding it hard to fall asleep himself. The people's excitement, mixed with their fear, smelled of sweat. Max thought the two emotions were perilously aligned. When to feel excitement? Fear? What if the two were confused? That was when danger crept in.

Across the room, Massimo Girotti lay down on a thin mattress. Lead actors like Massimo had been provided with slightly better sleeping accommodations, but no one complained. Most were just thankful to be alive. Max watched Massimo remove his black T-shirt and fold it next to him. He was taut and brown. The actor was the pivotal heartthrob whom Max had spent hours watching on the screen. He'd been in more films even than Marina. His features looked painted on, that was how perfect he appeared. His mouth was always pink as if he'd just finished a lollipop, and his heavy-lidded green eyes always seemed to be searching for something. Max looked at the stubble on Massimo's face and touched his own cheeks. It would take Max days to grow what Massimo produced in hours. He moved his eyes to the left and was startled to see the man next to Massimo staring at him. Max turned away, embarrassed. The man was Massimo's assistant and he'd just caught Max staring at his boss. He'd probably tell De Sica that Max was a weirdo and to keep him away from the movie star. The assistant caught Max's eye again, staring. Max lay down, shut his eyes, and pretended to sleep. The feeling—excitement or fear?

Halfway between wakefulness and sleep, Max thought of Bastian. He realized that he'd not thought of him once in the last few days. *That* was progress. He'd carried Bastian Fisher with him, through the hours and weeks, his dreams and daytimes; the young man from camp was an integral part of Max's inner fantasy world. Now, with luck, Bastian would fade from memory. The war may have one positive consequence: to drive the boy Max loved from his mind, replaced with new experiences, a new world.

BASTIAN HELD A SHOT GLASS in his hand. It contained water. He and the bartender, Leo, had a deal. Leo would discretely fill his glass with water over the course of the night, and at the end of the evening, Bastian would give him a few extra lira. All the while Bastian kept his back to a group of SS officers and his ears alert. He'd found the spot almost a month before. Each day his patience was tested. Would the men show up, would they say anything useful, would he finally be able to send worthwhile news to Clark? Now, he sat and waited for them to appear.

Since the incident in the alley, Bastian had been working eighteen-hour days, trying to find a source for information and attempting to block out what he'd done; the pulling of the trigger, the blood as it rivered toward him.

Each day he visited new locations where the officers gathered until he'd found this group. Mostly they just talked about women and played cards, but once in a while they'd speak of the war. Not for the first time, Bastian was thankful his father had made him learn German. It probably had saved his life more than once over the course of the war. That didn't make him feel any more affection toward the miserable bastard. It had been almost six years since he'd left home and his hatred for the man still burned inside of him.

When the officers were at the bar, he'd put on his show, drinking his shots. A drunk man was not a dangerous man. The Nazis ignored him completely after the first few encounters. They'd checked his papers and been satisfied by the results. With his golden hair, he looked more like them than an Italian Jew. Once they decided he was not a threat, they didn't even seem to notice he existed.

Every hour or so Bastian would play-stumble to the bathroom. There he'd jot down anything useful he'd heard before he forgot it. He knew keeping the leather-bound notebook could be dangerous, so he developed a code for himself. If they ever suspected him and found the pages, they'd find badly worded poetry. Bastian copied the useful bits, in plain language, into another journal, which he kept safely in his flat. It still didn't feel like anything he'd collected would be valuable to Clark, but he hoped the pieces would start to make sense and he'd have something for the general.

There were troops in Anzio, close to Rome. In the ten days the army had been there, Bastian could have walked there and back many times. That meant the Germans had either been waiting for them, or the Americans had moved too slowly. Bastian had heard Clark talking about Anzio back at the beachhead, how important it was to ensure the element of surprise with a swift attack. If the troops didn't move fast, the Germans would occupy the mountains and trap the Americans in the basin of the reclaimed marshland. Bastian had read in one of the papers that it was not Clark, but Lucas who was leading the attack in Anzio. Maybe Lucas didn't have an understanding of how important speed was in this particular mission. Whatever the reason, the Americans had yet to reach Rome. Bastian wanted to have something to give Clark, to help the army in their arrival to the city, or to help troops in other locations fighting the Nazis.

The feeling of inadequacy made Bastian dangerous. He didn't like to exist in a state of rest.

Often, when the men were deep into a story about a female conquest, or reminiscing about their childhood in Germany, Bastian allowed his mind to wander in and out of their conversation. More often than not, he went back to that night in the alley. It'd been more than two months; he still saw the face of the dead man clearly when he walked down the empty streets, when he lay down at night. It was true that Bastian had killed numerous men in the war. He counted them at first, wanting every life to matter, to be regarded and calculated. There were too many now. Some, he wasn't sure if he'd killed or only injured. Perhaps no soldier truly knew his number. In war, the lines blurred together. What was right? What was wrong? Bastian had no solid understanding of it anymore. The rule of war was kill or be killed. Was he in his right to kill that man in the alley? Whether he was in the midst of battle or not, he was still in a war. Did he have to be on a beachhead or inside of a tank to take aim at someone? Were the edges of right and wrong so intertwined in an impossible, endless figure eight that it didn't matter anymore?

It felt like it should matter, but Bastian could not say if it did.

He heard the bar door open, pulled his cap lower over his brow and concentrated on the mahogany bar top. He'd trained himself not to look up, to not appear interested in who was entering the bar. Without turning his head, he knew it was them. Their voices were now distinct.

"My fucking back hurts," The Nazi he had come to know by the name of Raeder said. He was the oldest of the three. Most of his sentences contained the word "fuck"—or its German equivalent. His graying hair was slicked back and parted at the side. His nose looked like it'd been broken several times. He wore a neat, trim mustache that flirted with his thin upper lip. When he walked, his right leg lagged slightly behind his left; a war wound from the First World War, Bastian suspected.

"All you do is complain." That one was Eichmann. Bastian thought he was meaner than the other two. Once a woman had come into the bar. After the officers checked her papers, Eichmann backed her into a corner and shoved his hand under her dress. Bastian could do nothing lest he break his anonymity. The other two squawked and watched, laughing at her pain. Afterward she went sobbing from the bar. Eichmann shoved his fingers under the men's noses and laughed until Raeder swatted his hand away.

The third man, Wolff, was the quietest. Sometimes Bastian was not at all sure that Wolff wanted to be there. He was young, around Bastian's age he guessed, and looked the most like Bastian himself, only six inches taller, with narrower shoulders. Wolff joined in with the other two, but often had a far off look in his eyes. He never said more than a sentence or two at a time. Bastian decided Wolff was the weakest link and if it ever came to it, could be used to his advantage.

The men sat at their usual table and Leo brought them each an amber colored beer and a shot of Schnapps.

Raeder and Eichmann drank their shots right away while Wolff sipped his. He did everything at a slow pace.

Leo returned to the bar and Bastian pointed at the whiskey on the shelf, indicating that he wanted a shot, a real one. Bastian didn't know how many more nights he could sit on his stool and listen to their nonsense. Nothing they talked about mattered. He took the shot of whiskey and ordered another. Behind him the men laughed. Leo looked at Bastian uncertainly. Did the bartender know what Bastian was up to? He threw his head back and drank the second shot.

He didn't know if he could be careful any longer.

"Did I ever tell you about Margot, that pretty young thing I fucked?" Eichmann asked.

"Many times," Raeder replied. "She was barely thirteen. She cried until you made her scream. That one, right?"

Bastian drank one more shot while Eichmann giggled gleefully like a schoolboy. They were sickening. *Thirteen.* His sister was thirteen when he'd left her. Just the thought of that man *looking* at her, let alone placing a finger on her, made Bastian feel ill. That girl, Margot, may have had an older brother too. She deserved protection. Bastian had failed Ilsa. He'd left her.

He spun around in his stool, too fast, and looked at Raeder's face. The man wore a smug grin. Wolff had his head down. Bastian stood and sauntered over to the trio. Eichmann and Raeder placed their hands on their guns. Wolff looked up from his drink.

"Do you want to hear about the last woman I bedded?" Bastian asked, slurring his words for effect.

"Fuck off," Raeder said.

Instead Bastian came closer and placed his hand on Wolff's shoulder. "Come on men, let me join in on the fun." He was pushing too hard. He didn't care. Hungry for information he said, "I can swap stories like the best of them. I have a few you can whet your appetite on."

Eichmann looked up at him. For a second, Bastian thought he was going to invite him to sit down. Instead the Nazi officer stood and drew his gun. In one swift movement Bastian grabbed Wolff by the shoulders and pulled him up, using him as a shield. Eichmann fired before Raeder could even stand. The bullet passed through Wolff and into Bastian's shoulder. They groaned in unison. Wolff fell to the floor, clutching his chest. Now Raeder was up and had his gun trained on Bastian.

They didn't expect him to react, not with a bullet in his shoulder. The officers looked at each other and grinned. The moment was long enough for Bastian to pull his own gun and aim it at Eichmann's head. At the close range, pieces of the man's skull exploded and splattered on Raeder and Bastian. Blood streaked Bastian's vision.

Leo came from behind the bar, a broken bottle in hand.

Raeder watched Eichmann's body slump to the floor. He cocked his gun and raised it at the young blond man who'd spent so many nights sitting on that stool. He'd told the other two more than once that they should watch out for him. Raeder took pride in being right, as he pulled the trigger. From behind him, a sharp blow to his head. Raeder collapsed next to his fellow officer. A trail of blood ran from his hairline into his ear.

Leo was the last man standing.

The sounds of moaning and gurgled breath filled the bar. Leo looked at the men scattered around his floor. Each was bleeding. Eichmann and Wolff were dead, the other two injured. Leo decided he still had time.

The last thing Bastian remembered was being dragged behind the bar. His shoulder ached like it was being crushed beneath a heavy boulder. The floor of the bar was cool. It lulled him into a deep, black sleep.

***

Two Italian former military men sat in a Catholic church with their heads near one another, looking over a map of Rome. They'd joined the army together and later defected together when Germany occupied Italy. Each had pledged to die for what they thought was right. In the church, a make-shift hospital had been assembled on their orders. Men, mostly, occupied the white-linened beds.

Inigo Campioni and Luigi Mascherpa had grown up together in a small village outside of Rome. Each had promised the other's mother when they joined the military that they would protect one another. Mrs. Campioni and Mrs. Mascherpa were now both dead. The men wondered what their mothers would think of their defecting, of Hitler and his plan. Country first?

"There," Inigo pointed to the map. "I've heard from several people that important meetings happen there with high ranking officials."

"All of the homes are gated in that area. How would we get through? No, we need to attack out in the open. There is more of a chance of success that way," Luigi said.

"There is more of a chance of innocent bystanders that way," Inigo said, sighing.

"Sacrifice is necessary, you know that."

Inigo did know. They both did.

Leo rushed into the sanctuary. He was out of breath. Inigo and Luigi stood and greeted their friend.

"What's happened?" Luigi asked.

"At—the bar ..." Leo said, inhaling sharply, trying to regain his breath. He slumped onto a chair and rested his palms flat against his knees. "Remember those officers I've been telling you about? The ones who come to the bar all the time? Well, two are dead and I have the other one tied up in the storage room."

Inigo and Luigi looked at Leo in question. "Well, what the hell happened?" Inigo asked.

"That other man, the one who looks German and comes into the bar and has me fill shot glasses with water—he happened."

"Is he still alive?"

"Yes," Leo said, finally able to breathe. "But he'll need a nurse. I need help getting him here."

Without another word, the two put on their coats and followed Leo out of the back of the church. They ran through side alleys and dimmed streets. It was past curfew. It would do them no good to be captured now. Not when they had a potential goldmine at their fingertips.

When they arrived at the bar, Leo and Inigo went to check on Raeder, tied up in the storage room. Luigi, who had some medical training, knelt down first to Eichmann and Wolff. It didn't take long to come to the same conclusion as Leo. They were dead. It didn't matter, they would get the same information from Raeder as they would have from the other two. Luigi went behind the bar. The man was unconscious. He inspected the wounds. It appeared that one bullet had hit his shoulder, but not gone the whole way through, and the other had grazed his arm. Luigi tried to remove the man's jacket to inspect the wound more closely.

Without help, it was impossible. He would need to be taken to the hospital anyway. They could examine him more thoroughly there.

Leo and Inigo reappeared. "Raeder will need a few stiches," Leo said. "I hit him pretty hard with the bottle. For now, he's going nowhere. Once we get this guy to the hospital we'll move Raeder to a secure place for questioning."

Inigo asked, "Are you sure we should deal with this one first?" He pointed to the man on the floor. "Shouldn't we take Raeder somewhere? He could be invaluable."

"This man killed two piece of shit Nazis. We take care of him first," Leo said.

Luigi pulled him up and slung him over his shoulder. "Who is this guy, anyway?"

"No idea," Leo said as they exited onto the street.

CHAPTER 14
FEB 1, 1944

THE THREE MEN TOOK TURNS carrying the limp body through the darkened streets of Rome. It was past curfew. Every few blocks, when one of them was tired, they would hoist him from their shoulders to one of the others. It was hard work and there was a constant fear of being seen. Once, they heard gunshots near their location. They took an alternate route, making the journey longer. At the church, they took him to the basement where the makeshift hospital was set. There were forty beds in all and around half of them were occupied.

Leo, who'd carried the man the last leg of the trip, laid down the body on the closest bed. The three looked at each other, satisfied. Inigo motioned to a tall nurse and she came over.

"Ilsa, we need to get back out there. We're leaving this young man in your care."

She gasped and took a step backwards. "It's him."

Inigo looked at her in alarm. "Who?"

"What is his name? What do his papers say?" Ilsa asked.

Leo opened the man's jacket and felt around until he found the man's identification. "It says his name is Bernardo Lombardi. Born in Rome."

"No," Ilsa said, sounding surer. She lifted his shirt. There was a thin scar on his right side from one of the first times their father had used the belt on him. She traced the raised skin with her finger. "This is my brother."

The three men looked at her, stunned. They knew she was in Rome to find her brother. Bastian was his name.

"I suppose he could have a fake ID, like many of us," Leo said. "The only thing I know is he's been tracking three Nazis for a month and I'd bet gathering information on them. Tonight, something happened. It was like a switch. He just decided he didn't want to wait anymore I guess. Two of the three SS officers are dead. We need to get the third to a secure location for questioning. Now, if possible."

"That's him, alright." She touched the penny around her neck. "He was always able to flip back and forth like that. A gift and a curse."

"You're alright then?" Luigi asked.

"Yes, of course. Tend to your business. I will take care of my brother."

Ilsa gave Bastian a shot of morphine to help with the pain and keep him knocked out, then stared at him for a long moment, unable to act. He looked almost the same. It was unbelievable, yet it was true. She had found her brother. He'd aged a little, though not as much as her. When he left her she was a little girl. Now she was a woman with a dead fiancé. She could not think of Eliot. Each time she did, it felt like someone was sitting on her chest. No, she needed to concentrate on her brother. He wore a beard now. It framed his face, made him look a little like their father.

She inspected his wounds. The bleeding had mostly stopped. All her life she'd gone to him for protection—

from their father, girls who pulled her hair, or boys who teased her. It was her turn to protect him now.

A bullet was lodged in his shoulder. She called another nurse, Helen, over to help her turn him. Ilsa didn't know if she should leave it in or take it out, she didn't have enough experience to make an informed decision. She and Helen examined the injury together. For the hundredth time since coming to Rome, she wished Clara was there.

"It will have to come out," Helen announced.

"Are you sure?"

"As sure as I can be without an x-ray. You'll have to trust me."

Ilsa preferred to trust Helen over herself. She'd been a nurse far longer than Ilsa, had removed many bullets from many men.

The doctor's schedule was erratic; he came when he could get away safely. They could not wait for him. Helen anesthetized Bastian and Ilsa picked up the scalpel. Her hand was shaking.

"Would you like me to do it?" Helen asked.

"No. I can do it." Ilsa steadied her hand and made an incision to widen the gash. "I don't see it. What should I do?"

Helen wiped the blood that seeped from the cut. "You'll have to put your fingers in," she said. "I've done it a few times before. I guess some men have bad aim."

"What does that mean?" Ilsa asked.

"I'm sure the gunman was aiming for his heart."

***

Hours later, Bastian awoke with a groan. He didn't know where he was. The room was dimly lit. Was he still in the bar? He turned his head to the side and saw a bed next to him. A woman with high cheekbones, freckles, and fair skin lay there. Her eyes fluttered open and she smiled at him.

"You're awake," she said.

Her voice hadn't really changed. She was taller, more beautiful, but still scrawny and a little boyish.

"Ilsa," he said.

A grin spread across her face.

"Am I dead?" he asked.

She laughed. That sounded the same too. "No. You were shot, but I fixed you."

"*You* did?"

She looked at him, indignant.

He stretched his hand to her. It hurt. "I only meant the last time I saw you, you'd barely grown out of playing with dolls. Now you're fixing bullet wounds."

Bastian studied his sister as she sat on the edge of the bed and smoothed his hair away. It was so good to see her. So many times he had wondered if they'd ever meet again. He had assumed he would die in this war, one way or another. He wanted to know everything about her life, his parents. More than that, though, his body wanted to sleep. He drifted off with his hand in hers.

When he awoke for the second time, the room was brighter and it took him less time to orient. It still felt like a dream, though, and Bastian didn't know where he was exactly. Ilsa was sitting in a chair next to his bed, asleep. How had she found him? Or had he found her?

Ilsa opened her eyes. Bastian smiled at her.

"So, tell me," he said. "How are you?"

Ilsa looked away. He watched tears seep from her eyes to her chin. It was a little too pointy for her face. He thought it made her even more beautiful.

"What is it?" he asked. "Is it Mom?"

"It's so many things," she said. Ilsa told him about their father. How he'd died. Bastian became stiff at the mention of him. She thought he would soften when he heard about his death; he only said, "Good riddance." She knew the two of them had shared a few good memories together. Those would never outweigh the pain he'd caused Bastian. She knew that too.

When she talked about Eliot, she began to cry again. Bastian pulled her to him with his good arm and she lay next to him on the bed. She told him everything. How they'd met. Their first kiss. How he'd proposed. She showed him the flower ring and the penny that hung around her neck.

"I think this thing has kept me safe," she said, holding onto the coin in her palm.

"I don't believe in luck," he told her.

"Then why did you give me your *lucky* penny?"

He grinned. "Maybe I believe in it a little. Hey, if I'd had that, maybe I wouldn't have gotten shot."

"Maybe you deserved to get shot," she said, looking away.

"Ouch, Ils. Why would you say that?"

"I asked you to promise to stay safe and alive. And you go and get yourself shot, doing what? What have you been doing?"

"I'm still alive." He took her hand that was grasping the penny. "I'm sorry. I'll try not to get shot again."

He always thought he was so smart. Ilsa squeezed his hand. "You need to sleep now. When you wake up next time, I want to be filled in—with the truth."

Bastian nodded and yawned. His body felt like he hadn't slept in his lifetime. Everything was heavy, stiff. As he drifted off, he thought of his father. The man was dead. The world was a better place as far as he saw it. Many men didn't deserve to live. He may have been one of them himself.

FILMING *La Porta del Cielo* was exciting, yes. But, Max soon discovered, it was also tedious. After four days of rolling cameras they'd only completed the opening sequence. There was a lot of waiting and standing around. The extras and many of the actors and crew had nothing to do for long periods of time. Some found a quiet corner in the sanctuary and read. Some, Max saw, found dark corners in which to touch and kiss. The dozen or so children ran around the church and the courtyard, chasing one another and making the most of their adventure. Their parents, when not otherwise occupied, yelled after them, shushed them, or sent them to the basement where they wouldn't disturb anyone. In the one short week they'd all been together, they'd formed a family of sorts and a life complete with routines, connections, and work.

In the mornings, most gathered at the long tables set up outside the kitchen and ate together. Lively conversation ensued about the film or the state of the world. Max felt like those who'd been living in constant fear were able to take a breath. They were out of danger, for now.

This morning, Max sat with Luca at one of the tables. Luca was re-reading a letter from Angelica while they ate breakfast.

"I'm still not sure what to write back," he said.

"Well, if you don't write soon, she'll be mad at you. It sounds like she is safe and doing well," Max said as Luca folded the letter and placed it in his pocket.

"I guess so."

"What's wrong?" Max asked.

"This is all just so ridiculous." Luca put his face in his hands. "A man should be able to be with his wife."

Max turned and looked around the room, spotted Jareth, Massimo's assistant. For the last few days, he and Jareth had been catching one another's eyes.

"Are you listening to me?" Luca asked, looking up and following Max's gaze.

"Of course. I'm sorry. Yes," Max said. "People should be with the ones they love."

Luca shook his head at Max and sighed.

"What?" Max asked.

"Sometimes I just can't figure you out."

"What does that mean?"

"Just what I said," Luca answered.

"Well," Max said, "I can't figure myself out half the time, so you're in good company."

They offered each other a smile. The room was quieting as people made their way to the courtyard where they would film again today.

"Ready to go?" Luca asked.

Max looked down at his half-eaten serving of eggs. "I think I'll finish. I'll meet you out there. Maybe today we'll get through the opening sequence finally and move to the first real scene."

"Here's hoping." Luca got up and made his way to the stairs.

Max turned his attention to his breakfast. He felt a prickling at the back of his neck and when he looked up, Jareth was standing there. He was a full head taller than Max and had rounded cheeks like a baby. When he smiled, he looked like a winged cherub, like the ones painted in cathedrals around Rome.

"Hello," Jareth said.

"Hi," Max said. For a moment, both were silent. "Do you think we'll get to Massimo's scene today?"

Jareth scratched his head, sighed and sat next to Max. "I think they are hoping to shoot one of the night scenes this evening. Massimo is nice, but needy. I like it better when he's busy."

"How long have the two of you been together?" Max asked.

"Together as in?"

"Um …." Max had thought he meant how long had Jareth worked for Massimo. Now he wasn't sure. "I don't know."

"You don't know what your questions was?" Jareth asked.

Max stood, his eggs still on his plate. "I should catch up with Luca."

Jareth stood too. "How long have the two of you been together?" he asked.

"We've been friends since college." Then Max added, "Me, his wife, Angelica, and him, I mean."

"I see." Jareth said. He leaned toward Max and plucked a loose feather from his shoulder. "From your pillow maybe? Or perhaps you are keeping birds?"

"Pillow," Max said, scarlet in the face from Jareth's touch. "I really should go. I'm supposed to be working."

Jareth took one step back. "Until we meet again, then."

Max nodded before he turned and left.

***

The day was long and productive. By six p.m. they'd finished the opening sequence and set up Massimo's evening scene. The night before, Max and Luca had finally gotten their hands on a script and read it. It explained the structure they saw the crew building in the courtyard; it was the interior of a train. Much of the action would take place on this set so the details needed to be perfect. The story followed a group of pilgrims, each one with an illness, on their way via train to the Church at Loreto. At the church, each character hoped to find health and redemption.

The scene they were filming that evening was between Carlo Ninchi and Massimo. They played two factory workers, one blinded by an accident the other had caused. Max believed this scene showed their relationship before the accident. Though it didn't appear that De Sica was filming in order, so Max was not sure. All of his previous movie experience came from darkened theaters and books.

"All right everyone," De Sica said, addressing the cast and crew. "Let's see if we can get this in one shot and then all go to dinner. Now, Carlo and Massimo this scene is right before—"

A loud gunshot cut him off.

They were used to hearing guns through the day and night, but this one was close. Too close.

Seconds later, a group of men burst through the church gate, guns raised in the air. Max saw at least a dozen Nazi officers led by a very tall, thin man with droopy eyes. Panic spread. Everyone outside scattered through the courtyard. Some ran toward the church, others ducked between trees and columns. Max was standing next to a little girl and Marina. He scanned the rushing crowd for Luca and could not find him.

"Max," Marina said frantically.

He grabbed their hands, Marina on the left and the little girl on the right and ran toward the church. He didn't know if the people who rushed around him were Germans or Italians. The three ran into the building.

"This way," Marina said. She pulled them to one of the confessional boxes and yanked the door open. "In here."

Max had only enough time to see a uniformed man hit someone across the face with his baton. There was chaos and screaming. Marina jerked the door closed.

"But we have to help," Max said.

"We must save this little girl and ourselves," Marina said.

Max had almost forgotten about the clammy hand in his palm. He leaned down in the small, dark, crowded confessional. The girl was crying. She had an innocent face, clean of any lines to mark her.

"It's okay," Max whispered, pulling her into his jacket to quiet her. "What's your name?"

She pulled her face back. "Anne Marie."

"Don't worry, Anne Marie," Max said. "Everything will be okay."

He could feel Marina looking at him. How could he possibly know that? Outside the confessional, they heard people screaming and crying. Men's deep voices yelling commands in German echoed in the sanctuary. Max drew the girl close as Marina looked out the small keyhole.

"They are taking people," she said.

Max moved his arms around the girl's head to block out what Marina was saying.

She continued, "There are at least a dozen already rounded up, men and women alike."

They heard three gunshots in succession. Anne Maria wept into Max's jacket. Were people dying right outside these doors? His people? He'd brought them here, thinking they'd be removed from danger, but he had put them in danger instead. Nothing he did was enough. His body was shaking, he realized, and he stilled it for the child.

The shouting faded and soon order was returned to the church. "They are leaving," Marina said.

"Alone?" Max asked.

She turned to him. He could not see her shake her head "no," but he knew her response. A few minutes later she said, "I think it's safe now. Let's go."

They opened the door and saw a sea of people converging in the vast room. Max tried to count their numbers. He could not tell how many were missing. De Sica was there and they were gathering around him.

"My child," one woman shouted. "Did they take my child?"

"My brother," another said. "I cannot find him."

"How many did they take?"

"I thought we were safe."

"Why did they come for us here?"

De Sica quieted the crowd. "I will send people," he pointed to several of his crew members, "around to every corner of the church to gather the others." The four men scattered in different directions. "Once we are all together, we will see who is missing and inquire with Lieutenant Pietro Koch about how to get them back." When De Sica said the man's name he felt like he was spitting poison from his tongue. "I had the unfortunate pleasure of meeting him just now. He came convinced we were harboring fugitives."

A murmur spread through the crowd. That was exactly what they were doing. They would no longer be safe.

He quieted them again. "I am going right now to the Vatican to straighten this out. We will do what we can to get our people back. In the meantime, Max Amsel—"

Max stepped forward, startled to hear his name called. "Yes, sir?"

"You have a manifesto of everyone working on the film, correct?"

"Yes, sir." Max had been diligent about writing each name down.

"Please retrieve it and we will have a roll call to see who is missing," De Sica said.

Max did as he was told. As he made his way toward the sleeping quarters where he kept the list, he realized that he'd still not found Luca. He turned around himself several times, looking for the familiar face of his friend. He was nowhere. If Luca was gone, Max would never forgive himself.

Max found him leaning over a pregnant woman near the makeshift beds. He ran toward him. "Luca!"

Luca stood and they embraced.

"For a moment, I thought …."

"Don't think it," Luca said. His eyes were bloodshot. "This is Silvia. I didn't want to leave her."

"I fell," she said, clutching her belly. "I don't know if the baby is all right. It hasn't kicked since the raid."

Max attempted to wipe the worry from his face. The woman looked to be close to term. Her dark curls fell over her cheek, covering half of her face. She couldn't be more than twenty years old. "Please, come upstairs. We are taking a count to see who was arrested."

While Luca helped Silvia up, Max grabbed the manifesto. When they climbed the stairs again, more people were in the central nave. The crowd spoke in frantic tones as families and loved ones tried to find one another.

Max moved to the middle of the circle, near De Sica. "Sir," he said addressing the director. "I have the list."

He patted Max on the back. "Good boy. Will you read it? I must go to the Vatican right away to see if I can find out any news."

"You want me to read it?" Max asked.

"Of course. It was your brilliant idea to keep track of everyone in the first place." De Sica addressed the crowd again. "Everyone!" They hushed and he continued, "Max will read off the names. For those who are missing, I will do everything I can to help. While I am gone, everyone stay inside. Lock the gates and bar the doors."

De Sica and two of his assistants left. Once the building was secured, everyone gathered around Max. He started at the beginning of the list. Each time he checked off a name, heard someone in the crowd yell "Here," his heart leapt. But when there was silence, or wailing for someone missing, he thought he might give up.

Early on he discovered a child's mother had been taken. When Max called her name, he heard a small voice in the crowd, "My momma. That's my momma's name. Where is she?" No one came forward. The little boy said his father hadn't come to the church with them, that "the men in the black boots came for him." The child had no one. An older woman stepped up and said that she would care for the little boy until his mother returned. The child was now an orphan, like Max.

In all, sixty-two people had been taken. Some seemed to have no one. When Max called their names, he heard nothing. No one claimed them. Others had families, friends, husbands, and wives that were left. Silvia's husband was one of the people taken. Their worst loss, though Max tried not to qualify one human life over another, was that their only doctor was gone. He was an older man, could not run as the crowd scattered through the basilica.

Max calculated that the Nazis dragged forty-two men and twenty women from the church. None of the main actors were captured. Had De Sica intervened? Or had they been lucky? The little girl, Anne Marie, found her uncle. He'd taken over her care after both of her parents were arrested in the October roundup. Anne Marie had hidden inside a bureau while her family was loaded onto trucks. Story after story emerged as they went through the list. People talked of near misses, of everything they'd endured before coming to the church for sanctuary. With each name, each story, Max could feel himself depleting. It was too much to be responsible for all of these people.

Six extras had suffered injuries from the chaos. It looked like two might need stitches, and one young man dislocated his shoulder when he tore from the grip of a German soldier. Silvia still had not felt her baby kick.

"What will we do about the sick?"

"What if more people fall ill? He was our only doctor."

"No one will come to help us."

They all looked to Max for a solution and the voices overwhelmed him. The pressure was insurmountable. He felt like he was underwater. He thought he might collapse when Luca stepped up.

"It is not up to Max to find a solution. What are your suggestions?"

A woman wearing a dark green shawl over her shoulders stepped forward. "There is a secret hospital, in a church. It is run by, and for, resistance workers. I don't know if they have any doctors, but they may be able to spare a nurse."

"Yes," Luca said. "Yes, let's go there."

A man came forward and touched the woman's arm. "I will go, Vi," he said. "It's safer for me." He looked at the crowd. "I will leave in the morning. I don't want to risk leaving tonight."

It was decided the injured would last the night and that the man, Anthony, would go in the morning to the hospital. After, the room quieted faster than Max imagined possible. Everyone was exhausted and scared. Many of them left for bed in pairs and groups, with no dinner. Luca walked Silvia downstairs, leaving Max to sit in one of the pews alone.

Jareth lingered on the other side of the church. Max turned from him. There was no room for pleasure in this new world. He did not deserve it.

IT HAD BEEN FOUR DAYS since Bastian was shot, but his body could not tell. Every bit of him still ached. Pain medicine was hard to come by, according to Ilsa. The hospital was a secret from the Germans, so they couldn't go requesting supplies.

Bastian lay awake and listened to Ilsa breathing each night. She was a bundle of questions, wanted to know everything about the last five years. Could he really tell her of the people he'd killed, did she really wish to know?

"What was it like?" he asked Ilsa as the sun rose outside the makeshift hospital. "After I left."

She offered him a smile, but he could see her meaning on the other side of it. "We made it through. Once I was out of the house I really only worried about Mother and you, of course."

"You don't have to worry about me," he told her.

She laughed, a wide, open-mouthed laugh. "Says the man who was shot only days ago."

"I have a question, Ils. In those months after I left, did anyone come looking for me?"

It was an odd question. Bastian had some friends in school, but none of them knew where he lived, as far as she knew. Like her, he had avoided bringing people over. Ilsa remembered when she found out at school that he was telling everyone their father was dead. Instead of being angry or denying it, she joined in on the fabricated tale. It was a happier story than the one they lived.

"I don't think so. Were you expecting someone?" Ilsa asked.

He sat up in bed so he could see her face. His heart thudded in his chest. "No one named Max?"

Ilsa looked at him, her eyebrows knitted tightly together in concentration. The name sounded familiar, but she couldn't place it. She was sitting in a chair, hugging her knees to her chest. Bastian thought she looked small again.

"You sent me a letter that he wrote. Did he ever write again?" Bastian asked.

"Oh, that boy. I vaguely remember the letter. No, I never heard from him again. Why? Who was he?" She looked intently at her brother. He always had so many secrets.

"He was no one. Just someone I knew from camp."

She stood up at this. "If you knew him from *that* place, then he wasn't worth knowing. It's because of people like that this war is happening. Because no one tried to stop it before it started. Because we fed into it like it was a good thing. It's because of people like him."

"You don't know what you're talking about." Bastian shifted in bed, painfully, so that he no longer looked at her. "He was a good person."

She turned to leave and said, "I thought you said he was no one."

***

Ilsa expected that every piece of her would be ecstatic when she found her brother, and it was mostly true. But at the corners of her happiness was resentment, a little bit of anger. She could taste the emotions through her smile. Somehow during their childhood Bastian had managed to hold her close, while at the same time keeping her an arm's length away. He was doing the same thing now. Her brother was so full of secrets, of motives she didn't understand. It made her ache for Eliot, for his open warmth and sincerity. Despite their differences, though, Ilsa thought her fiancé and brother would have gotten along.

She watched him sleep as daylight shadows slid across his face, marking the hours. He looked much the same. His face was longer, leaner. But his smile had not changed; it was full and heartbreaking as ever. Perhaps it was the area around his eyes that was different. The lines on his face told a story she didn't know if she wanted to hear.

Did she appear just as changed to him? Could he pinpoint on her face or body where the shift had taken place? Personally, she thought a piece of her spirit had been altered. Could her brother see that part of her? He used to be able to.

Ilsa watched his chest rise and fall, counted the number of breaths. She thought of Clara and her mother. The night Bastian was carried in, she'd written to both of them, telling them simply, "I've found him." No return letters had yet arrived.

Behind her, heavy footsteps. Anthony—one of the resistance workers she'd seen around the hospital—

rushed in, out of breath. Two other nurses went to him, as well as Ilsa. Their voices rose in hurried tones.

Bastian awoke and sat up in bed. Ilsa and two others were talking to a stocky man with broad shoulders. He watched Ilsa take a small, almost imperceptible step forward. As if she was volunteering for something.

The other two nurses went back to their patients and Ilsa stayed to speak with Anthony. She stole a glance at her brother. He was straining to hear them, she could tell.

"How far is this church?" she asked Anthony.

"Not far. It's the Basilica of Saint Paul Outside the Walls."

"You're filming there?" Ilsa asked, surprised.

"By order of the Pope." Anthony shrugged his shoulders. "So, you can come?"

Ilsa looked back at Bastian. He was sitting up, but was pale. She motioned to Anthony to walk with her toward the bed. "Bastian, this is Anthony. He is an Italian resistance worker. Anthony, this is my brother." Ilsa turned to Bastian. "There is a large group of people staying in a church—there was an incident. They need a nurse."

"Okay," Bastian said, pushing himself further up in bed. "And?"

"And I'm going to go with him to see what I can do to help."

"No," Bastian half shouted.

"I'll be back as soon as I can," Ilsa said.

Anthony took one more step forward. "They took our only doctor in the raid. We'll be needing someone long term, if you can."

Bastian worked to swing his legs to the floor. After so many days of immobility, they felt like lead.

"What are you doing?" Ilsa tried to gently push him back into bed.

"If you're going, I'm going," Bastian told her.

"Absolutely not. You're not well enough yet to travel."

"Ilsa," Anthony said, "if I may. The space where we are staying, it is safe."

"Must not be that safe if you just had a raid and people were taken and others were hurt," Bastian spat, attempting to put the pieces together.

"True," Anthony said in a calm voice. "Still, it is one of the safest places in Rome. I only meant that if you are able to travel there, with Ilsa, we should be able to keep you both safe."

Ilsa put up a hand. This was nonsense. Her brother could not go. She would not allow it. She was about to say as much when she looked over at Bastian. He was already sliding his belt into the loops around his pants. He had that look in his eyes. Ilsa knew that look. He would be going with her, no matter what she said.

She sat on the edge of his bed while he dressed and Anthony gathered supplies.

"We've just found one another," Bastian said. "I can't lose you again."

"We'll have to walk slowly," she said, nodding. "You have stitches and they will rip if you move too fast."

"We can take side streets and stay out of sight," he assured her. "I can find the way."

"I've lived here almost as long as you, dear brother. I can also find the way."

Bastian submitted to her. He was in too much pain to argue.

Anthony reappeared with a bag over his shoulder. He handed another to Ilsa. "This should be enough medical supplies to get us started. I will come back later for any personal belongings you need. The priority now is to get to the church."

"Another church?" Bastian asked as he heaved himself to his feet.

"Yes, we're making a movie."

"A movie?" Bastian asked.

"It's rather … complicated. Or perhaps it isn't. Either way, time is of the essence," Anthony helped Bastian out through the basement door and into the sunlight.

They walked for a while in silence. So many questions swirled around Bastian's head. Who would make a film in a war zone? Was this new place really safe? When would the Americans come and help to end this mess?

It was late morning and few people were on the streets, huddled into jackets despite the mild weather. Everything felt colder since the Germans had occupied. A shop here and there was open but most were closed, some even boarded up. They didn't see any SS as they made their way to the church. Anthony said it was only a few blocks. Everything on Bastian's body burned as if he were being held to a fire. He didn't know how much further he could go.

"So," Anthony said in a quiet tone, breaking the silence. "How do two German-American siblings end up in Italy, in the middle of a world war?"

"Long story," they answered in unison.

They laughed and the movement ached Bastian's shoulder and side. He was thankful to hear Ilsa's laugh anyway.

"How much farther?" Bastian asked, leaning more fully onto Anthony.

"We're here," Anthony said.

Bastian looked up and found himself outside a massive basilica. He'd been in Italy long enough to know that this church was part of the Vatican. That's where the inhabitants' protection was coming from.

Intricate iron gates stood guard outside. Bastian extricated himself from Anthony's grip and leaned onto one of them. Anthony pointed to something for Ilsa to look at. A pain gripped Bastian's shoulder and he collapsed onto the cold stones. He stared up at the blue sky for a moment, then succumbed to the pain and closed his eyes.

CHAPTER 17
FEBRUARY 5, 1944

MAX SAT ALONE in the courtyard. It was rare in the church to find a space that was unoccupied. After the October raid in the Jewish quarter, people had clung together. They wanted to be with loved ones, whether long loved or newly loved, in crisis, Max didn't think it mattered. In the last week, small families had formed within their strange new world on set. People who didn't know each other before, now shared meals together. Those who'd lost someone found another who suffered a similar fate. Children who'd been afraid to run and play laughed joyfully in resounding halls. And now sixty-two members of this new family had been taken.

Max buried his face in his hands and rubbed at his eyes. Sleep had not come to him last night. Each time he closed his eyes, he heard the gunshots, so close they could be going through him. He heard the screams, felt Anne Marie shaking in his arms inside the small confessional.

"Max," Luca's voice said.

Max lowered his hands and looked up. His friend looked just as bad as Max felt.

"I wanted to let you know I've just come from the sick ward."

Sick ward: a new word in their new world. They hadn't needed a sick ward until yesterday. The worst they'd seen in the last week were scraped knees.

"Silvia is doing okay. The nurse found the baby's heartbeat. She says—the nurse, I mean—that Silvia will likely have the baby soon. She's already at thirty-eight weeks. Did you know that?"

"Huh?" Max had allowed his mind to wander away from him again.

"Did you know? When you recruited Silvia, did you know she would likely have her baby at the church?"

Luca had an edge in his voice that made Max look him in the eye. "I don't know. I guess I didn't think about it."

"You didn't think about it? So, you thought it would be okay for her to have the baby in a church with no doctor?" Luca's voice rose.

"We had a doctor." Max was deflated. He couldn't be angry. Luca was right. Had he thought at all about the four hundred plus lives he was forcing together? What if someone were seriously ill? A few stitches after a raid was nothing. Someone could have been shot. "I'm sorry, Luca. What do you want me to say?"

Luca sat down next to him. "Nothing. I'm sorry. I'm upset because I received another letter from Angie." Max looked up at him in alarm. "No, it's good news actually. She's pregnant."

Max wanted to smile and congratulate him but he couldn't. Who would bring a baby into this world? "Is she okay?"

"She's fine. I'm just even more worried now ... and being around Silvia and thinking of all of the things that could go wrong ... it's made me a wreck. I'm sorry.

"What happened is not your fault. Anyway, the nurse seems great. She's young but competent. She brought a good amount of supplies and she's stitching people up. We should be okay now."

Max nodded, not believing his words. "We should be okay now," he repeated.

***

Despite the raid, the filming continued. The actors loaded into the simulated train car wrapped in coats. One had a bandage around his head, a prop. Max watched the actors as they said their lines. It was a surreal world he'd entered into. When he watched a movie, he was immersed. Hours after it was over, often days, he'd still think of the characters as if they were as real as Luca. He'd dream about them, interact with them. Filming *La Porta del Cielo* was the same way. As he watched a scene being made he lived in an alternate Alice-down-the-Rabbit-Hole kind of world where he wasn't sure what was real and what was imaginary.

In the makeshift train, Maria Mercader, who was rumored to be De Sica's mistress, adjusted her gray coat and pinned up hair. She looked nervous. The young boy next to her, who played her brother, stared off. His name was Cristiano and in the movie, he was crippled, confined to a wheelchair. He had thick dark eyebrows and had already taught himself how to brood. A ticket stuck out of his pocket with the number "28" written on it. All of the actors who played someone needing to be healed by the shrine at Loreto had a similar ticket.

"Maria," De Sica said over the murmured din of the actors. "Place your hand on your brother's leg."

She did as she was told, giving him a steely glare. Perhaps the lovers had a fight, Max thought.

"Very good, Maria. Thank you, dear. Is everyone set?" he addressed the crew. With a nod from each of them he yelled, "Action."

The scene progressed. Max found himself engrossed as it unfolded.

"Maria," the boy said. "What if Loreto is unable to heal me?"

"Hush. Everything will be fine."

"But what if I never walk? What if I can never play with the other children? I would rather be dead."

"Claudio," she said, turning to him. "Do not talk like that. Never wish death upon yourself."

Beside Max, someone quietly cleared his throat. He looked up to find Jareth almost shoulder to shoulder with him.

"Hello," Jareth said. Max nodded, not meeting his eye. "Would you like to take a walk with me?"

Max looked at him this time. "Sure."

They made their way through the back courtyard where the filming was taking place, into the church near the sanctuary. Max saw several people kneeling at the pews, their hands together in prayer. They continued through the long central path of the church. Sunlight reflected off of every surface, painting mosaics on top of mosaics. That such beauty in a time like this could exist was a comfort to Max. The Nazis had not destroyed everything.

They walked through the central nave and exited onto the wide portico that overlooked the front courtyard. Beyond it, they could see the street and a few people milling about. The statue of Saint Paul stood erect and weathered, white against the mostly green backdrop.

The day was cool and Max pulled his coat tighter around himself.

"So …" Jareth said.

They strolled around the porticos, the huge columns rising to the sky around them. It was a beautiful spot to get to know someone.

"How long have you worked for Massimo?" Max asked.

Jareth laughed and Max feared he'd asked the wrong question. "It's a bit more complicated than that."

"How so?" Max asked.

"Massimo and I were childhood friends. When the war came to Italy, my family left. But I didn't want to leave. Rome is my home. I didn't want to run from it."

"So, you're Jewish," Max said.

"Does that matter?"

"Not to me. But you still didn't answer my question."

Jareth smiled at him. "When De Sica decided to make this film, and you had the idea about the extras—"

"How did you know it was my idea?"

"That's why Massimo came to me. He said I could act as his assistant and help out on the film. I had no interest in actually being in the thing."

"Why not?" Max asked.

"Stage fright. Ever since a bad experience in grammar school acting in a rendition of Grimm's fairy tales."

"That's too bad. You'd look good on screen." Max blushed when he said this. He hadn't meant it the way it came out. Or perhaps he had.

"So, Massimo was nice enough to think of an old friend," Jareth continued, "and here I am. No need to ask how you got here since it was your idea."

"Do you think everyone knows?"

"Not everyone. But many people do."

As much as Max dreamed of a life in film, he didn't want to be famous. This was as close as he would likely ever get.

"It's an amazing idea you had, Max. I think you will save many, many lives."

Max faltered in his step. The tears came in an instant. He was incapable of seeing the lives he'd saved. All he could see were the lives that were lost; the October roundup and now, sixty-two from the cast and crew.

"What's the matter?" Jareth asked.

"If I saved any of these people, then I also damned the ones who were taken last night. It's my fault they're gone."

"That's nonsense. If you hadn't brought us together, who knows where we'd all be right now. You're not God, Max. And, if you believe in him, you are also not Jesus. We are not your lambs. We came here because we thought it was a good idea." Jareth grabbed Max's hand. The gesture felt intimate, dangerous. He dropped it again.

Max wiped at his face. "You're right. Of course, you are." Max felt foolish for crying in front of him. And for allowing Jareth to see his weakness—his complexity. "Let's talk about something else."

"Why, hello!" Jareth said in a bright tone.

Max looked up and saw a pretty young woman sitting on one of the benches with a cup of tea. Her face looked vaguely familiar but Max could not place her.

"I'm sorry," she said. "I just needed to get some air."

"No need to apologize," Jareth said. "You're the nurse who came to help us, right?"

"I'm doing what I can," she said. She stuck her hand out to the men. "I'm Ilsa."

"Jareth," he said, taking her hand in his.

"Max." Her palm was soft, like a child's. He could not shake the feeling that he knew her from somewhere.

"Where have they been hiding you?" Jareth asked.

Max may have been imagining it, but it felt like Jareth was flirting with her. Had he been wrong about him?

"I was at another church-turned-hospital. I guess this is more of a church-turned-film set."

They both laughed. Jareth had a bright smile on his face.

"You're American, right?" Max asked, wanting to break in.

"Yes. A New Yorker."

"Maybe that's how I know you."

"You know me?" Ilsa asked, surprised.

"Maybe not. You look familiar. Like someone I know. I'm from New York too. Do you have any sisters?" He could have gone to school with her older sister. She looked several years younger than him.

"No sister, just a brother. Bastian."

Max's face went white, then red.

"Are you okay?" Ilsa asked. She offered him a seat next to her on the bench.

"Ilsa!" Luca came running through the courtyard. "It's time, Silvia is having the baby, I think. She's in a lot of pain. You need to come now."

She jumped up from her seat, knocking the cup to the ground and shattering it. Jareth's head swiveled from Max, who still looked ill, to Ilsa, whose eyes were wide with terror.

"You go. We'll clean that up," Jareth said. "Then we'll come find you to see if we can help."

Ilsa was gone before he finished his sentence, running through the courtyard with Luca by her side.

Ilsa darted through the doors into the church and nearly tripped running down the stairs but Luca caught her arm. When she found Silvia lying on a pile of blankets on the floor, sweating and moaning, she understood the gravity of the situation. Ilsa had never delivered a baby. She was trained as an Army Nurse. There was no need to learn such a skill. If there were a bullet to be extracted, or an arm or leg to be stitched, sure. But a baby?

Silvia must have seen the hesitation on her face. "You can do this, right?" she asked.

Ilsa nodded her head in affirmation. Silvia was pale. Sweat dripped from her forehead, down her neck.

"Luca, get some more pillows so she can sit up. And any clean sheets or towels you can bring." Ilsa didn't know much, but she suspected Silvia was close to having the baby.

"Where—is—my—husband?" the woman cried through labored breaths.

Ilsa looked to Luca for help. He knelt down next to Silvia and took her hand. "He was taken last night, remember?"

"It's too soon," Silvia said, straining and lifting her head. "He should be here. When will he be back?"

"We'll find him as soon as we can. For now, you have to worry about the baby," Luca said.

She let out another long, low moan.

"Go," Ilsa said to Luca, sending him away to get supplies.

She adjusted how Silvia was lying and tried to speak in reassuring tones as she examined her. Ilsa shook when she saw the crown of the baby's head coming from between Silvia's legs. "The baby is ready to come out," Ilsa said. "You will have to push."

"When will he be back? When will he be back?" Silvia was sweating more profusely.

Ilsa moved to her head and touched it with her palm. She was burning up. Tears streamed down her face.

"I can't do this alone," Silvia said.

"You're not alone," Ilsa told her. "I am here. And Luca will be back. And soon you will have a beautiful baby. But you have to push."

Silvia turned her head and looked at Ilsa. "Why am I bringing a life into this wretched world?" Her voice was quiet.

For a second, Ilsa stumbled. It was a question she'd asked herself. She took a deep breath and closed her eyes. "Silvia. You are bringing a life into this world because you will make it better. We will work together to make it better." Ilsa didn't know if she believed it. She did know that Silvia and the baby could die if she didn't push.

***

Max sat on the bench, stunned, as Jareth cleaned up the broken glass. How was it possible that Bastian's sister was here? In the church? What did that mean? He ran through multiple scenarios; nothing made sense. He didn't even know Bastian had a sister. Yes, of course he did. She'd sent him that letter. A long moment passed while Max dove into the recesses of his mind.

"Who is he?" Jareth asked, taking a seat next to him.

"Who?" Max asked.

"Her brother. When you heard his name, well ... I've never seen anything like it. You looked like you'd seen a ghost."

"A ghost," Max half laughed.

"Jareth," Massimo stood before them. "I need you, please."

Jareth looked from Max to Massimo. "I'll be right there."

Massimo turned and walked back in the direction he'd come from. Jareth took Max's hand in his own. He rubbed it with his thumb and forefinger.

"Good luck with your ghost," he said as a good-bye.

Max watched him walk away, his palm tingling. Then he remembered that a woman was having a baby and that Jareth said they'd help. Max stood and hurried through the church, hearing cries before he reached the room. They were the cries of a baby.

It was a pink little thing, and bloody, shaking with its wails. Ilsa had handed the infant to Silvia, who lay exhausted on a pile of blankets and pillows. She cried as she held onto her newborn. Next to her sat Luca, red-faced and wild-eyed. Max smiled. Despite the war, the hatred men were capable of, the deeds that would haunt the world forever, life was still possible; they could create it, if they wanted to.

He felt a light touch on his shoulder.

"Max?"

Every memory, each moment they shared, seemed to flow over Max like a raging sea as he stared up at him. He was still a head taller than Max, having also grown himself. Max often wondered if he would recognize Bastian in a crowd, if he ever saw him, or if the boy he held in his dreams was not the same one with whom he'd spent an unforgettable summer. He searched Bastian's face. This was a face he would always recognize. He was so handsome, it was almost painful to gaze at him. Max had to look away, struck.

"Max," he said again.

His voice was the same. Like a pebble smoothed by water, it eased Max.

"Bastian."

CHAPTER 18
FEBRUARY 8, 1944

MAX SAT IN A CHAIR next to Bastian's bed. They'd both dozed off. The room was quiet. The cast and crew were filming a long sequence at the "train station" where everyone was needed. He'd barely slept since Bastian appeared, so he gladly took the few moments of peace.

When Max awoke, Bastian was staring at him. That Bastian was here in the room with him was still unbelievable, even three days later. Despite the information Bastian had shared as he'd drifted in and out of consciousness—that he'd joined the army, was sent around the world to fight, landing finally in Sicily and then Italy, Max had a hard time with the realization that this man who consumed his thoughts for years, was really there, next to him. Max's heart had not stopped furiously thumping since they'd reunited.

"How are you feeling?" Max asked. "Ilsa said the gunshot wound is less infected than yesterday. She thinks you'll be okay."

"That's what I hear," Bastian said. He reached his hand toward Max. In the empty room they allowed their fingers to brush against one another. Max looked, sounded, felt, exactly the same to Bastian. The last few days had been blurry, unreal. Each time Bastian closed his eyes, he was sure that he'd dreamt finding Max, that he was still lying in a pool of his own blood in the bar. But when he opened them again, he'd always find Max there, next to him. It hurt too much to cry, though that was what he wanted to do; more than anything he wanted to wrap his arms around Max and weep, and beg forgiveness for what he'd done.

Max, as graceful in his humanity as ever, had not brought up the topic of Francesca, of that last night they'd shared together. With the war, everything they'd seen, perhaps that night didn't matter anymore.

They heard footsteps and Max drew his hand away. They both looked up. Ilsa approached them from across the room.

"How are you feeling?" she asked Bastian.

"Good. Better."

"Max," Ilsa turned to him. "I need to talk to you."

At the tone in his sister's voice, Bastian sat up. "What's going on?"

She hesitated, then said, "Silvia's baby. She needs medicine. Penicillin, I think. It's not widely available, definitely not something I have. It's something you have to get from a hospital, and even there ... with the war ...."

"Okay," Max said. "I'll go to a hospital. Give me a list of everything we need and I'll get it."

"No," Ilsa said. "We can't just ask for it. The Germans have taken all of the major hospitals, where the supplies would be. This is dangerous. I only wanted to ask who you think might be able to go."

"Give me a list and I'll get it," Max repeated.

"No, you won't." Bastian said.

Ilsa took one step backwards. "Let's see how the baby is by day's end and then talk again." She left and Max turned back to Bastian.

"Why did you say that? Why wouldn't I go?"

"Because it's dangerous."

Max smirked. "You've told me about all of the stupid, dangerous situations you've put yourself in over the past years. I can't get medicine for a sick baby?"

Bastian didn't answer him.

"I don't want to fight with you, please," Max sighed. "I'm tired of always having to fight."

"I'm sorry," Bastian said.

"You talked about taking the train here. The SS stopping you and how they killed that man. Do you know his name?" Max asked.

"It was David. Why?"

Max breathed deeply. "It's just that a friend of mine, a professor, he and his family were headed to the hills, like many others. I wanted to make sure it wasn't him or one of his relatives. I think about them all the time, hope they're safe somewhere. I helped print forged identification papers for them, for safer travel. I was in the Jewish Quarters the day of the roundup."

Bastian reached for Max's hand again and this time Max let him hold it, fully. "I was there, too." Bastian said. "I watched, felt helpless."

The two of them had been so close to finding one another that day. What had kept them apart?

Max withdrew his hand again. There was no privacy in the church basement. He knew Hitler was not only rounding up Jews. Max had been able, in part, to repress his fears that the Nazis would come after him too. But with the man he loved in front of him, Max could not deny who he was and what that meant for his safety.

"I received a telegram a few months ago from my Uncle Franco in America," said Max.

Bastian twisted his face involuntarily. He didn't think he liked that man.

"He told me my mother died." Max looked at Bastian for a reaction.

He sat up in bed, reached for Max. "I'm so sorry." Bastian didn't know what else to say. Max had now lost both of his parents. What could he say or do to comfort Max? "Ilsa only just told me my father died recently too." The words left his mouth before his mind had time to catch up. He watched the news dawn on Max.

"What do you mean? You told me all those years ago your father died in a factory fire."

Bastian turned in bed so he was looking straight at Max. "I know I said that. He did, in some ways. A piece of him did."

"You sat on the train with me while I cried and you told me the whole story. How the factory had burned—the people who'd jumped, those young girls who'd been locked in the stairwell …. The images have stayed with me, even through this war and devastation. Now you're saying you lied to me? While you held me in your arms and I cried for my dead father. How could you do that?" Max had raised his voice. He was standing and Ilsa was there, staring at them. "How could you do that?" Max repeated.

Bastian lay back in bed. "I don't know," was all he could say. He wasn't ashamed. If Max understood what his life had been, he would not question him.

Max left, Ilsa behind him, following him out. She caught his arm as he rounded the stairwell into the church.

"Wait. Can I talk to you, Max?"

"More lies from the Fisher family. No, thank you."

She stepped back, stung by his words. "I just wanted to explain why he would make something like that up."

Max sat on a pew and waited until she joined him. He could not look at her. The doors to the church were open and the room was cold. A few birds flew around near the intricate mosaics of the Popes.

"Our father was a terrible man," she began. "To my mother and me, he was cold, but to Bastian, he was cruel. He slung insults and painful words at him until Bastian learned to cope somehow … then the beatings started. His rough outer exterior—it's been built up from years and years of abuse."

Max looked up at her and said nothing. Outside he could hear a scene being filmed. The sky was overcast and made the interior of the church spread out in shadows and tricks of light.

"There *was* a factory fire, by the way—many people died. And it was our father's fault. That's when it got really bad. I think Bastian wished so many times our father were dead, that in some ways, to cope, he thought of him that way. It doesn't surprise me he told you Herr Fisher was gone. I told people the same thing."

"Would you have comforted them while they cried on your shoulder and talked about their own dead father, one who had *actually* died?"

Next to him, Ilsa shrugged. "I don't know what I would have done. Pretending our father was dead … it was part of the way Bastian made it through."

"It doesn't matter," Max said.

"It does. To him. The way he looks at you … I can tell how much he cares about you."

"I don't even know him. He's just someone who I spent one summer with six years ago." Max tasted bitterness in his mouth. He brought his finger to his tongue and it came back red with blood.

"Ilsa," Luca ran up the stairs. "The baby. I think she's worse. She's burning up. What should we do?"

Max looked at Luca and hardly recognized him. He was thinner and looked half-crazed. He'd taken on caring for Silvia and the baby.

"She needs medicine," Ilsa muttered. She bit her fingernail and looked at Max.

"Make me a list," he said to her. "I'll go tonight."

CHAPTER 19
FEBRUARY 8, 1944

MAX ALLOWED HIS ANGER to fuel him as he wove through the mostly dark city. He'd spent years thinking about a man he knew nothing of, a man who had lied to him at one of the most critical moments in his life. What if everything he'd shared with Bastian, everything he'd felt with him, was also untrue?

Trash littered the streets and there was a smell. Urine? Though it was cold, he was sweating. He wore a uniform, similar to those worn by the SS, and it itched. He clutched the list from Ilsa in his palm.

Earlier in the night, he'd stood in front of a mirror in the uniform and saw at a life his father may have wanted for him. Max believed if Herr Amsel truly knew what this war and the Nazis had brought, he'd be on the side of the Allies. Then again, Max didn't know his father. He could not say.

Anthony, the person who'd brought Ilsa (and as it turned out, Bastian) had found the uniform for him. It had been worn several times, by different resistance members. Each returned after their mission, unharmed.

"Maybe the clothes are good luck," Anthony had said when he handed them over to Max.

"Do you still believe in luck?" Max asked.

"There is very little I believe in anymore." Anthony

said. Before he walked away he added, "Good luck anyway, for what it's worth."

***

Max spotted the hospital ahead of him. The red brick building loomed two stories higher than the others around it. Someone in the church who had worked at the hospital drew Max a map. He was to locate a side door around the back of the building. He circled the area, watching for Germans. When he saw no one, Max took shelter behind a large bin used for hospital trash and monitored the entrance. While he waited, he thought of what Ilsa had told him about her father, his abuse of Bastian. It did not surprise Max to learn of this. Certainly, Bastian acted the way he did for a reason. No one was that slick, that sure of themself. It was simply a mask he'd been wearing.

With this realization, Max wondered if he and Bastian were more similar than different. If his own father had been so cruel, would he have lied to his friends? Maybe. Max chastised himself for how he'd reacted to Bastian. He was angry, yes. But he should have said good-bye. If something happened now at the hospital, after all that Bastian had gone through to find Max …. He felt sick with guilt, and even thought about turning back. Then he remembered the baby, the painful, agitated way she'd cried, and her red face.

Max went to the door. It opened with a slight creak. He was completely still as he held onto it and listened. He found the stairs and went straight to the sixth floor where they kept the medical supplies. While he climbed each step, his body skirting the wall, he thought of the baby, of the people he may be able to help with the medicine. He wanted to turn back. Twice he had to stop and press his hand against his chest to calm his thudding heart.

For the past three days, as he sat next to Bastian, his heart had pounded in a similar way. But not with fear, instead with excitement, thrilling, undeniable, love-filled excitement. While Bastian slept, Max wrote and rewrote their future together. In his mind, everything was easy. A movie. They were in the third act, the lovers reunited, having been separated by war. They had grown and matured while they were apart, become who they were meant to be separately so that they would have a future together. Right? He'd spent so many years scripting his life, Bastian's return. What was real now? Planned? What was already decided with their fate?

There was a lock on the door of the medicine closet. He'd been warned of such. Inserting one of Ilsa's hair pins into the keyhole, he moved his hand in a circular motion. Max was in an open hallway, exposed to anyone who may pass. After struggling for several minutes, he heard the lock turn.

The room was small, but held hundreds of vials with liquids, pouches with powders, jars with creams. Max was tempted to throw everything he could into his sack, though it would do no good if he came back with items they couldn't use. He inspected each label carefully. It was difficult to find the penicillin. After what felt like a long time, he located it toward the back of the room. There were only three vials on the shelf. How many did she need? Max took two of them. He thought only for a second about another person who may need the same remedy. He found the morphine and the Sulfanilamide powder. He plucked several other vials with long names from the shelves.

Max was out of the building and back on the street in moments. The bottles clicked softly against one another as he walked back to the basilica. He unbuttoned his coat, part of the uniform scratched his chest. He never wanted to wear the thing again. Max was not meant to be a soldier, didn't want to be one. He wanted to live in a simple world, though he was starting to wonder if perhaps that world didn't exist.

When he returned, Ilsa was thrilled and administered the drug right away. By morning, the baby's coloring had improved, she'd stopped wailing, and her fever was down.

"Thank you, Max," Ilsa said, embracing him. From across the room, Bastian stared at them. Instead of going to him, Max climbed the stairs to find Luca. A red rash had spread over his chest from the uniform.

THEY HEARD THE PLANES flying overhead before they saw them. Max was with Silvia and her baby in the courtyard. The infant, still nameless, felt fragile and small in his arms. The baby was better since Max had brought the medicine back a few weeks before. Spending time with the tiny life made him feel better about the state of the world.

Silvia was the first to hear the engines of the planes in the distance. She took the baby from Max to search for Luca. It took less than five minutes for the basement of the basilica to fill with people. Those who had survived the San Lorenzo bombing knew what was coming.

Max's eyes searched for Bastian in the room. Instead he found De Sica. He sat with Maria at one of the breakfast tables; their heads leaned close together. They did not hide their clasped hands.

Max approached them.

"Sir," Max said.

"Ah, Max," he said. "Don't worry, we'll be fine. Maybe they won't even drop a bomb. Can you still hear the planes? Maybe they have gone."

For the moment Max did not hear them. Though that may have been because of the quiet roar from hundreds of people who now occupied the basement.

"No, sir. I wanted to ask again ... about the people who were taken." Max had already questioned him twice before with no resolve.

De Sica sighed and shook his head. "I'm sorry, I've not found out any information."

"But isn't the Pope intervening?"

"I will keep working on it, Max. In the meantime, we will make the film and protect those who are here." He turned back to Maria, and then said. "By the way, I heard about your trip to the hospital." He patted Max's back. "Brave boy."

The building shook and the people in the room collectively held their breath.

"Vittorio!" Maria gasped, shoving her face into De Sica's chest.

The bomb had dropped close to them. The baby cried and some of the children joined her with their own wails. Max searched, desperate. He was not looking for Luca, or Ilsa, or Silvia and the baby, or Marina. He was looking for Bastian. By the time the second bomb dropped, Max spotted him.

Bastian looked to be frantically searching for someone too. His sister stood by his side clutching his arm. Max ran to them. Bastian pulled him into an embrace, just for a moment.

"I should find Silvia and the baby," Ilsa said to them, watching.

"No," Bastian said. "We should stay together."

"We are together. We're all in this basement together. I'm not going far."

Bastian kissed her cheek and she was off.

Max watched her go, surprised that Bastian had relented so easily. The last several weeks, he'd barely let Ilsa out of his sight. Max figured Bastian was afraid she would do something stupid and brave, like her big brother.

When Max was not on set helping with the film, he and Bastian spent time together. Sometimes in silence. Max did not bring up the story about his father again. Once in a while Max spotted Ilsa staring at them from across a room. They didn't touch, only lingered close when they were able, their breathing in sync with one another. Max had still not adjusted to seeing Bastian each day, to sharing meals with him, laughing with him, as if all of the time in the universe had not passed between them since they were last together, as if each of their worlds had not changed irrevocably.

Another bomb rocked the basilica. That made number three. It sounded like the explosions were getting closer. Pieces of plaster cascaded down from the ceiling. People covered their ears and eyes, imagined themselves somewhere else. Some screamed, most cried. There was constant movement. Max thought of ants climbing along a hill, hundreds of tiny lives scurrying away from a foot ready to squash them.

"Come on," Bastian shouted through the pandemonium. "We need to take cover." Bastian grabbed Max's hand and led him toward the hall with the long tables. Others had the same idea. There were at least a dozen people shoved under them. "Here," Bastian pulled him down to the floor and under the table. Another bomb fell. Bastian didn't know if it was closer or farther away. A hush took over the basement. Four so far. How many more did the Germans have for them? When the Allies dropped bombs on San Lorenzo, thousands had died. Bastian did not want to become another statistic. He kept hold of Max's hand in his own.

"Max. Look at me, please." Bastian said. He needed to say the thing he hadn't, in case they were about to die.

Max hadn't realized he *wasn't* looking at him.

"Max. *I'm sorry*. I know I never said those two words to you. I know that. But I'm sorry. Can you forgive me for what I did all those years ago?"

A fifth bomb. The high pitch whistle accompanying each became easier to identify. More of the ceiling crumbled above their heads. They could hear things falling in the central nave. More ancient relics destroyed by war. The crowd oscillated between panic and resignation. After all they had endured, was this how they would die?

"Max, look at me!"

Max turned to Bastian and held his stare. "What do you want me to say? You slept with my mother. My *mother!* The same night you and I ... why? Why did you do that?" It was the first time Max had said the words aloud. They came out shrill and teary. He'd asked Bastian a thousand times, but never out loud. It was freeing to finally say it; a weight lifted. He'd carried those words with him most days and they grew heavier as the years went by. "I loved you."

A sixth whistle. A sixth bomb. Bastian pulled Max to him. Pressed his lips to Max's. For a solitary second, they were alone in their intimate moment. The world held its breath, waiting for the bomb to land.

***

Ilsa stopped partway across the room when she heard the sixth bomb coming. She clutched the lucky penny in her palm, the chain pulling at her neck. She saw Bastian and Max, under the table, their lips together. She could not look away. Every piece of her said this was a private moment. It was not meant for her. Ilsa blinked several times. Something she couldn't identify bubbled inside of her as she tried to adjust to the reality. She slid onto the floor, clutching the penny. "Eliot," she cried. It felt like her heart was breaking, all over again. Had it been a bombing like this that killed him? She brought her knees to her chest and cried into them. She was alone.

The building seemed to shift and sway. Another collective intake of breath from the crowd. The engines droned, then shifted. The planes were flying away. People let out tiny gasps and sighs; their bodies pulsated. Every vein full of blood yelled out, *We're still alive, we're still here!* The air raid was over.

Ilsa watched Max crawl from under the table. People began to move again, to find each other. Light filtered into the basement. The air smelled of sweat and sulfur. Once Max was gone, Ilsa went to her brother.

"Bastian," she said, helping him up. "Are you okay?" She could tell he'd been crying. She didn't know the last time she'd seen tears rim his eyes. They embraced.

"I'm fine, of course. How are you? Did you find Silvia and the baby?"

"Yes. They were fine when I left them. Right before the last bomb went off," she added. He looked down at her and brushed stray hair from her face. Ilsa reached around and took the penny from her neck. "Here."

"Why are you giving this to me?"

"I just think you need it more than I do. I don't know why. I just have a feeling."

He ruffled her hair. "You're not having death visions of me are you, Kid?"

"I really am too old for that nickname. I was almost married." She was petulant in her adult request.

"I know," Bastian said quietly. "But it makes me feel better when I say it."

"Let me help you." Ilsa said. She went behind him and worked the clasp on the necklace. "Now it's yours again."

Bastian touched the penny. It felt like an old friend. "Do you know how I got this?" He asked.

She didn't. In all the years, Ilsa had not thought about it. He told her it was a lucky penny and she took it as that. Her brother's word had been gold. "No. Tell me."

***

Bastian and his father walked down the crowded streets of New York together. They were going to the hospital. His sister had just been born. At three years old, Bastian already considered his relationship with his father complicated. If asked to put it into words, he would not have been able to say what that meant. He could have said that often Daddy yelled and it scared him. And that when Daddy was loving, he was the only one that mattered. And that when he was mad, Bastian hid under the bed because it felt dangerous not to. He would have said that the good days outnumbered the bad. The family was excited for a baby sister. And, Bastian would have said that he was ready to protect that baby if more good days turned to bad.

Something shiny on the ground caught the child's eye. Bastian bent down to inspect it. It was a brand-new penny, minted 1924. On the front was Lincoln's proud profile, his nose and chin jutting outward. *In God We Trust, Liberty,* and the year, *1924,* were imprinted on the front. Bastian flipped it around. *One Cent* was stamped in big letters above the two wheat stalks framing the words *United States of America.* It caught the light and shone brighter. Bastian offered the penny to his father.

"How about you keep it?" Herr Fisher suggested.

Bastian was shocked. A whole penny? Just for him?

"Think of it as an early payment for being such a good big brother." Herr Fisher bent down to his son on the street. "That's your job now. To protect your sister and be a good brother, okay?"

Bastian nodded his head, overcome and excited about the responsibility. His father kissed his forehead. Bastian clutched the penny in his small hand. He would keep the coin forever. As a reminder of his duty to his sister. As a reminder of the last time his father kissed his forehead. As a reminder of when the good days outnumbered the bad.

CHAPTER 21
MAY 3, 1944

B ASTIAN AND MAX sat near the Trevi Fountain and watched. They did a lot of that these days. Either they were watching the movie being filmed, or they were in the city, watching people, gathering intelligence for Bastian to send back to Clark. He still had nothing for him. Everyone expected that the Americans would have come by now. It had been eight weeks since the Germans had bombed the Vatican and Saint Paul shook. The Allies were still in Anzio. It was spring again and yet no tanks rolled onto their street in victory.

The movie was almost complete. Max regained some of his wonder as he watched the project come together. With the war, the lost lives, the bombing of the church, Max questioned his devotion to movies. Did something as inconsequential as film belong in this new world? It was De Sica who'd helped him see his misconception.

"We need film, and music, and art, more than ever now," De Sica had said. "These mediums help us remember that we are humans living in a world filled with monsters. What we are doing here is not frivolous. It is saving us, our humanity."

Max knew the director was right. It was why he gravitated toward the sphere of film in the first place. It made him feel like he was not alone, like he belonged to something. The worlds created on the screens, the stories told, were important.

When they were not filming, Bastian would drag Max out into the city. He thought two people, sitting and talking, looked less suspicious than a single man lurking. Plus, it gave them time together outside of the basilica. In the last eight weeks, while they'd run out of film and waited for the Americans, Bastian and Max had again found their natural rhythm together and fallen into their old pattern, the one that had come to them so easily years before. They spent almost every waking moment together. They took too many risks.

Having been born exactly one week apart, they'd spent their 23rd birthdays together just weeks before. Still, Bastian felt like he was seventeen again with Max. The fear from before, his fear of discovering new feelings, had transformed into excitement. He wanted to have experiences with Max. He wanted to be opened up to possibilities and a future. Despite the war and dangers surrounding them, he saw clearly that together they could make a life. Whenever Bastian tried to broach the subject, however, Max brushed him away.

Max wanted to talk of tedious things. He didn't want to feel like Bastian was moving mountains with his words. After so many years of wishing for him, of imagining what it might have been like if Bastian had stayed in his bed that night, Max didn't know how to live in the reality of having him by his side.

"Max," Bastian said in a whispered tone. "Is that the same man we saw here yesterday?"

Max looked at the graying hair, the clean-shaven face. "I'm not sure. I can't tell."

Bastian opened the book on his lap and roughly sketched the man's face onto a blank page.

"His chin is pointier than that," Max said, looking at the drawing. Bastian redid the chin and Max nodded. "That's better." He gazed around at the few people who stopped to stare at the Trevi Fountain. Two SS officers sat at a café across from them. "Remind me what we're doing here again?" Max asked.

It began to sprinkle. Max covered his head with an old newspaper he'd found and been reading. The headline, now covered in rain, read, *Americans Land in Anzio*.

"I am trying to finish what I started," said Bastian. "Clark sent me here to collect information. I haven't sent him shit. What if intelligence that I gather helps the Americans get to Rome?"

Max gave him a bemused look. "You think very highly of yourself, don't you?"

Bastian took the paper from Max's head and smacked him on the arm with it. Max replaced the paper with his hat.

"No, really. Before I was shot, I heard some information from those three officers. I just need a few more clues to piece it all together. I think I might have something then."

"Why don't you just send what you have to Clark and let him decide?"

Bastian snorted. "It doesn't work that way. Come on, let's find shelter somewhere. It will look suspicious if we sit here in the rain."

They walked quietly down the dirty streets. Rome had become a dumping ground when the Nazis arrived. They left their trash on the street and there was no government to pick it up. "How much longer do you think we'll have to live like this?" Max asked.

"Do you mean in a Catholic church? Or in the middle of a war?"

"Both, I guess. The film is almost finished. What if De Sica decides it's too dangerous and sends everyone home, to their death?"

"Then you, Ilsa, and I will find another safe place."

Max stopped walking. "What about everyone else?"

Bastian grabbed his arm and pulled him onward. "You can't save everyone. It's childish to think you can."

"So, I'm a child?" Max asked, louder than he intended.

They ducked into an alley and Bastian placed his palm on Max's cheek. It was warm, despite the rain. "Of course not. But my main concern is making sure I don't lose you or my sister. If I can save anyone else along the way, I will certainly try."

"Bastian, I am not a child you need to save anymore. And if you think of me that way, well then we can't be … whatever we are."

"You have an incredible heart. I just don't want to lose you because of it."

Max smiled and pulled away from him. He was a grown man now and he would do what needed to be done. They kept walking, heading toward the church. "What will you do, after?"

"After?" Bastian asked.

"After the war is over."

"I suppose I'll go home. There is nothing here for me," Bastian said.

"There is nothing *there* for me. My parents are dead. At least here I have some family."

"Family you haven't seen in months. Family you never talk about. Come on. *I* am your family." Bastian hesitated. "I've heard, in some cities, some men are more open about … we could live our lives together maybe somewhere."

"I don't know if we have a life together," Max said flatly. After all they had been through, the betrayals and secrets, Max wasn't sure what was left to bind them.

Bastian looked at him, pained. "Ilsa told me she wants to go back to the States. I have to go with her. I hope that you come."

Three uniformed officers walked down the street opposite them. Max saw Bastian touch something at his side. He had a gun. "Just keep walking. Don't make eye contact," Bastian said.

Max examined the men under the brim of his hat. One looked familiar. When they passed them he quietly said, "Bastian. Was that …?"

Bastian stopped, frozen in his spot.

Max yanked at his arm. "We have to keep going." He could feel Bastian fuming next to him. They jogged the last block as the rain poured down, drenching them. When they were safely in the church, they turned to one another.

"So, it was?" Max asked.

Bastian nodded his head gravely. "It was him. It was Hans Mandel. The last time I saw him, I was punching him in the face and then running through the woods with you."

"Do you think he saw us?"

"No," Bastian said, his voice shaking. "If he'd seen us, we'd be dead."

T HERE WERE MORE PEOPLE in the streets today. The sun shone and Bastian wiped sweat from his brow. It was their first summer weather of the season. War or not, the people wanted to be outside. The SS officers walked in pairs and trios down the streets. Max and Bastian looked discretely at each face, searching for Hans. They'd not seen him since the first sighting.

"This way," Bastian said, pointing to Via Marmorata. They veered off Via Ostiense and onto the new street.

"Are we going back to Trevi?" Max asked.

"Yes, I have a feeling about that café. Last time we were there, I thought I heard something."

"Like what?"

"I'm not sure," Bastian said. "A name, of an operation perhaps, that I heard from the three Nazis at the bar once or twice."

They walked the several miles in quiet contemplation. Max thought of Bastian's lips against his own, their bodies pressed together. Their one and only kiss since they'd reunited was the day of the bombing. His lips were just as Max remembered, soft and full. Locating a private spot in the church proved difficult. They hadn't discussed the idea of finding a secluded place where they could be alone, but each looked for options as they went about their day. Interaction outside of the church was out of the question. Max had read articles that talked of roundups of homosexuals. No, he didn't believe he and Bastian would ever find a place to be together, not in the way they wanted. Perhaps they'd had their love affair in New York and that was the end of it. He told Bastian on the day of the bombing that he'd *loved* him. Did their love live in the past tense only?

As they walked toward Trevi Fountain, Bastian also thought of Max. The man who was right next to him somehow felt very far away. He'd talked of them being together after the war, the two of them. And what had Max said? *I don't know if we have a life together.* When they were beside one another in their comfortable ease, Bastian knew exactly why he'd spent the last six years trying to get back to Max. When they'd been apart, a life together didn't feel quite as possible.

Bastian still didn't believe that he himself would make it through the war. He'd come so far, yet something told him he wasn't meant to come out alive. This feeling carried over from Bastian's childhood. Maybe it was from the nights in which he wished for death, to escape his father and his household. Maybe it was his brazen disregard for his own life, and often the lives of others. Whatever the reason, there was a piece of himself that had accepted death, as if it were a sealed fate. Max, on the other hand, *had* to make it through, because if he didn't, it was guaranteed Bastian would not survive. Is that what love was? Not wanting to outlive a person?

They turned right onto Via delle Muratte and made their way to the fountain. The pair leaned against the iron railing and looked out on the surrounding streets. The square had many people milling about. On a bench opposite them sat two lovers, both dark haired and brown eyed. They were whispering in one another's ears and laughing. A typical scene in their atypical life. Max gazed at the lovers.

"Bastian," Max said.

"Shhh. Wait one minute. I want to hear them." The same two officers Max and Bastian had seen for several weeks in a row sat at the café, talking. Every few moments, the officers looked around themselves.

Bastian left Max's side and strolled closer to the officers. Too close for Max's comfort. Max watched Bastian walk into the café and order a drink, listening with his back to the men. He stayed for several minutes, sipping his coffee. Max saw his body stiffen. Bastian set his glass on the counter and walked slowly back to Max.

"We need to go. Now," Bastian said.

Max's face flashed in alarm.

"Don't worry. It's good. I think I put a piece of the puzzle together." Bastian led him down the street toward Via Rasello. They were going the opposite direction of the basilica.

"Where are we going?" Max asked in a forced whisper.

"I have to get back to my old apartment. My notebooks are there and I need to look at them to see if I'm correct."

"Correct about what?" Max asked.

"About the information I've found."

"Can't you just tell me?"

Bastian stopped walking. "It's too complicated to explain. After we get to the apartment and we're *alone* ...." The word struck both of them and caused Bastian to falter. "When we're alone I can explain it. My apartment is right near Piazza Barberini. Not far from here." There were often SS around his building and it could be dangerous to enter after being gone for so long, but Bastian needed to check the notebook. Now was his chance to prove himself to Clark, to truly help with the war effort.

"Is it safe?" Max hurried after him. For a moment he felt like he was back at camp, scurrying along after Bastian, always trying to catch up.

"Yes and no. As safe as anywhere else, I suppose."

Bastian stopped. He flung his arm out to halt Max in his path. From the side street marched a crowd of SS Officers. There were at least fifty of them, making their way toward the narrow street of Via Rasello and singing. A crowd gathered. Bastian and Max listened to the words and cringed.

"Es zittern die morschen Knochen / Der Welt vor dem großen Krieg …."

The rotten bones are trembling / Of the World for the great War …."

Max and Bastian watched them march. On the second refrain of their song, a sudden blast shuddered through the street. A bomb exploded, sending bodies into the air. Dead German soldiers littered the ground. Limbs were torn away. Max gasped from the smoke, coughing as Bastian pulled him further away from the scene. The Germans opened fire in response and more bodies hit the ground. Screams and cries echoed off the stone walls as people scattered on the street. SS officers ran after the onlookers, pulling at their hair, their clothes, whatever they could get their hands on. Between the people running in all directions and the bomb blast residue, it was difficult to know who was shooting whom. It felt like a perfectly choreographed movie scene, complete with wails of pain, bloody limbs and faces, terror filled eyes and desperation. It was not a movie however, it was real life. More real than any movie Max had ever seen.

"In here." Bastian yanked Max into an apartment building entryway. They both doubled over, coughing from the smoke. Once they recovered, they hovered behind the wall and watched the bedlam, helpless. "You're bleeding," Bastian said, pulling Max's face near to inspect it.

"I'm fine." Max swiped at the blood on his cheek. "What are we going to do?"

"We're going to get out of here, unharmed if we can."

"No. We have to stay. Maybe we can help," Max said.

Bastian was exasperated. He looked at Max as if he were seventeen again. "How? How could we possibly help?"

Max turned away from him and back to the scene, where the gunfire had died down. The unharmed officers were rounding up people in the street to arrest them. Everyone was a suspect. Blood and insides spilled onto the cobblestones. The carnage didn't look real. Max saw a little boy, lifeless among the bodies and gasped.

Dozens of people were lined up along a large building. Max and Bastian ducked into the entryway farther when several SS ran past.

"What do you think they'll do with them?" Max choked. Bastian only looked at him in response. "We *have* to do something!"

Two uniformed men stopped outside the doorway, just out of view. Max and Bastian held their breath.

"Aufrunden jeder, das Sie finden können." They were rounding up anyone they could get their hands on.

The men moved on, forcing more people against the building. The air smelled of blood and rot. Those who were lined up stole glances at their neighbors and at the bodies on the ground. The ones who were brave cried quietly.

"We have to do something. These people are innocent," Max pleaded.

Two trucks, much like the ones that had taken the Italian Jews away during the October raid, pulled up in front of the gathered crowds. The men with guns grabbed everyone on the street, rounding them up indiscriminately. Anyone who was seen was taken. The officers shoved men and women alike until they climbed into the backs of the vehicles. Once everyone was loaded, the remaining officers did a sweep of the area. Clothes, fingers and toes, parts too mangled to identify; carnage spread across the narrow street.

When the trucks pulled away, Max exited the building and followed them. Bastian had to run to catch up. Max ducked in and out of side streets, attempting to trail the trucks.

"Wait!" Bastian said, chasing after him. He got hold of Max's arm. "Stop, Max! We can't save them."

Max pulled away and continued to follow. The trucks sped onto a main road, Via Venti Settembre, and he picked up speed along with them. Halfway down the block he stopped, Bastian yanking his arm. He pulled Max onto a side street, away from the main thoroughfare.

"Do you know how incredibly stupid that was? What if they saw you chasing them? How do you think that would have ended?" Bastian's face was red, with sweat pouring from his forehead to his neck and back. He punched his fist against a building. Blood oozed from his knuckles.

Several SS hurried down the street in front of them. Max and Bastian pressed their bodies against the building. The rough-cut stone dug into their backs.

One of the officers said, "We are to meet at headquarters for instruction. I hear they are sending all of us out to round up any suspects."

"How will we know who the suspects are?" another asked.

"Anyone we find on the street is a suspect," he responded.

When they were gone, Max exhaled deeply, but Bastian was panicked. "Ilsa—she went back to the hospital church to get more supplies. She's out there right now."

The two ran, walking when necessary to avoid distrustful eyes. Few people were on the streets. Had word of the attack and roundup already spread? Barely a patrolling officer was left. The SS had not been turned loose on the city yet.

Bastian ran into the church and Max stood guard outside. Moments later, Bastian pulled a frantic-looking Ilsa out the side door. "It's only three blocks to the basilica," Bastian said. "We can make it."

They ran onto another street and stopped cold. A group of officers were loading three men onto the back of a truck. Behind them a door opened. They were pulled inside a café.

"Here!" a voice hissed. An old woman dressed in black stood in the shadows of the shop. They all watched as the men were put onto the truck. Two officers climbed into the front while the others continued down the street.

"How many of us dead?" they heard one of the officers ask.

"More than thirty, last I heard," another answered.

"And Herr Hitler has ordered ten executed for every one of ours that died?"

"Correct."

"We'll pull from those we already have imprisoned, but we'll need to retain more from the streets to meet the quota."

The pair turned and disappeared.

"Ten for every *one?*" Max uttered in disbelief.

"Thank you," Ilsa said to the old woman. They shook her hand and slipped from the shop.

No one spoke during the three blocks to the church. Ilsa hurried along behind Max and her brother. Over the months, she'd watched Bastian and Max's relationship with interest, wonder, and hesitation. The two did not touch, yet they were inseparable. As she lay awake at night, she questioned whether she'd imagined the kiss. In this world, almost anything seemed possible. But this? She worried about Bastian all the time. His constant roaming of the city, distracted by Max at his side. He was not taking precautions. This incident proved her point perfectly.

While her brother and Max had been wandering all around Rome, Ilsa was thinking about what was next. She wrote and received letters from her mother. Frau Fisher missed her children and wanted them to come home. Ilsa promised her that as soon as they were able, they would come back to America. It sounded like her mother was rebuilding her life, shaping it into something she'd always wished it had been.

Ilsa walked to the gate of the basilica. Beyond her, she could hear a scene being filmed in the front courtyard. She stopped. "Aren't you two coming?"

Max was walking away. He stopped and turned to Bastian. "I don't know if I can help, but I am going to try. I watched a thousand loaded onto trucks in October and did nothing. Where are those people now? Gone. Dead."

"When it's safe, we will go to my apartment for the notebooks," Bastian said, dismissing Max's words.

"When it's safe, it will be too late."

Bastian buried his face in his hands for a moment then faced Max again. "But this information—what if what *I* know can help the war effort?"

"These people need us *right now,*" said Max.

"Think of the bigger picture, Max."

"You just want to run to Clark so you can be the hero of this story," Max said, staring him in the eyes. "You are only thinking of yourself. I'm going."

"I'm thinking of *you.* I want to keep you safe," Bastian shouted at him.

"And everyone else?"

Bastian said nothing.

"Exactly. You will do anything to save Ilsa or me. I know that. But there are more people in this world than us." Max walked away from him and ducked down a side street.

Bastian threw his arms up in frustration. Ilsa reached out for him. He'd forgotten she was there.

"Promise me you won't leave the church," he said. "And don't let anyone else leave. They are rounding people up on the streets."

Ilsa grabbed his arm. "Then don't go. Stay here with me."

"If you stay inside you will be safe."

"And you?" She was crying now. "Who will keep you safe?"

Bastian looked beyond her to the church. "Go inside. Please." Her hand fell away from him. He held the penny between his fingers, closed his eyes with a wish, and took off after Max.

CHAPTER 23
MAY 24, 1944

EARLY AFTERNOON LIGHT filtered through the windows of the car. It was parked off the side of the road, hidden behind trees. Moments earlier Max and Bastian had watched four truckloads of victims drive up the hill to the Ardeatine Caves. Two cars packed with SS officers followed the trucks close behind.

Bastian rubbed his sleep-starved eyes. The two had spent the night gathering information where they could. They learned enough to know that the massacre was to be executed at the caves.

"How will we get there?" Bastian had asked the previous night. By this time he was resigned to helping Max. Though any obstacle, like the lack of a car, caused him to argue his case against the attempted rescue.

"We can borrow a car from my family."

"You want to wake them in the middle of the night?"

"No. I know where they keep the keys."

It was hot inside the car. Bastian cranked down the window. He was thinking of Ilsa. She was smart enough to listen to him, but a piece of him was still terrified he would find her among the others in the trucks. Her stubbornness and drive had brought her to Italy, back to him. He only hoped it would keep her in the basilica.

Bastian gazed at Max who appeared to be in his own world, contemplating his fate. Bastian knew he did not want to live in a world without Max. Maybe Bastian would be remembered as a hero. Maybe no one would know what'd happened to him.

Max's curly hair fell over his left eye, and Bastian tucked it behind his ear. "You'll need both your eyes to survive this," he attempted a joke.

Max faced him from the passenger seat.

"You said you loved me, Max. Do you still?"

"If I said 'no,' would you let me go to the caves alone?"

"No," Bastian said, turning away. "Even if you don't love me, I love you." It was the first time he'd said those words to anyone other than Ilsa and his mother. Perhaps he'd said "I love you" to his father, in the before time.

Max placed his hand on Bastian's neck so that he turned to face him. "I've spent almost every day since we parted trying to convince myself I didn't love you, that I hated you instead, that you meant nothing to me. It will take some adjusting to rewire my brain. To believe that you are real. And honest. And that you truly love me." He paused and lowered his eyes. "I don't want you to risk your life today because you love me. I want you to risk it because you still believe in the good in people. In yourself. Because I do. I believe in the good in you."

Max pressed on the back of Bastian's neck, pulling his face toward him. They kissed. The moment was imprinted, like a stamp on a coin.

In the distance they heard two gunshots. They separated from one another.

"Are you sure you want to do this?" Max asked. Bastian nodded his head in confirmation and then they exited the car together.

They walked down the dusty street. At the top of a hill, they could see the caves, stone tops covered in grass. The gray rock looked too serene of a place for what was about to happen. At the bottom of the hill they ducked into a furrow of trees.

"Let's take cover here and see what we can find out first," Bastian said.

They listened to the voices that carried to them. Prisoners were pulled from the trucks to sit en mass outside the caves, their hands tied behind their backs. They sat on the grass in terrified silence. The only noise came from the cluster of SS gathered in two groups, one inside the caves, the other near the vehicles. The men near the cars were taking drinks from a bottle in turns. Some appeared to already be drunk. They laughed loudly and slapped one another's backs. Then they grabbed three wooden cases from the car and headed up the small hill to the caves. All of the officers disappeared inside.

"Let's go," Max said, stepping out of the tree cover.

Bastian grabbed his arm. "I'm sorry," he said.

Max looked at him, confused. Then a sharp pain overtook him and all was dark.

"I'm sorry," Bastian said again as he laid Max gently down among the trees, concealing him. The bump on his head where Bastian had hit him was already swelling. He would be in pain tomorrow, but at least he'd be alive.

Bastian left the tree cover. He gasped. An intake of breath sharp enough to make his heart hurt. Standing in front of him was Hans Mandel.

Hans raised his gun. "Who are you? What are you doing here?" Hans looked around himself, wondering if there were more people lurking in the trees, then steadied his hand and aimed.

"Wait!" Bastian half-shouted, not wanting to bring attention and more SS to them. In German he said, "I was sent to help. I'm late. Don't tell anyone."

Hans eyed him with suspicion. The man wore no uniform, but he looked like one of them. Then, as if watching a film backwards, it dawned on him. He knew this man. He looked at Bastian Fisher and laughed in delight.

"What luck!" he said, laughing harder. "I mean, how is this possible? Remember the last time we saw one another?" Hans leveled his gun again. "My aim may be even better than yours now, Fisher."

"I'm flattered you still remember me." Bastian's eyes flicked to the side, involuntarily. Hans followed the glance.

"Who's in there?" he said, extending his arm toward the trees. "Come out of there!" Hans took one step forward.

Bastian's gun was still strapped to his ankle. He didn't think he could get to it in time. "No one's there," he said, taking one step backwards toward Max.

"Liar, liar pants on fire." Hans laughed again and pushed past Bastian. "Eeny, meeny, miny, mo, catch a tiger …." He peered through the tree cover. "Wait … really? Is that the same scrawny kid from camp whose side you never left?"

Bastian stiffened.

"So, the rumors were true? I said it couldn't be right. Anyone with an aim like that …." He faced Bastian. "I guess I was wrong. Bound to happen once."

"Leave him alone."

Hans laughed again. It was high-pitched, unnatural. "As if I could? I will do *this* for you though. I'll kill you first, so you won't have to watch him die. Young love and all." He turned to peer at Max again.

The instant was so fast, Bastian wasn't sure he'd succeeded. He grabbed Hans's short hair and pulled him back. In one swift movement, he yanked the gun from Hans's hand and placed it to the man's skull. Bastian dragged him behind the trees and once there, he didn't hesitate for a moment. The blow from the shot knocked him backwards, and pieces of Hans's skull spattered the front of his shirt. Blood gushed onto the grass, staining it dark red. The body thumped to the ground. Bastian quickly looked around. The victims on the hill remained quiet. The officers stayed inside the cave.

He pulled Hans's body farther inside the tree cover and laid him next to Max.

"God damn it." He tried to catch his breath. At least if he died today, it would be with the knowledge that Hans Mandel was dead too.

Bastian was covered in blood and skull fragments. He looked down at Hans's uniform. The back of his shirt was stained, but it looked better than what Bastian was wearing. He stripped Hans's clothes off. After he'd shed his own clothes and put on Hans's he shoved the body as far away from Max, but still under the cover, as possible. If he lived, he'd retrieve Max. If he died, well then he could only hope that the Nazis would be gone when Max awoke. Bastian dug a small hole next to Max and put the gun in the ground, covering it with dirt.

When he exited again, the scene at the Ardeatines remained unchanged. He moved toward the back of the caves where he could be hidden, but could see the action. Bastian still hadn't worked out how he would save a single person when the Nazis started taking victims into the cave. They gathered them in groups of five and led them inside by their ropes. Two officers stood in the entrance, watching. Bastian recognized them from photos Clark had shown him. They were two high-ranking officials—SS Officers Erich Priebke and Karl Hass.

"Where have you been hiding?" he asked under his breath. If he'd been able to track them down, he could have had information for Clark months ago.

The two officers gave orders to the others. Bastian watched more men filter in and out of the caves, guns by their sides and cognac in their hands. He heard the command, "Niederknien," *Kneel down*, from inside the caves. Five guns went off. Those waiting to be executed began to cry. Another round of five was gathered.

One of the officers staggered and fell as he attempted to drag a woman into the cave. Another man immediately took his place and picked her up. Bastian thought the officer might have fainted. Or he was drunk enough to pass out.

During each round of executions, the officers disappeared inside. This was Bastian's opportunity. He slipped along the outer edge of the caves to the dwindling throngs of people. There had to be more than three hundred of them, Bastian thought. Several people were placed just beyond the sight line of the caves.

Bastian covered one prisoner's mouth, a young man around his age with dark eyes and held his finger to his lips. "Voglio aiutare," he whispered. *I want to help*. He was able to gather three people without notice.

Gunshots rang out from the cave. "Hurry!" he whispered as he guided the trio down the hill.

He untied them. "Run!" he said. Two followed his direction.

The third, a middle-aged woman with sunken eyes looked at him. "My son," she pointed to a young man who sat near the edge of the cave. "Please save him."

Bastian waited until five more were taken in and then rushed up the hill. This time he was only able to grab two. The woman's son and an older woman. The prisoners ran down the hill in front of him as five more shots echoed off the stone walls. The young man ran into his mother's arms. She held him for a moment, and then they were gone.

There were two more at the edge of the cave who would be easiest to save. He sprinted again, timing his movement. Some of the prisoners noticed him and cried out, but he put his finger to his lips. He knew he could not save them all. At least fifty had already been taken to the caves. He grabbed two more and thrust them down the hill.

Behind him a deep voice yelled, "Halt!" Shots resounded near him.

"Run!" Bastian screamed to the two a few yards in front of him. He looked back.

An overweight man was chasing them down the hill. The officer took aim at the prisoners, but his shots missed. "Halt!" he yelled again.

More officers were gathering. People were turning around in their restraints to watch. Shouts arose. Bastian thought he heard his name being called.

The officer chasing him slid on dewy grass, weaving. His drunkenness was Bastian's only hope.

That was his last thought as Bastian was struck by a bullet. His body slammed into the ground, blood soaking the back of his uniform.

The officer stopped, out of breath; the young man didn't appear to be breathing. He looked around for the escapees. "Scheiße," he screamed to no one in particular. He kicked at the body, but it didn't respond. He huffed back up the hill, swearing all the way.

The Nazis continued to drag people into the caves, five at a time, a bullet into each of their brains.

***

Max's hand went straight to the swollen spot on his head when he woke. "Damn it, Bastian," he muttered, knowing exactly what had happened. He propped himself up by his elbows, but he was woozy and fell back down. His head ached and felt heavier than it should. He touched the bump again. "Damn it, Bastian." He tried to sit up, leaned to the side and heaved. He lay back down and concentrated on his breathing. After a few more moments he sat up, successfully this time.

Max saw Bastian's discarded clothes before he saw the body. The dead man next to him was stripped down to his underwear. Max trailed his gaze up the body until it landed on the man's face. Hans's blank eyes stared upwards, unblinking. He was white and chalky. Max reached out and touched his arm. He was still warm. The back of his skull had been blown apart.

Max stood, wanting nothing more than to get away from the now-dead Hans. He pushed himself from the ground and felt something hard buried in the dirt. He bent down, still dizzy, and picked up a gun. It was lighter than the rifles at camp had been. Outside the tree cover, he heard a man yelling. "Halt!"

Max peeked out and saw Bastian running down the hill. Two others were several paces in front of him. Bullets whizzed through the air.

"Run!" Bastian yelled. His voice sent shivers through Max.

The officer was gaining on them. Max aimed the gun. "Halt!" the man called again. The two people in front of Bastian ran into the woods and Max watched them disappear. Before he could re-aim the gun, a single shot pierced through the screams.

"Bastian!" Max called out.

Max watched Bastian's body fall violently to the ground and tears streamed down his face as he watched the motionless form. What was the last thing he'd said to Bastian? He couldn't remember. Max didn't know why it was so important, but he was desperate to remember. He pressed his fingers into his stomach and cried quiet tears. Was it *Let's go*? Or *I'm sorry*? No, that was the last thing Bastian said to him. *I'm sorry.*

The officer lumbered back up the hill. A chilled quiet fell over the remaining victims. The crowd had shrunk. How many had been killed? How many had escaped? How many lives could justify Bastian's death? After a few moments, the officers seemed to forget about the boy at the bottom of the hill. They continued to march people into the caves, five by five. Max watched, unable to turn away. There were less than two hundred now, huddled near the cavern.

Nobody sent so much as a glance Bastian's way. Max hurried to him. Somewhere within him, Max wished they would shoot him down, next to Bastian. Somewhere bitter within him hoped they wouldn't.

"Bastian," he whispered frantically. "Bastian, please."

Five more shots.

Blood bloomed like a delicate flower on the front and back of Bastian's uniform. Max pawed at the floral patterns before hoisting him up so that his body leaned into his own. He took him by the waist and dragged him into the cover. Bastian's blood covered Max's shirt. He felt for a pulse and pressed his hand over the wound in an attempt to staunch the flow of blood. It was good news that he was still bleeding, right? If he were dead, wouldn't the blood stop flowing? His body and mind were too disoriented to have a clear thought. Max couldn't find a pulse but didn't trust himself to be sure. He ran and grabbed Bastian's shirt that lay next to Hans. He could use it to put pressure on the wound.

Max lifted Bastian's arms over his shoulder and made his way to the car, though it was slow going. When he placed him in the passenger seat, he thought he heard a moan, but when he leaned his ear to Bastian's mouth, he heard nothing. No breath sounds, no groans.

Max could hardly see through his tears as he raced back to the city. He pressed the shirt to Bastian's wound and the blood bubbled over, running down Max's fingertips. He didn't know what else to do, other than take Bastian's body back to Ilsa, back to the basilica.

Bastian had survived almost six years in the army, Max thought, but he couldn't survive six months with him. In the middle of a war, he'd come to Max. Alive.

He looked over at his friend's body and wept. He had done this.

THE TIRES SCREECHED as Max pulled up in front of the basilica and flung open his door.

"Help!" he yelled toward the courtyard. "Help me, please!"

Three men appeared at the gate. They recognized Max and ran to his aid.

"What's wrong?" one asked. He stopped fast when he saw Max, covered in blood.

"It's not me. It's Bastian. He's been shot."

Max opened the passenger door. One of the men inhaled sharply.

Bastian's pallor was like something out of a book or a movie; unreal and inhuman.

The men lifted his body from the car and hurried him to the church, through the courtyard, and into the central nave. By the time they were in the sanctuary, Ilsa was there.

She held onto the edge of a pew and steadied herself. "Lay him here."

The men placed him gently onto the marble floor.

"Gather towels and blankets. And the sulfanilamide powder." She kneeled next to him. "Fast. I need to stop the bleeding." With swift efficiency, she removed his shirt and pressed her hands to his chest. Moments later, one of the men was back with towels and the powder, which would help prevent infection. Ilsa sprinkled the powder onto his chest and then replaced her hand with the cloth.

"It's good that he's bleeding, right?" Max asked. "It means blood is still pumping to his heart?"

Ilsa glanced coldly at him. "Nothing. Nothing is good about this. Why did you let this happen?"

Max fell into a seat on the pew. Her eyes watched him for a moment, fixed, before she looked back at her brother.

"Why did you make him go with you? Why did you do this?"

Max had no defense.

Ilsa kept one hand pressed to Bastian's chest and reached the other toward his wrist. Around his neck was the coin. It looked bent, twisted.

"I think ... I think I feel a pulse," she said.

Max felt any color left in his face drain away. He lay down on the pew. More than anything, he wanted to be of use, but he couldn't will his body to do anything other than lay on the cool wood. He thought of Ilsa's words. They formed a blanket around him, tucking Max in tightly so he couldn't budge.

Why did you do this?

***

Bastian's mouth was parched. He opened his eyes and tried to coat his throat with saliva. Lying next to him on the floor was his sister, her mouth turned down in a grimace in her sleep. He saw something of his mother's resolve and stubbornness in her. Ilsa had experienced too much pain in her short years and Bastian knew he'd thrust some of that hurt onto her. Disappearing for a year, joining the army, getting shot—twice. She'd taken all of that in and wore it on her face.

He reached his arm across the short distance between them. It hurt to move, but he wanted her to see that he was alive. With his other hand he felt the neat row of stitches on his chest. He suspected there was a matching string of them on his back. As he moved his hand from his stitches back to his side, he brushed the coin around his neck. He inspected it with his fingers, unable to move his neck downward. The coin felt chipped or bent, damaged in some way. It had come in contact with the bullet, and the bullet had won.

He found Ilsa's hand and squeezed it. She bolted upright and looked around. When she saw he was awake, she began to sob. He pulled her the best he could toward his body. Ilsa gently laid her head next to his on a small stack of pillows. Bastian had tears in his own eyes. They fell from his cheeks to his mouth, coating it. It felt good to be able to swallow again.

"Max?" he said in question.

"He's fine," Ilsa answered.

They fell asleep like that, their heartbeats thudding next to one another.

When Bastian woke again, Ilsa was there with water and a moist rag on his forehead. He drank the water gratefully and tried to sit up.

"Don't you dare," she said. "You might pull your stitches if you move too much."

He lay his head back down on the pillow. She looked younger again, not as worn down by him.

"Thank you for stitching me up."

"Again," she said, offering him a smile.

"Yes, again." He laughed a little, but it hurt so he stopped. "My lucky penny. It was damaged, feels like."

"Not so lucky I guess," Ilsa said.

"Maybe its luck just wore off."

"Maybe I used it all up?" she offered.

Bastian looked at her. "I wouldn't say you've led such a lucky life."

"Look at how bad it would have been if I didn't have the damn coin."

Her smile. It was what separated Ilsa from their mother. The two women may have looked alike, but Ilsa's spirit was large enough to fill the basilica. Bastian always thought that when she was born, she'd been put into their family for him to protect, to save. All along it was she who protected him, saved him.

"Thank you," he said.

"For what?"

"You know for what."

She kissed his forehead. It felt like they'd finally figured something out.

"When you're better," she said, "and the Americans arrive, and this war is finally over, let's go home, okay?"

"Okay," he said.

"Promise?"

"Promise."

***

Max watched Bastian sleep as he'd done the past five days. His coloring seemed to improve a little each time. Max spent time with him when Ilsa was not around. She still wasn't speaking to him, and he didn't blame her.

Max had thought that Bastian was gone. He'd brought her a dead sibling. Why should he be forgiven?

Yesterday, from across the church, he'd watched Bastian sit up against a stack of pillows and smile. Max didn't think he'd ever see that smile again, the smile that made Bastian's face almost unbearably handsome.

All those years ago, they'd shared a night that changed Max's life. Since boarding the ship to Italy, he'd thought of himself and Bastian in the past tense, as if they could not exist in the present, in the future. The life they'd experienced together was unreal. The life they'd lived together was fiction. Like a movie. Too bittersweet and painful, or too full and consuming to be real. Meant to last for a short time only.

THE LEAFLETS DROPPED from the sky on the morning of June 4, 1944. Max was in the front courtyard, watching a scene that would never make it into *La Porta del Cielo*. They'd run out of film a week ago. Unbeknownst to the actors, there was nothing in the cameras.

"What's this?" Luca said, grabbing at the paper falling from the sky. The scene stopped and the actors peered upward. Luca read the words aloud, as the others silently stared at their leaflets, dropped by the Allied troops. *"It is time to stand shoulder-to-shoulder to protect the city from destruction and to defeat our common enemies. Citizens of Rome, this is not the time for demonstrations. Obey these directions and go on with your regular work. Rome is yours! Your job is to save the city, ours is to destroy the enemy."*

"What does that mean?" Max asked.

De Sica stood next to him. "It means we've done it, Max. It means the Americans are here and are going to take our city back." He looked at the actors and crew. "That's it, everyone. It's a wrap. No more. Go inside. Find someone you love and tell them the news. The Americans are coming."

Max watched everyone file toward the church in awed perplexity. Was it really over? Luca stayed next to him.

"We've done it? It's over?" Max asked.

"Looks like this portion almost is, anyway. You did good, Max," said Luca.

"Except for the sixty-two we lost in the raid," Max said.

Luca turned Max's body so he was looking directly at him. "Damn it, Max. When will you get it? You can't save everyone." He went to go, then turned back. "By the way, I'm fine. Angie and the baby are fine. She's due in a few weeks, you know, since you haven't asked. Since it feels like you've barely talked to me in months."

"I'm sorry," Max managed to say.

"It's fine. I want you to be happy, but I can't figure out what you want. You should be ecstatic right now. We're being *liberated.*" Luca threw out his arms. "You did well. This was your idea and now we're safe." He hesitated. "Is it Bastian? Who is he, anyway? You gave me half an explanation when he showed up and then for the last three months, watching the two of you, stuck together like glue, and then you disappear overnight and when you come back, you're covered in blood. Who is he? Who is this man to you?"

It was the eternal question in the Eternal City. Who was Bastian to Max?

He met Luca's eye. "I think he's someone I love."

Luca nodded at him. "You need someone to love." He turned to go again. "I'm going to find Silvia and the baby to tell them the good news and to write to Angie."

Max wanted Luca to say more, to give his approval of Bastian, of the person he wanted to love.

"I'll see you later, okay? Stay inside. Don't go on any more rogue rescue missions," Luca said, a smile on his lips.

Max nodded at him. He sat on the ground and stared at the fake train station. The movie was over. The war in Rome was over. *Liberated.* What did that even mean? He should tell Ilsa and Bastian.

It was over.

***

During the night, they heard a few gunshots. No more than usual. Max and Bastian sat on a bench in the courtyard when they saw an army of SS march past the basilica. They were not singing this time. The soldiers at the end of the line dropped sheets of paper every few yards as they retreated from the city. Once the marching men were out of sight, Max retrieved one of the notes.

The struggle in Italy will be continued with unshakable determination with the aim of breaking the enemy attacks and to forge final victory for Germany and her allies.

Bastian and Max wondered aloud in what state the Germans would leave the city. Would they wake in the morning to find the Colosseum a pile of stones? The beautiful Trevi Fountain blown to pieces? None of the previous actions of the SS indicated any other outcome. They'd all but destroyed the spirit of the Italians. Would they decimate their historical relics as well?

"Tell me again," Max said, "about what happened at the caves." He'd made Bastian tell him twice already. He needed to hear it again.

"No, Max. I don't want to."

In the week and a half since he was shot, Bastian had grown more quiet and contemplative. For the first time he was thinking of his future; he could have a life after the war. He didn't want to recall its ugliness anymore.

"Please, once more. I won't ask again."

Bastian relented. Max was not convinced that he was telling him the whole story. Each time Max searched for holes in the narrative. Could he have helped if he'd been conscious? He would never truly know.

"After confronting Hans and killing him, I saved seven people from the massacre at the caves. As I was running away the last time, I was shot, very near to my heart, Ilsa tells me. That was the last thing I recall."

Max remembered every moment after that shot vividly. He would see the blood coming from Bastian's chest in his dreams and nightmares for the rest of his life.

"We need to let someone know about all those people out there," Bastian said. "They need to get a proper burial."

Max nodded in agreement.

"I have to lie down now. I've been sitting upright for too long."

Max helped him inside. Bastian felt the warmth of Max's body against his own. The two of them had come to an impasse. Bastian felt like he knew what was next, but he had no idea if Max would be around for it. For life after the war.

As Max helped him into bed, Bastian thought about how his entire life, up until this point, had been a war. A war with his father, a war with himself and then, a war for his country. He was tired of fighting. He wanted to make peace with the man who'd beaten him. It was too late to do it with Herr Fisher himself, but was there peace to be found anyway? And more than anything he wanted to find a peace within himself. He'd fought against his attraction to men so fiercely that for most of his life he'd convinced himself the battle didn't exist. Until Max. Max had made him see the truth of himself. For that he'd always love him.

***

The morning of June fifth started peacefully. The people of Rome obeyed the leaflets that were dropped on them and stayed inside. They let someone else fight the war. They awoke to find their city much as they had left it the night before, much as it was before the Nazis occupied it. Empty of SS.

Then came the first Jeep, quietly into Rome. The Americans did not bring fanfare, but the Italians brought it to them. Over a million people flooded the streets. Shops closed. Crowds converged on every inch of the city, cheering, waving, and throwing roses into the trucks as they passed through the streets. The feelings of joy were overwhelming. People, young and old, stood together and watched. The Germans were gone. Jews who'd gone into hiding in attics and churches came into the sun next to their fellow Italians. The soldiers tossed American flags to the crowds.

Max watched at first from the basilica, and then joined the people in the streets. Bastian was resting. There was rumor that the Pope would speak later and Max knew Bastian would want to be there.

Trucks driven by American and British soldiers passed through the roads. Max examined each of their faces, looking. Some stopped and greeted the Italians, received flowers and embraces, while others continued through the street.

After some time of waiting and watching, a truck with four men drove by slowly, the crowds cheering them on.

They stopped and got out. The American officers shook hands, hugged women, and kissed babies.

Max saw the man he was looking for, someone obviously important who sat in the back of a truck and waved while another man drove him: Lieutenant General Mark Clark. He was tall and slim with a round face and broad shoulders, just as Bastian had described. Despite all of his warring, he had kind eyes and when he smiled, it extended to his whole face. General Clark exited the truck to shake hands and smile.

"General Clark?" Max shouted, coming across the street toward him.

Clark turned when he heard his name. He waved at Max.

Max edged his way through the crowd in front of him. "Sir," he said, "I need to talk to you."

Clark smiled and shook Max's hand. The man next to Clark said something in his ear. The officers gave a final wave and walked back toward the truck. Max shouted after Clark. "It's Bastian Fisher," he said over the cheers. Clark turned sharply to him.

"I need to see about one of my men," Clark said to the others. The three men nodded and followed him.

"I'm Max," he said, shaking the General's hand. "I know where Bastian Fisher is. I thought you'd like to know, too."

Clark ran his fingers through his hair and laughed. "Of course, that kid isn't dead. Where is he?"

Max explained the best he could as the five of them walked to the basilica. He knew only in part what had led up to Bastian's fight at the bar, him getting shot the first time, but he could fill in what happened after Bastian came to the church with Ilsa.

"She found him?" Clark asked in wonder. "That family is something."

Max nodded. He told the General about the Ardeatine caves last. Clark and his men stopped walking and throngs of people passed by before they were able to come back together. "Bastian says you need to get people out there to bury the victims properly," said Max. "I don't know if the Italians know about what happened. It was all very fast."

"And he was shot. Again. And lived … again?" asked Clark.

"That's right," Max said.

***

Clark told Bastian that he would receive a Purple Heart for heroics.

"I thought I'd get you here sooner," Bastian told the General.

"You took out several high-ranking officers at that bar. I heard about it, just had no idea it was you. And your friend here," he indicated to Max, "told me about the seven you saved at the caves."

"You need to send someone out there," Bastian began.

"Don't waste your breath. I'll work with the Italians on it to give those people a proper burial," said Clark.

"Also … do the words 'Operation Drachenhöhle' mean anything to you?" Bastian asked.

"Max," Clark said turning to him. "Can you give us a moment?"

Max nodded and left.

***

Later, Bastian and the men came outside. Bastian saluted each one and they did the same in return. He held the stitches at his chest and smiled.

As he was leaving, Clark asked, "What's next for you, Fisher?"

Bastian looked at Max. "I'd like to go home, sir."

"Home? Okay."

"Both my sister and I." He pointed to Max, "And him if he'd like to."

"I will do what I can to get the three of you on a plane or a ship as soon as possible. Most likely it'll be a couple of weeks, but I'll do my best to make it happen even sooner." Clark and Bastian saluted again. "If you want to watch the Pope's speech, I can hitch a ride for you."

"That'd be great, General. Thanks."

When Clark and his men had gone, Bastian said, "Wow. A Purple Heart."

"Well, I told him everything you did," said Max.

"You didn't have to do that."

"I know, but you deserve it. To be recognized."

"How about what you did? Saving all of these people, convincing me to go to the caves."

"So you could be shot," Max said.

"Well," Bastian said, smiling, "shit happens." He pulled himself into a chair. "Will you go home with us?"

"I haven't decided," Max said.

"I have to go, you know. I promised Ilsa."

"I know," said Max.

Outside, the crowds continued to cheer.

***

Max, Bastian, and Ilsa were packed into Saint Peter's Square with half a million others. Clark had gotten them near the front. Ilsa and Max stood on either side of Bastian, trying to prevent him from being jostled too much. He was healing; nonetheless it still made Ilsa nervous to be there. She understood though; witnessing Pope Pius XII's speech was worth the risk. She saw how much Bastian wanted to believe in something. Despite the fact that all three of them felt like the Pope could and should have done more during the Nazi occupation, they still wanted to be a part of the history being made.

When Pius came onto the balcony of Saint Peter's, the roar of the crowd was deafening. He began to speak, his voice booming through a microphone. The crowd fell rapt with silence.

"In recent days we trembled for the fate of the city. Today we rejoice because, thanks to the joint goodwill of both sides, Rome has been saved from the horrors of war. Yesterday's fear has been replaced by today's new hope; instead of unimaginable destruction, Rome has been granted salvation. The Eternal City has been saved by divine mercy inspired by the intent of both belligerent parties to seek peace, not affliction. We thank God, the Trinity, and Mary, Mother of God, for saving the Romans." The Pope bowed to his city. "Sursum corda!" he cried. "Lift your hearts!"

Max, Bastian, and Ilsa watched as Pius left the balcony to lively cheers.

"That's it, I guess," Ilsa said.

"That's it," Bastian said.

She hugged her brother. "Time to go home?"

Bastian looked at Max. "Time to go home."

***

The car was waiting to take them back to the basilica. Bastian stepped in first.

"I think I'd like to walk back," Max said.

"Okay," Bastian said, starting to get out of the vehicle.

"No, you don't," Ilsa told him. "You can't walk all that way. I'll go with Max and you get back safe and rest. You've pushed yourself hard enough already today."

Bastian agreed and Max and Ilsa watched as the car pulled away with him inside. They walked together, neither one speaking. It wasn't until they were halfway back when Ilsa said, "I saw the two of you, you know. During the bombing. Under the table."

Max flushed. That moment had been private. Then again, how could it have been with hundreds of people sharing the room with them? "Okay," he said, uncertain.

"I didn't know that about Bastian." She was quiet and Max had to lean close to hear her over the people on the street. "I thought I knew everything about him."

"I don't think I could ever know everything about Bastian," Max said.

Ilsa agreed. "There have always been pieces of him that were unknowable, true. But I thought I *knew* him. His soul, you know. Who he was at his core. Maybe now I do."

"And you don't like what you see there?" Max asked.

"I don't like the life he'll need to live because of it. It will be hard no matter what he chooses. If he hides who he is, he'll be miserable. If he doesn't, he risks condemnation from the world at large. I do like how happy he looks when you're together. I like that you make him happy."

"He thinks that in the city, we'd be okay," Max told her.

"He's delusional," she said, not unkindly. "That doesn't mean you don't try, though." She put her hand on his shoulder. "You are coming back to America with us, right? I don't know how he'll cope if you don't."

"America," Max sighed. "Maybe. But not New York. I don't want to go back there. Maybe Los Angeles. To make films." If his life were like a movie, then Los Angeles seemed like a suitable home. From what he'd seen, nothing was entirely real there.

"That's a start, at least." Ilsa said.

***

Max wanted to have a life with Bastian. But the war had taught him something different than it taught Bastian and because of that, their love seemed an insurmountable objective. Max saw the destruction and pain. The war had left so much ugliness. He was afraid it had coated his heart.

For Bastian, the war had given him a new outlook, of what life *doesn't* have to be. Max only saw what life already was: dirty, stark, and unforgiving.

That night, the two of them lay next to one another on Max's bed in his unlit apartment. Ilsa stayed at Bastian's place, said she would start packing his things. Just like that, the life they'd known for the past year was over. They were expected to … what? Find jobs, start families? Was Bastian to block out the men he'd killed? Max to forget the people he'd lost?

Outside the people still cheered, laughing and talking into the night. In the dark room, Max and Bastian shared their first moment alone since they'd been reunited, without mortal threat surrounding them. Max didn't know if they could exist in a state of rest.

"Clark came back later today when you were visiting your family," said Bastian. "He said he can get us a ride out of here by next week."

Max said nothing.

"You'll come, right?" Bastian asked.

Every piece of Max's body vibrated as he absorbed the surreal changes that were happening. He grasped at the new reality before him. It would take more than a week to remember what it was like to exist in a world without war. He felt lost, empty. In his life, death had signaled transformative change. With the death of his father, he'd found love in Bastian, only to be catapulted to a foreign land where he was expected to start over. After his Nonna, the Germans came. Then, with the death of his mother, he'd taken hold of his life for the first time and helped to make something happen for someone else. Whose death was to propel him into this next chapter?

"Then what happens after that? After we arrive in America?" Max asked.

Bastian was tired—of Max's endless questions, of the unsettled nature of the world. He didn't know their future, could not comprehend their past, and was barely able to come to terms with the reality of the present. He used to believe that he'd been built for war. Now, he wanted nothing to do with the endless, tormented fighting of man. He wanted to become another person, a better person. He wanted Max and himself to have a life together beyond the war against their parents, their country, and themselves.

"Do we need to know what happens next?" Bastian asked.

"If this were a movie," Max started, "we would be in act three. That's when the story wraps up. Everyone finishes their popcorn and goes home."

Bastian reached for him in the dark. "This isn't a movie."

Max supposed Bastian was right. They didn't know, or need to know, what happened next. The life they chose to lead, or not lead, was not pre-scripted. They could do with it what they wanted. The thought comforted Max as he drifted off to sleep, next to Bastian, their hands intertwined in a bouquet of fingers.

And once the war was over, a war that had attempted to take away people's humanity, their spirit, their faith; once grave stones were carved and the dead remembered; once the ever-gnawing hunger was dampened and bellies were almost full again; once children were born who had not lived through it, Max and Bastian would have this night, this moment, precious and maybe ill-conceived, it could not be taken away.

A NOTE FROM THE AUTHOR

In April 2015 I traveled to Rome, a long-time dream fulfilled. While there, I toured The Papal Basilica of St. Paul Outside the Walls, the only Vatican-run Basilica outside of Vatican City. The guide had a fascinating story to tell; a movie had been made right there in the church by the famous Italian director Vittorio De Sica during the Nazi occupation in World War II. According to the tour guide, the movie, *The Gates of Heaven* (or in Italian, *La Porta del Cielo*) had aided in saving the lives of hundreds of Italian Jews living in the city at that time. Accounts claimed that De Sica continued filming, even after they had run out of actual film. I left the church, repeating the story to myself. It followed me from the basilica and out onto the streets of Rome. There were many untold stories of World War II, and this was one I wanted to explore.

The same day I read an NPR article titled, "Nazi Summer Camps in 1930s America?" that featured a blurry photo of young blond men, crouched in the grass, rifles in hand. The article read, "Healthy, happy, high-energy guys—against the bucolic backdrop of the Catskill Mountains in eastern New York—pitch tents, get muddy, play checkers, shoot rifles, box and wrestle one another, raise a Nazi swastika flag...."

Thus Max and Bastian were born. I did not see their entire narrative from the start, but I saw them. Two boys, who meet at a Nazi-American camp, fall in love and somehow reunite in Rome during the filming of *La Porta del Cielo*. I wrote their character profiles and part of the outline on the plane ride home from Rome, a few days later.

Then began the research. Though Max and Bastian are totally fictional characters, most of what transpires in the book is based on real events. The camps, spread throughout America, were real. The round up in the Jewish Ghetto happened on the same day in history as in the book. I read several accounts of a woman claiming a baby who was not hers to save him from going to the concentration camps. The attack against the Nazis, executed by the resistance, happened as it did in the novel, and the consequential aftermath, The Ardeatine Cave Massacre occurred as well. Three hundred and thirty-five people were killed. I did change the dates of these two events to fit into my timeline. Many of the Nazis and Gestapo I've named were real; however, they were not necessarily in Rome during the occupation. The film, of course, is real. Though there are varied accounts of how many lives were saved, it is mentioned in several sources. All of the text from the leaflets and newspapers is real. Much of the timeline is also accurate.

What made World War II so unique, in my opinion, was that though the devastation and inhumanity seemed insurmountable, people were still fighting, still rising up, still risking their lives, often for people who they did not know. There are many true stories from war to be told, this is only one of them.

Angelle Petta